CODENAME: ECLECTICS

JACK STRAW

CHAPTER 1

"Are you sure they stole him?"

"Yes."

"And are we sure who they are?"

"Pretty sure."

The slightly balding heavy-set man behind the large desk leans back in his black leather office chair, steepling his fingers in front of his face. He looks at the younger man standing in front of his desk between glances at the television screen mounted on his office all near an American flag. "Pretty sure? What the hell does that mean?"

Brian Temple, the man expected to respond, knows he must give a calculated and short response. He's worked as the top administrative assistant to Secretary of State Eugene Harberts for over a year and he is fully aware of the cabinet member's two most famous traits: volatility and a short attention span. A lengthy answer can set him off, and causing volcanic eruptions is not good for one's career. "Ninety nine percent certain," Temple said.

"Based upon?" Harberts said, almost absent-mindedly, keeping his eyes on the TV monitor.

"We're receiving intel as to Jasper's whereabouts."

Harbert sits forward in his seat, holds both arms out in front of him, extended with the palms up in a look of bewilderment. "Well, then go pick up Jasper and get the asshole back here. It's not a big deal."

Temple raises his right hand in a small fist and coughs lightly into it. He feels perspiration forming on his slender five-foot eight-inch frame, clothed in his navy blue Capitol Hill Clothiers suit. He takes a moment to again prepare a response. He Looks at Harberts who is six foot and two hundred and fifty pounds, dressed in a white sport shirt, black pants and cowboy boots that he has now propped on his seventy-thousand-dollar desk. The man somehow manages to look both intimidating and ridiculous, like a genetic mix of Conor McGregor and Louis Anderson.

"Well, Mister Secretary,"Temple began, "Jasper was carrying certain documents with him when he ...disappeared. So, it is kind of a big deal."

Harberts pulls a Rum Crook cigar from his pocket and lights it with a wooden match he retrieves from a buffalo head match holder and ashtray set on his desk.

"Of course, he was carrying documents. He's a goddamn State Department courier, "he said. He looks quickly at his aide, then nods back to the television. "You know what, Temple?"

"What, sir?"

Harberts points at the screen with the lit cigar. "That fat boy lost all that weight and he still ain't a hair on Barker's ass. Price is Right is just not the same. Yes sir, Bob Barker was the man. Old bastard was so ancient and leathery, he looked like a shoe tongue with a Q-tip head for hair," he said. "But, he was still throwing the strap to the show gals after a full day of getting physically mauled and jumped by every bun-haired, dimple-assed housewife that showed up on the program. And not once did he ever forget to tell us to get old Fido's nuts cut so he wasn't knocking up the neighbor's poodle. Hell of a guy."

“Sir,” Temple intervenes.

“Huh?” Harberts says. “Oh, yeah. So, what was it we were yakking about?”

“Jasper being kidnapped and missing documents, sir.”

“Oh yeah, that’s right. Well hell, Temple, we can always get another courier. Besides, what was he carrying, the menu for the dinner for the ambassador from the Ivory Coast?”

“Uh, no sir. He was delivering the Fake Election Dossier to the White House.”

Harberts’s eyes widened, “Holy shit,” he hissed. “Where the hell was security? Who was covering him? Get their boss on the phone! He did have somebody with him, right?”

“Oh yes. Calvin Wasyl was with him, sir,” Temple said.

“One Secret Service guy? That’s it?” Harberts yips.

“No, not exactly,” Temple said. “Wasyl is not with the Service…or at least, not that Service.”

“What?” Harberts asked, a little quieter now. “Who is he? FBI? Marshall?”

“No,” Temple says. “He’s with custodial and maintenance services.”

“He’s with…He’s a janitor?” Harberts rises from his seat, placing his hands palms down on his desktop leaning into Temple’s airspace, “We sent a janitor to guard the dossier? Are you shittin’ me? Where was the Secret Service detail?”

“Guarding the menus for the Ivory Coast dinner.”

“Oh great. Well, hopefully they were sober enough to do that!” Harberts leans back in his chair again. He looks back at this TV. “Can you believe this?” he said.

“Which part, sir?”

“That broad just put a $6.99 price on that macaroni and cheese. How goddamned stupid can you be? It’s not even Kraft. Maybe I should call the President,” he said, reaching for the phone.

"No can do, sir."

"Why not?"

"He's in his personal quarters, sir. I believe he's Tweeting."

"Tweeting? Goddamn bird impressions?"

"No, sir. He's messaging the public."

Harberts leans back in his chair. "Christ. He'd be better off doing crow cackles. Can't someone take that damn phone away from him?"

"He is the President, sir."

"Yeah, he is. Amazing isn't it? What's he going on about now?"

"He's responding to a CNN report."

"About what?"

"About a cabinet member calling him a peckerhead, sir."

"Which cabinet member did that?"

"The report says you did, sir."

"Really? Don't remember that."

"Probably best that you don't, sir."

"Oh, well. So who the hell has Jasper, anyway?"

"Ricardo Reyes."

"Who?"

"Ricardo Reyes, the head of the Mexican and Central American Drug Cartel and Home Health Care Delivery Services Incorporated," Temple said, reading from a file then lays it on the Secretary's desk.

"Incorporated?"

"Delaware corporation. Tax purposes. Anyway, sir, they say they will kill Jasper and Wasyl and expose the dossier if we don't meet their demands."

"Wasyl?"

"The janitor, sir"

"Hell of a threat. Do what we say or we'll kill your janitor," Harberts said as he stands up and walks across the room and takes a seat on a full-sized brown sofa.

Temple takes a moment to look around his boss's office, with its wall hung African hunting trophies, honorary degree plaques, plush carpet, and the large framed photograph of Harberts and Merle Haggard's bus driver drinking beer while sitting on wooden horses.

"Could call the FBI...hell, better not," Harberts mumbled. "Sure was easier back in the old days. Years and years ago. Had a real director then. A real man of action. The kind of agent you could count on."

"You mean Hoover, sir?"

"What?"

"J. Edgar Hoover. Is that who you are talking about, sir?"

"Get your head out of your butt crack, Temple. I'm not talking about Hoover, goddamned cross-dressing gargoyle. I mean that other guy, Ethan or something."

"Ethan, sir?" Temple said. "I'm not following you, Mister Secretary."

"Oh hell, don't you know your history? How'd you get this job anyway, kid? Was your dad a huge donor or something?"

"Actually, yes, he was."

"I'm talking about that Zimbles or Zombie guy, you know, Ethan, or whatever," Harberts says, somewhat exasperated.

"Sir," Temple says in disbelief. "Are you talking about Efrem Zimbalist Junior?"

Harberts stands up, slaps Temple on the back and strides over to his desk and takes a seat again.

"That's the guy. Now that was a Federal law enforcement officer."

"Uh, no sir. That was an actor."

"Yessiree, my boy. Much bravo on that guy. Hell of an FBI man."

"It was just a TV show, sir."

"And his daughter was hotter than three days in hell," Harberts winks.

Temple retakes his position in front of his boss's desk. "Uh, sir. Maybe we should revisit the topic at hand. Jasper...dossier...drug cartel," Temple said.

"Of course my boy," Harberts said. "No White House, no FBI. How about the CIA, maybe they can help."

"Probably not, sir. They're still a little upset about that comment the President made on Fox."

"What comment?"

"The one about them being so ineffective, they couldn't sneak up on a dead man."

"Oh, yeah. Sensitive bastards, aren't they?" Harberts taps his fingers rhythmically on his desk top. "Hey," he said, "What are their demands, anyway? Aw hell, it doesn't matter. We can't be doing business with the cartels. Unless they got oil. How about the Vice President? Maybe he's got some ideas."

Temple shakes his head. "Sorry, sir. Won't work. He's out on the speech tour getting ready for his campaign for the White House next election. Not available."

"Presidential campaign? What a waste of time. Hell, nobody even knows who Paul is."

"Mike, sir."

"Mike?"

"Mike, Mister Secretary. The Vice President's name is Mike."

"No shit? Who the hell is Paul?"

"No idea, sir," Temple takes four steps to a camouflage-colored chair, sits down and crosses his left leg over his right knee. "Mister Secretary," he says, "maybe we could try the military. Quite possibly they could get some intel from Mexico on how to handle Reyes."

Harbert's jerks his head away from his TV viewing to stare at Temple. "Mother Mary and Joseph, boy. Hell no, we can't call the military! My God, the Head of the Joint Chiefs, old General Pickens wants to nuke everything south of El Paso already."

"Because of illegal immigration, sir?"

"No, no. Nothing like that . He had some houseboy named Miquel for a while. Turns out, Miguel was playing 'Muzzle the Weasel' with the General's mail-order Korean bride. One day, the old five-star fool walked in on the two of them in an impromptu session of canal diving. He ran the boy off. Kept the wife, though. Says she's permanently damaged. Won't let him do the belly bump now unless he dresses like a matador and hums Ricky Martin songs during the mating dance. Tough deal."

Temple stands up. "Well, that leaves Homeland Security, sir."

"Sit down, Temple."

Temple sits.

"Let's get something straight here. Sometimes you don't know shit. Hell, Homeland Security is just another agency on the gameboard trying to build up their monopoly money. Give Congress a good reason why they exist. Right now they're over at a budget committee meeting trying to convince some Wisconsin Senator that we are about to be attacked by Iraq, Afghanistan, Iran, and Pakistan, not to mention some Australian outback aborigines that threaten to drop dynamite strapped wombats onto the Washington Monument, and a radical new terrorist organization call Nova Scotians for Clean Air. Busy people."

Temple said, "Well, sir..."

"No," the secretary interrupts. "Don't even say, 'NSA'. They're probably listening in on newlyweds' phone conversations while they clutch their driveshafts to the point of carpal tunnel. It's pointless."

"Sir, that's not what I was to say," Temple said, rising slowly from his seat. "There is one group we can contact. Someone totally outside the beltway."

Harberts looks straight at this assistant. "I was afraid you were going to say that. Are you serious?"

"Yes sir, I am."

"Temple, those people are a mess. A political nightmare. It gives me a cold chill just thinking about it. This could all turn to shit in a hurry if that group of intellectual misalignments comes riding down the hill."

"The President likes them. And, they are his supporters, sir."

"Yeah, I know."

"We can still call the FBI, sir."

"Yeah, and I can pull diamonds out of my ass, too," Harberts said. "Do you have a way to contact them?"

Temple goes to a briefcase sitting on a small table along the wall under a stuffed jackal's head with a rat in its mouth. He removed a large file and placed it on the desk in front of Harbert's. The file is black, marked with gold letters that say, "Top Security – Eyes Only."

Harbert's opens the cover. Inside is a cover sheet. Codename: ECLECTICS. He looks at the Temple. "Where are they right now? Do you have any idea?"

Temple nods slowly.

Harbert's frowns slightly. "Why do I have a sudden tightening feeling in my colon?"

Temple shrugs slightly.

"Okay, my boy, fill me in. Where are they? What are they doing and how fast can we get in contact with them?"

"Well, Mister Secretary, I took the liberty to let them know they may be needed. Right now they are…."

CHAPTER 2

Skeet Jackson yawns and stretches. Or, at least he stretches as far as a 6'2", 210-pound man can stretch while driving. He pulls a CD out of the center console and pushes it into the dashboard player he'd had installed in the used Lincoln after he'd bought it. A little driving music by David Allan Coe, "The Ride."

"Can you turn that down a little?" Paulie asks.

"Nope."

Paulie looks at Jackson, dressed in his basketball shorts with an Iowa Hawkeye logo on the front. He's wearing a faded yellow shirt that has a hole on the chest just big enough to show some short hairs and a tan that matches the one on his legs, arms and face. His feet are protected by a well worn pair of New Balance shoes and socks so short you could barely tell they existed.

Paulie said, "Hey, I've got a call on the hotline."

"You call your phone the hotline?" Skeet asks.

"Well, it's the one they gave me. What else would I call it?"

"You gonna answer it or just let it buzz?"

Paulie puts the phone to his ear, "Yes, this is me." He turns to Skeet and whispers, "It's him!"

Skeet shrugs and starts humming along to the music.

"Yes, sir," Paulie said. "Uh, well yes, I received the instructions. We're headed there right now. Prepared?" Paulie looks at Skeet while raising his eyebrows. "Well, uh, I think we're prepared. Russian? Uh, no sir. The guy with me? He's from Iowa, sir. Okay," Paulie looks at Skeet, "Do you speak Russian by chance?"

"Nope," Skeet replies. "Dated a French teacher once, though."

Paulie speaks back into the phone, "He doesn't speak Russian but he did date a French teacher. Uh, I'll check." He turns back to Skeet. "What was her name? He says might know her. Uh, wait. He says never mind.

Turning his attention back to the phone, Paulie jots some notes on a piece of paper, then disconnects.

Skeet said, "So where are we going?"

Paulie said, "The Last Dive. It's a hotel along the coastline about 40 miles ahead."

"Last Dive? Bet that's a nice place."

"Actually, it's pretty nice. It's a place where politicians and their close, you know, secret friends meet."

"Hey, ain't that the place where that congressman fell out the window or something?"

"Yeah, sure did. You see, the hotel is built right on the edge of a cliff, so the windows on the east side look right down into the Atlantic."

"So the old incumbent just fell out the window?"

"Well, he didn't just fall."

"You mean he was pushed?"

"No, no, nothing like that, "Paulie said. "You see, he and Dory Stoopen, a local call girl, were doing a little afternoon conjugal conga, and in all the excitement, they got too close to the window and, well, out they went."

Skeet smiles. "No kidding, so she really was a fallen woman?"

Paulie rolls down his window, retrieves a cigarette from his pocket and lights it. "Yep," he said. "And apparently the unfortunate incident befell right at the apex of the event, if you catch my drift."

Jackson grabs the cigarette from Blumenshine's lips and pitches it out the window. "That does give a whole new meaning to coming and going, but how, might I ask, would you know that little sensitive bit of info?"

Paulie frowns, watching in the rear-view mirror as his newly-lit tobacco bursts into a thousand sparks on the road behind the car, highlighted by a fading early evening sun. "It was in the photo," he said.

"What was in the photo?" Jackson asks.

"The look."

"The look? What look?"

"You know, the look a guy gets right at that moment," Paulie says, rolling his eyes up in his head, opening his mouth wide and shaking his entire body convulsively in demonstration.

Skeet stares at his friend's display a tad too long and drives partly off the road. "Holy shit, Paulie," he says after recovering control of the car. "I don't know what happens to you at that moment, but what you just did reminds me of the flinching and jerking my Grandpa did the time he hiccupped and swallowed a whole chaw of Skoal."

Paulie composes himself. "You know what I mean."

"Where the hell did this picture come from?" Skeet asks.

"It was on the front page of the Capitol Evening News. Showed them both stark naked going out the window. Of course the more sensitive areas were blacked out," Paulie says.

"Of course," Skeet says. "Is this a Washington thing, taking photos of lovers leaping out windows?"

Paulie pulled another cigarette from his pocket, which Jackson quickly grabs and dispatches, just as he did with the prior one. Paulie sighs loudly, "Dammit, stop that, and no, it's not a Washington thing. Apparently, he had a camera with a timer set to catch periodic moments of the event and, as luck would have it, their ecstasy induced exit is now a part of photographic history."

"Wow," Jackson exclaimed. "That's a helluva drop from what I hear. Did it kill 'em both?"

"Never found Dory. The congressman bobbed up down the coast a ways about a week later, all puffed up and bleached out, lookin' like the Pillsbury Doughboy after an extended microwave engagement," Paulie says, shaking his head slowly. "It was on Fox News, even."

"Wow, Fox, CNN, and everything?"

"Not CNN. Democratic Congressman."

"Oh."

Blumenshine looks at his friend and realizes why people seem to like Skeet so much. He's athletic and easygoing, and he has looks. Not movie star looks, just good looks. Paulie turns to look out his window, and as he does, he glances at the outside rearview mirror, catching his reflection looking back at him. He is definitely from a different mold, he isn't cool or easygoing, and women don't find him attractive, even though he does have movie star looks. The problem is his movie star looks amount to a strong resemblance to Wilford Brimley. The lines around his eyes seem to have deepened over the past few months. There was no mystery to the sudden aging. After all, the script for his life would make "The Walking Dead" look normal by comparison.

It had all begun when his mother died, leaving him a heavily mortgaged radio station and his wayward 50-year-old sister to care for. The latter came complete with an assortment of wigs, leather skin from daily tanning booth radiation treatments, and facial makeup that looked like it had been applied with a cement trowel. Ruth, the sister, claimed to be an exotic entertainer of the highest order, although she seemed to spend most of her professional time in truck stops, baseball stadium bathrooms and various alleys in D.C. where she claims she was entertaining the homeless by performing something she had personally choreographed called 'Dumpster Dancing.'

Occasionally, Ruth would come to visit, usually during a recuperation period from some social malady she claimed she had contracted from a toilet seat or unclean hand towel. During these times she would regale the family with stories of her romantic and professional exploits with various men named Big Earl, Panhandle Pete, and Jaundiced Jimmy Wheeler. She would continue with this monologue while chain-smoking Lucky Strikes until she would start to wheeze, which invariably was followed by a coughing spell so violent that it caused the ground in West Virginia to vibrate enough to register on the Richter scale and initiate phone calls from North Carolinians to late night radio show hosts with testimony that they had heard the mating call of a distant and lonely Bigfoot. At the end of this volcanic air expulsion episode, Ruth would grasp at the first piece of woven or felted material she could find, such as the tablecloth, and then orally deposit upon it a noticeable portion of expectorated phlegm. She would then closely examine the disengaged object for a moment before asking anyone in the immediate area if they were willing to check the item for blood specks because that was a sign of poor health...something she said she wished to avoid.

The previously mentioned radio station, which was part of the inheritance package, was a quarter million dollars in debt from collateralized loans. How this was possible was a total mystery to Paulie. After all, it wasn't a brick building with executives and secretaries and advertising salesmen working in small cubicles while airing top 40 computer music hits interspersed with witless commentary from DJ's whose education levels would make Jethro Bodeen look like an MIT graduate. Nothing that good. It was an internet station, and not that popular of an internet station at that. Paulie wondered who in his right mind would loan that kind of money to an old woman with only a computerized radio station?

Ruth provided the answer one night shortly after their mother's death as the two siblings were sorting through the deceased's belongings. It was simple, she had told Paulie between deep lung hits on a filterless cigarette. Henry Kepler, down at the Gays Creek Bank, had loaned their mother money on a regular basis because good old Ma had been handling his spiritual and physical needs, with the emphasis on physical, for quite some time. When Paulie expressed his doubts as to the accuracy of such a claim, Ruth validated the theory by reciting the story of Henry's unfortunate days of youth, and how that particular time period brought them to the here and now dismal debt problem.

It seemed that one slightly rainy afternoon many years ago, Henry Kepler was riding his new Stingray bicycle on Dogtown Road near its steepest part, known as 'Sheepshit Grade'. It was so named because of Norbert Ball's flock that crossed there daily as they headed home after a full shift of grass-eating, leaving evidentiary deposits as they roamed.

Apparently, as he descended at rapidly increasing speed, Henry's front tire came in contact with a rather imposing multi-layered clump of post-digested sheep food. The effects were quite dramatic. Henry's bike, with Henry attached, tumbled end over end, then sideways, then end over end again some three hundred feet until both ceased their fall against a large pile of boulders at the base of the hill, stopping only because the large gray rocks would let them go no further, despite the fact that rider and ridee were gaining air speed expeditiously at impact.

Surprisingly, Henry's injuries were not as severe as one might assume from such an unfortunate event, that is, until the local volunteer fire department arrived on the scene, responding from the annual West Virginia coal-mining and beer-guzzling festival to the call of assistance needed. The totally untrained and completely inebriated firemen excitedly began yanking at the bent bicycle, and jerking feverishly at the bike chains in their attempt to free the unconscious youth from his bondage, apparently ignorant to the fact that sensitive human body parts were entangled therein, and thus removing one testicle and dramatically damaging Henry's once-straight future mating appendage.

Henry was changed forever. He never married, and as far as anyone knew, never even dated after the traumatic incident. Apparently, the now-deceased Mrs. Blumenshine had somehow become his geriatric sex kitten in exchange for loans, but now that she was gone, he was demanding payment. There had to be some way to handle it, Paulie thought. He looked at Ruth, straddling the arm of the living room couch while rolling a homemade cancer stick, a paper in one hand and a can of 'Uncle Bert's Fine Australian Tobacco' in the other.

"Hey Sis," he said.

She spit a small tobacco flake on the floor, then plucked a second one from her tongue and wiped it on the sofa. "What?" she answered.

He petted her arm. She jerked away.

"You know, you could really help us out here," he said, still smiling.

She gave him a crinkled-up look, and with all the over-tanned leather that posed for skin on her face, she could really crinkle.

"Oh yeah?" she asked suspiciously. "How so, fat boy?"

Paulie sat on the sofa cushion. "Well," he began, "I was thinking, maybe you could help old Henry out. You know, just a little here and there. It might buy us some time."

Without missing an inhale or turning her head, she said, "No."

"Why not?" Paulie whined.

"No way, tubby brother of mine," Ruth said, rising from the arm of the sofa and facing Paulie. "Why don't you do it? He's probably desperate enough. He might be ready for a plump partner. Besides, what do you think I am, anyway?"

"Well you're…" he said.

"A dancer," she spat back at him. "Besides, Hairless Helen told me about him."

"Who is Hairless Helen?" he asked, raising an eyebrow.

"She's a lady who entertains gentlemen down by the pier in Gays River City."

"You mean she's a streetwalker, in other words," Paulie said.

"Don't be so damn arrogant," Ruth retorted.

"Well," he said, "my mistake. I just assumed that, due to the fact that the pier is also called 'Wine Piss Alley' because that's where all the skid row bums live, and the docks are full of underpaid, sex-starved illegals…well sorry," he said.

"Apology accepted," Ruth said, returning to her place on the sofa's arm to begin rolling another cigarette.

"So, Helen told you what, exactly, Ruth?" Paulie asked after a moment's silence.

"Huh?" Ruth said "Oh, yeah, Helen. Well, Helen prides herself in being totally professional and completely unbiased, so she entertains men of all persuasions courteously and competently."

"Uh-huh," Paulie said.

"Provided, of course, they are able to remit her standard twenty-dollar handling fee."

"Handling fee."

"Yes, handling fee. The normal operating fee for all professionals in Helen's field," Ruth said

"Which is…" Paulie inquired.

"Entertainment. So, Helen will not turn anyone away...almost," Ruth said, stabbing out the cigarette she just finished into an ashtray, then reaching into Paulie's pocket to grab one of his Marlboros which she then held up in front of his face. "Paulie, do you realize that the filters attached to the cigs you smoke are full of chemicals?" Ruth said with sincere concern eyeing the cigarette while again searching his pocket for matches. "Filters are bad for you."

"Uh, yeah," he said, "But they're cigarettes."

"Exactly," she said, twisting the filter off, placing the cigarette in her mouth, and lighting it with a match she then discarded to the floor. "Tobacco is natural! Filters are man-made. Christ, Paulie, when will you learn?"

"I don't know," he answered, his voice fading in confusion.

Ruth looked up in the air for a moment, as if gathering her thoughts. Apparently unable to find them, she looked at her brother. "What were we talking about?" She asked.

"Hairless Helen, her code of ethics, and how Henry Kepler didn't fit in," he answered, looking at the twisted-off filter Ruth had handed to him.

"Oh, yes, that's right" she began, "Well, Helen said that Henry showed up one night and offered her sixty dollars for an entertainment session, which of course, she thought was wonderful. I mean, triple time pay for the same work...well, you know how it goes."

"Not really, but go ahead," Paulie added.

"So she took the sixty, and all was well until Henry unwrapped himself. Well, let me tell ya, she told him no way, right off. Said after she got a gander at his goose she voided the verbal contract. She said she gave him the sixty back and offered him another fifty if he would let her take a picture of it. She was sure she could cut some kind of deal with those Ripley people over at the 'Believe It or Not' show. She said it gave her nightmares for a week."

Paulie just sat and looked at his sister, wondering how they had come from the same womb.

She turned and smiled at him. "So, the end of the story is that old Mommsy was taking care of Henry Kepler," she said.

"Good God," Paulie mumbled.

"Well, Paulie, you know people always said how Mom was so kind and generous, and we both know she was flexible about things." She took a deep drag of smoke. "And God knows, with Henry she must have been flexible." She exhales. "Real flexible."

Paulie shakes his head and suddenly he's back in the car. He glances at his friend, who is now signing along with the CD player on some song about a Redneck Mother. Jackson sees him looking at him. "Jerry Jeff Walker," he said, smiling, "Great beer-drinking music."

Paulie Blumenshine looks back out the window at the passing trees, cars, and houses. Houses probably filled with happy people with happy lives. Hell, the houses even look happy, almost smiling, if that was possible. His house didn't look happy, he thought. No, his house looked like it wanted to kick you in the sack when you walked up to it. Once you get inside, it's worse. He would look forward to these returning home encounters in a fashion he is sure was similar to how Iraqi soldiers in the Gulf War looked forward to daily visits from American Abrams tanks. One problem seemed to follow another.

Just recently, his son, Paulie Jr., had decided that he was gay. In this day of modern living, such a statement isn't in and of itself, all that shocking. But when the one hundred twenty pound, six foot college freshman with red hair, and endless freckles, told his father of his revelation, Paulie felt the fatherly need to inquire about this news at the dinner table that night. "Junior, I guess I'm a little surprised," he said in a reasonable parental tone.

"I don't know why you would be surprised, Dad," Junior said. "It was basically your idea."

"My idea?" Paulie said, raising his right eyebrow. "How could all this, uh, gay stuff be my idea?"

"Well, you always said that when something difficult comes along in life, I should make a decision and move on it," Junior said.

"Uh, okay. So, Junior, what was it that happened that made you realize you were gay?" Paulie asked slowly, almost fearing the response.

"I'm failing math," Junior said.

Didn't see that coming.

"Uh, math? You're failing math and that made you think that you're gay?" Paulie asked, confused, but oddly relieved.

"Let me clarify," Junior said. "I'm not sure I'm gay, probably not. But after I saw the results of my last math test, well, I had to come to a life-changing decision, and for some reason that's the first thing that popped into my head, so I'm going to go with it."

Paulie decided to let it go in hopes that the confused young man would become unconfused at a later time. That hope crashed and burned a week later, when Junior called his father at work and announced he was getting married, and to a man, no less. The future groom or bride's name was Art, and Junior was bringing him to dinner that night to meet the family. Paulie hung up the phone, expecting his next call would be from Maury Povich with an invitation to headline his next show.

That evening, when Paulie gazed upon his son's choice for a soulmate, he realized that he was even more dismayed than he thought he was going to be. Art, the fiancé, was much older than Junior, in fact he was Paulie's age, and the similarities to Paulie didn't stop there. He was short, overweight,and had very little hair, most of which seemed to grow from his ears. To top all that off, he seemed to suffer from some sort of palsy. Art had, a short time ago, discovered that he loved boys. As it turned out, Art's revelation was fine with his wife Alice, who had a discovery of her own during a recent home renovation. Her discovery was that she loved plumbers, electricians, carpet-layers, and any other tradesman who showed the right amount of butt crack while performing in home repair services.

At dinner that evening, during which time there was much male handholding and cooing, interrupted only by his sister's intermittent hacking, Paulie found himself mentally adrift in a sea of 'what the fuck?' This feeling was magnified near the end of the meal, which Paulie didn't touch, when Art stated that this was the last night that anyone was going to be able to call him Art. He said he had an appointment with the county judge in the morning to have his name legally changed. He said he was initiating the name change to make a statement. He went on to say that during a disastrous relationship he'd had prior to Junior, he had been physically abused, thus causing the need for a lifesaving operation. Therefore, in honor of the surgery that saved him, his name would now be...

"No, please," Paulie said, "No more surprises tonight."

"Quiet, Dad," Junior said in anticipation.

"Yeah, butterball, let the shakemeister spit it out," Ruth chimed in.

Art tremored and slowly stood , spreading two quivering arms out like wings, he smiled and gasped, "Semi-colon."

"Wonderful!" Junior said, clapping.

Ruth started laughing and slapping the table.

"Well," Paulie said. "I think that's all for tonight. I don't believe we can outdo that." Paulie started to rise from the table as Ruth then began coughing violently, probably due to the fact that she was attempting to smoke while laughing. She continued to cough and punch herself in the chest until she went into a mini-convulsion. Blindly searching for the tablecloth, she instead grabbed the first thing she could find, which happened to be a shirt sleeve, one that Paulie happened to be wearing. Once it was firmly in her grasp, she loudly deposited on it what looked like a miniature model for Steve McQueen's arch-enemy in "The Blob."

"Shouldn't be too much longer, should it be Blume?" Jackson asked his daydreaming partner.

"Huh? Oh, no, it's not too much farther," Paulie answered.

Skeet returns to his singing, which Paulie has to admit, isn't too bad. Jackson always looked fit and happy. He ran five or six miles a day. He had just upped it to seven miles, just for the hell of it, he'd told Paulie. 'Damn,' Paulie thought to himself. "I couldn't walk five or six blocks without a respirator." Two weeks earlier, after a complete examination, Paulie's doctor had told him he was overweight, smoked too much, drank too much, his cholesterol was through the roof, and his blood pressure was 190 over "Jesus Christ! Call an ambulance."

To continue that happy downward spiral, when he arrived home after his appointment that evening, somewhat depressed at his future prospects for living, he was met by his suitcase-toting wife in the doorway of his suburban home. She told him that she had found out the reason for their lack of sex, and it was good news for Paulie. It wasn't his fault after all, for being dumpy, homely, and totally unattractive to even the most desperate of women. No. It was a female condition called vaginal dysfunction, for which the only known cure was prickly pears and iguana liver oil massage. She closed by saying that at this very moment, she was departing for a therapy colony somewhere in the Nevada desert called the 'House of Sensitive Manipulation' in the company of the colony leader, a world-renowned genital malfunction repair specialist named Claude. Once there, she would partake in a recovery program by ingesting the aforementioned cactus plants and attending what she called 'Creation and Stimulation' therapy sessions that dealt with nude bonfire dancing and potato sack races with the medical staff, headed of course by Claude. She then walked past Paulie to a beat up red GMC pickup, complete with gun rack and gun, that had pulled into the driveway. Tossing her luggage into the bed of the truck, she got in the passenger seat and waved through the cracked windshield at her husband, while the driver, who had long dark, greasy-looking hair and matching beard, no shirt, and a black patch over his right eye, backed them out onto the street and away.

Only then did Paulie realize that this entire event had happened without him uttering a word.

"Hey Skeet, have you ever heard of something called vaginal dysfunction?"

"Hmmm, no. At least, I've never seen a commercial for it, "he responds. "If it was important, there'd be an infomercial, at least."

"Sheila says that's her problem," Paulie says. "She left a while back to get the cure for it with some fella named Claude who uses prickly pears to fix it. Gonna stay in the desert for a while."

"She's gonna live in the desert with a dude named Claude?"

"Yep."

"Do you know this Claude?

"No, why?"

Jackson looks out the corner of his eye at his passenger. "Buddy, ain't you a little concerned about some extracurricular activity in that scenario?"

"Naw, I guess not," Paulie said slowly. "She told me once, that no matter what, she would always save herself and her feminine property just for me."

"Whatever you say, but I'm not so sure I want a woman saving her feminine property for me after some stranger drove a small cactus down her street a few times, "Jackson said.

But Paulie hasn't heard him, his mind has left the car again. Looking back, he really hadn't seen Sheila's leaving on the horizon. What he had seen even less on the horizon was his mother-in-law moving in while his wife was moving out. How the hell had that happened? But it had. He could see her now, sitting in his recliner. A shriveled up, white-haired South Carolinian who believed deeply in reincarnation, a natural process that she hoped could somehow be abolished after discovering at a Tarot card reading at the county fair that Confederate General Stonewall Jackson had come back as the lead singer for Kool and the Gang.

Buela, the mother-in-law, had once weighed over 300 pounds, but thanks to a strict diet of bran flakes and prune juice, she had literally defecated two hundred pounds away. It was a feat so great that she was actually named Charmin Toilet Tissue Woman of the Year. Of course, there were some side effects to the epic loss of pounds. Due to the fact that she was eighty years old she had serious old-people's skin sag prior to the diet, but after losing weight equivalent in proportion to a baby buffalo, she no longer needed all the hide required to hold a tenth of a ton of cellulite. Therefore, she had an epidermic droop that was so severe that the tattoo on her upper arm of her daughter's caricature at birth, now looked like a map of Argentina.

On the bright side, she no longer needed to diet. She switched to eating large quantities of mixed nuts and nacho chips that she crunched loudly while smoking Swisher Sweet cigars and slurping down copious amounts of single malt whiskey that she drank from large plastic cups that she periodically used to soak her cigar-stained dentures. Sometimes simultaneously.

Paulie had now reached a point of either desperation or numbness. So much so, that he had actually begun slamming booze with the old creature. They would drink late into the night, listening to her Frank Fontaine records and watching Matlock reruns while she told him stories about her youth, like the time she lost her virginity to Billy John Johnson behind Uncle Bobby John Johnson's outhouse. She said with pride that Billy John had been so passionate that night that he gave her a hickey on her neck that remained to this very day. Of course, gravity had now pulled it down to her hip.

Paulie had cut back on the late night drinking-in-the-dark sessions with the old buzzard recently. He'd started losing interest after he picked up the plastic cup of Carls' Kicking Kentucky Bourbon and slammed it back, only to find that his mouth was being bombarded by dozens of tiny particles he was soon to discover were crushed cashew and almond bits, followed by the collision of his upper lip with the dentures that had crushed the aforementioned nuts. His immediate gagging was interrupted only by Fontaine's cover of 'Rawhide' and his drinking partner's call of, "That's my cup, dumbass!"

Back in the car, Paulie sighs.

"What's the problem, Blume?" Skeet asks.

"Do you think all of this will work, Skeet?"

"All of what?"

"Well, the Russians, the documents, the guy from Juarez, all of it."

Skeet reaches over and pats his friend's arm. "Sure it will," he says. "What could go wrong? As long as the Ruskies don't kidnap us and torture us for the papers, and a Mexican cartel doesn't shoot us and bury us in the desert, and of course, if the Feds don't indict us for the three or four hundred criminal codes we probably already violated, everything will smooth. Provided, of course, you have the only phone in America the NSA isn't listening in on, and Homeland Security doesn't have snipers stationed up ahead, I'd say we're in pretty good shape...mostly."

They drove down a long lane and came to a group of buildings overlooking the ocean. The Lincoln's headlights are now on due to the evening darkness and as they came to a stop they could see two people looking out the window at them.

"Well," Paulie says, "like Reagan said, there's the evil abscess."

"That's evil axis, Paulie."

Paulie stares at the man's face looking back at him. "There's a difference?" he asks.

As they slowly get out of their car, Paulie stops his friend. "This is really a big deal, Skeet."

"I know," Skeet says. "We could get shot, ya know."

Paulie thinks back to his family. His wife. His son. His deceased mother. His sister, and the last drink he had with his mother-in-law. "There's worse things," he said.

CHAPTER 3

THE RUSSIAN WOMAN scans the landscape as she looks out the picture window, awaiting the arrival of the two Americans.

"Any people coming yet, Olga?" a voice behind her asks.

"Nyet," she answers.

"Dammit Olga. It's NO! It's NO! Do not say NYET!" Her husband fires at her. "We are capitalists now! Talk like Americans. We need to blend in. Be like me."

She looks back at the man who calls himself Bobby, but whose real name is Boris. He is wearing a gray shirt, gray pants, and a gray fur hat. He is all gray. His complexion is even gray. His body is stocky and slow-moving. His head is large and square-looking, with large ears, a prominent almost bulbous nose, and a split between his front teeth. He has a brushed-back, flat-top haircut, and his eyebrows are so long and bushy that he combs them with a hair brush. It looks like Stalin, Lenin, and Khrushchev all decided to inseminate a peasant woman, shook hands, took turns mounting up, and then let the best sperm win. The fertilization race was apparently a tie.

"Yes, dear," Olga said, returning her gaze to the window. She actually likes looking out the window at the Last Dive, which she and her husband run as a business and occupy as a home.

Having the ocean just outside their back door was nice. Of course, after growing up in Krasnoyarsk, Siberia where she worked as a livery stable hand caring for retired Cossack horses in temperatures as low as 90 degrees below zero, the flooded basement of an east Arkansas outhouse would seem nice.

Times were bad in Siberia. She still hadn't gotten over the loss of Vlad, an ancient but beautiful horse that belonged to retired colonel Stanska, who was also ancient, but not so beautiful. Vlad wandered from his stall out into the mid-winter weather in the aforementioned temperature one night. When she finally located him standing near a large boulder, she threw a rope around his neck to take him back inside. However, unbeknownst to Olga, the horse had died several hours earlier of old age and exposure and due to the extreme temperature, he was now frozen solid. Ignorant of this information, the well-intended horse-saver gave the attached rope a jerk. Immediately Vlad's head snapped off from the rest of his body, which in turn, due to the sudden imbalance, tipped over onto the frozen Siberian ground, and shattered into pieces. One hundred and eight pieces, to be exact. Olga knew, because with the aid of her mostly toothless boyfriend Igor, they had loaded eleven burlap potato sacks with the body parts and then dogsledded to the home of Colonel Stanska to deliver the bad news.

When they arrived, the Colonel, a little 97-year old man who looked like a human raisin, was sitting near an old stone fireplace, warming himself, drinking vodka, and talking to a picture of Rasputin. While Olga was attempting to explain the unfortunate incident, the Colonel began using a stiletto to poke in one of the sacks of horse that she and Igor had brought in. Apparently a piece of Vlad had thawed sufficiently to allow it to be skewered, at which time the old soldier held it over the fire to roast. That's when Olga, somewhat startled, told the colonel that the meat he was cooking was Vlad. Suddenly, he started laughing hideously and began to disrobe. Item by item he threw his clothing into the fireplace, then broke out in a Russian folk dance, circa 1920. Olga whispered to Igor that it was time to leave, which they did, but only after Igor snatched a couple of pieces of Vlad the Russian Wonder Horse and put them in his furry pocket.

Olga longed to leave her home of ice and snow and go to America. Igor, being the feeble minded and cowardly socialist leg-humper that he was, told her these thoughts were foolish and probably dangerous. He would stand before her, pointing his tobacco-stained index finger at her nose while he lectured her for ungodly periods of time on the evils of America and anywhere else outside the Siberian oasis where they lived. When he finished with his diatribe, he would put his hands on his hips, nod once briskly, and flash a gaping smile at her. The oral cave in his head consisted of a lot of barren gums and two teeth, both of which stood side by side in the very front of his mouth on the top side pointing down, making him look very much like the famous American cartoon rabbit, but not as cute.

He would always leave Olga with the proposal that she should abandon all hope of happiness and become his wife, share his political ideals, move into his shack and provide him with dozens of little Siberianites, or whatever the hell they're called. That's not his offer verbatim, but that's how she took it. She managed to delay a decision on his tempting offer in hopes that something better would come along – like perhaps a fight to the death with a Sumo wrestler covered with weeping boils. She would have gotten a different boyfriend, but the pickings in Krasnoyarsk were beyond slim. Actually none.

Finally, one evening, while sitting in her one-room apartment, slamming fermented potato juice shots and staring at the handle of an old wooden soup ladle (while entertaining thoughts of using said soup dipper in an un lady-like fashion, for short but relatively intense distraction from her situation), she came to a decision. She would go to Igor's two-room shack, taking along her last bottle of vodka, profess her ongoing loyalty to the Slav people, strip naked, throw herself on the urine-stained mattress he'd had since boyhood, and consummate the agreement with her future husband.

They had never had such an encounter before because Igor never felt the time was right, and Olga really didn't find him attractive...at all. But Olga decided this was it. Tonight's the night. Her life seemed pointless. Her future prospects were dim. Besides, there was nothing to watch on her black-and-white TV, except a continuous broadcast of a military band marching around Red Square. Also, she was drunk, and of course, she still had vivid memories of the splinter-filled engagement she had with the previous soup ladle liaison. She felt certain that a similar encounter with Igor would be more enjoyable, if only marginally.

So, coat on back, hat on head, and gloved hands gripping the vodka, she embarked on her journey. The sky was dark, the wind was stiff, the snow deep, and the temperature had dipped to minus holy shit, as she made her way to her unsuspecting lover-to-be's home at the base of a frozen mountain, which, of course, the only kind of mountain they have in Krasnoyarsk.

When she arrived at Igor's she wanted to make an entrance. Throw open the door and surprise him. That was the plan. Knowing from previous experience that the door was only held shut with a chair leaning against it, she raised her fur-covered, booted foot, staggered a little, braced herself and mule-kicked the door with sufficient force to make if fly open, disengaging the weak hinges, breaking the door frame, and landing the wooden slab prostrate upon the floor. "Surprise!" She yelled.

And surprised he was. Igor, apparently not anticipating any visitors on this particular evening, had decided to dabble in a little sexual stimulus as well. However, he had opted for a session of 'mano a mano,' in which he played both parts. There he was, in the middle of the room, just out of reach of the fallen door, with a firm grip on his male mood enhancer with his right hand, while his left hand held a photograph near a lit candle on an old wooden table.

When the door crashed in, Igor let out a scream. First of surprise, then of pain, since his startled jump made him bump the candle, causing hot wax to flip onto his full-mast manhood. The photograph, which was instantly too close to the candle flame, ignited, burning his fingers and causing him to drop it to the floor. Then, simultaneously clutching his fried pleasure-partner and emitting a high-pitched yelp that caused a dog sled team five miles away to bark, he sprinted past Olga, out into the Siberian winter evening, totally naked.

She stood there for a moment, listening to Igor's cries fade into a distant night, dumbfounded at the events that had unfolded before her. Then she gathered her thoughts and did what any woman would do when she had interrupted her man in such an embarrassing situation, knowing that he was in peril of losing his life, or at least several body parts from the extreme conditions...she grabbed the burning photo to see what he was whacking off to. After extinguishing the edges of the picture, she used the flashlight she'd brought with her to study the photo that her nearly-betrothed had been using as a workout aid for his prostate exercise.

"Shit," she said to herself as the person started to come into focus. "I don't believe it."

It was bad enough that she had walked all the way here tonight to let dumbass Igor the Adventureless have his way with her, and that she had even decided to stay in Unpleasant Valley and be sired by him, releasing upon the boring populace even more boring populace, but this was too much. She moved an open jar of Humpback Whale Lubricating Jelly from the only chair in the room and sat down. It was one thing that Igor had decided to release his army of mini Igor's by hand onto the old wooden floor of the shack, which, judging by the looks of it, he had done quite often. But the photograph was too much. A Vladimir Putin look-alike, flashing a smile and a left butt cheek at the camera, dressed only in army boots and a standard Russian fur hat. Hmm, maybe it wasn't a lookalike. No, had to be. Probably.

Olga got up, dropped the picture and thought to herself that maybe she should track Igor down out in the freezing night, but suddenly remembering the horse dismemberment with similar temperatures, she figured to hell with it. Besides, the object Igor was holding as he ran past her would not have qualified him for any Member of the Month Club. In fact, the phrase "hamster dick" came to mind. Oh well, there was the vodka, there was the hot soup, and a hotter soup ladle. I am woman. Hear me roar.

Boris broke into her memory track.

"Do you see anything yet?" he asks.

"No, I told you, I'll say when I see, and I don't see yet, so I don't say yet," she answered. She looked again at the man she had married. She married him because he said that he would take her to America. That was the only reason, and he had done just what he said. He brought her to America. She had met him in a small town near the Ob river after she left her roots behind and journeyed out one morning with an old man driving a rendering works wagon full of frozen animal carcasses. Boris hadn't exactly swept her off her feet, but he had intrigued her with his endless stories of his life in Moscow and his career with the KGB.

After a while she noticed all the KGB stories seemed to happen in the men's room. Odd, Olga thought, that the espionage masterminds of modern day Russia would hold their top-secret meetings in a toilet. Finally, after prodding, Boris admitted that he was actually the bathroom attendant on the second floor of the Secret Police building. However, he told her, that did require a certain security clearance and that he had held that level of clearance for nearly twenty years until he was let go when it was discovered he had attempted to order winter fishing gloves made of genuine antelope skin, which he had found in a Bass Pro Shop magazine sent to him from an American place called 'Missouri.'

But, he told her, before he was terminated, he had discovered what he was certain was a secret code. The code, he said, was on a piece of two-ply toilet paper that he had observed attached to the bottom of the shoe of a KGB agent, who was passed out on a toilet seat from a midday vodka overdose. Boris had actually laid on his back and pushed himself under the stall door to retrieve the item without disturbing the drunken spy. He then placed it in a plastic bag and carried it in his wallet to this very day in the hope of discovering someone, someplace, who could decipher the faintly-written, coded message, which he could then use to regain this position with the KGB. Maybe even move up the professional ladder. The third floor john was his goal.

He was certain the paper contained critical information, although he admitted it would be difficult to read, due to the fact that it had probably been urinated on. He offered to show the prize possession to Olga, but she declined, asking him to leave it in his wallet until some more appropriate time...like maybe after she died.

Overall, being married to Boris had been an adventure, albeit not an erotic one. On the night of their wedding, as Olga disrobed rapidly and headed to the marital mattress to receive the cure for virginal scourge she had been strapped with all these long years, her new husband announced that he believed that sex should only be used in procreation. Furthermore, due to the fact that he was not prepared to have little Boris boys and girls running around yet, there would be no penile/vaginal activity at this time. He made this statement like a prison warden reading a death warrant to a person about to be gassed. Olga received it the same way. The disappointment Olga felt only magnified by one hundred as she watched Boris strip his clothes in order to put on his nightshirt. It was then that she discovered that, unlike Igor, Boris carried a male stem so prominent that it was easily comparable to the one dearly-departed Vlad the horse carried, which she had admired many times. From afar, of course.

In the following months, she learned to just sigh and go to sleep, being a dutiful but physically-deprived wife, who would only occasionally clutch her hips to the heat radiator in their small apartment that would vibrate wildly as the temperature rose.

Back at the window now, Boris stands near her.

"They should be arriving soon," he said. "I must prepare." Then he turned to walk away.

Olga can see her reflection in the window. She was perfect by Russian rules. That meant she was dumpy by the American standards. She planned to correct that, and had actually begun dieting. She would become a beautiful American woman, and Boris would find her irresistible. Someday, she told herself, someday. In the meantime, if the opportunity arose, she would not cheat on him. Well, at least, not again. The first time really wasn't cheating, at least not quite.

After all, it had been such a crazy, spontaneous moment. Landing in the airport in New York. People running here and there, amidst all the excitement. Boris had gone off in hopes of getting directions to the Russian Embassy and acquiring some transportation. Olga sat and watched the luggage spin around on some machine, while listening to the airport announcements being made. The young man sat down beside her and introduced himself as Dale. He struck up a pleasant conversation with the 30-year-old Russian woman all dressed in black. She thought he was nice looking, even though he had a silver dot on the left side of his nose and a similarly-colored piece of metal shaped like a spike sticking through his tongue. His hair was short and black, and his voice had a high quality to it. He was wearing a light green jacket that said 'Jets' on it. He looked very slim, and to Olga, very attractive.

At first, Olga had wished that Boris would hurry back, but now she was hoping he wouldn't. She and the young man were enjoying a talk. Actually, her visitor did most of the talking. Olga just listened. She would nod occasionally while she took in the sight of her new friend, from the brown cowboy boots up to the blue jeans, to the jacket all the way to the dark blue eyes that were staring back at her, causing a familiar flutter in her stomach. Suddenly she felt his hand on hers and was immediately taken by how soft it felt. The soft hands pulled her from her seat gently and he walked her across the airport, leading her into a public bathroom, where she knew that she, a married woman, shouldn't go. She felt helpless and knew the moment was in control. Her guide opened a stall door and took her inside. Olga and the stranger embraced and clutched and kissed. Olga abandoned all of her Russian values and decided this was it. She would finally know. She was going to do it. The pace of their action became near-frantic. Olga became the aggressor, moaning and squeezing and groping her young lover.

It was during the moaning, squeezing and groping that Olga noticed something was missing - a penis. She couldn't locate the young man's penis. After several attempts, a totally perplexed Olga decided to address the issue.

Olga whispered in his ear, "Where is penis?"

"What?" Dale said.

"Penis," Olga said "Where is?"

"I don't have one," her lover responded.

Olga, still physically searching during the conversation, in hope of discovery, wondered how this could be. "Were you hurt in war?" she asked.

This brought a loud laugh from her partner, as well as from someone sitting in the next stall.

"No, I'm a girl, silly," Dale said.

Suddenly, Olga felt the heat of passion turn to the cold of confusion.

"Girl?" she said. "But, I am girl, too. I was hoping for a man with penis."

Dale smiled, "Can't help you there. But we can still have some fun. That's what lesbians do."

"I'm not Lesbian," said Olga.

"Oh, I'm sorry," Dale said. "I just assumed. I mean, the way you're dressed and the way you...well, I just thought..."

"No. I am Siberian. I have never even been to Lesbia."

A voice from the next stall said, "Hey, either of you know an eight-letter word that means to hamper or impede? Starts with an E."

"What?" Dale asked. "Are you weird or something? What's that supposed to mean?"

"Hey girlie," the woman's voice shot back. "I'm just taking a dump here, doing the Times crossword. You two are in the same stall, looking for missing sex organs and trying to get directions to the capital of Lesbia...so who's being weird here?"

"Encumber," Dale said.

"What?" The stall neighbor asked.

"The word is encumber," Dale said. "Eight letters, starts with an E."

After a moment of silence, the woman responded, "Hey, you're right. Thanks." Olga had released Dale from their entanglement, and opened the stall door and left. Olga returned to her seat where the stark realization set in.. Her sex life, or lack of one, was making her suicidal. Well, maybe not suicidal, but damn depressed. It was like being stuck in libidinous neutral. She had started with a person with a small penis that he didn't want to share because he was using it himself, to a person with a large penis that didn't want to use it at all, to a person who was more than willing to utilize a penis, but didn't have one available. I am dying of virginity, she thought.

The headlights of an approaching car refocused her to the window. It was the Americans.

"Boris, they are here. Are you ready, comrade?" She called out.

She felt his hand on her shoulder. "Yes, I am ready."

CHAPTER 4

It was obvious to Biff Brinkley, radio show host at XWAK, that Herbie Crow and Danny Waitman had lost their freaking minds. They could have just walked into the sound booth and told him to get out of the way and he would have complied. It was if he gave a rat's ass about this job anyway. Instead, they crashed in like they were storming an imaginary beachhead and popped him on the skull with whatever the hell it was they popped him with, and then tied him to a chair to immobilize him while they took over the broadcast booth. A little extreme, to say the least. During this little physical exchange, he had discovered a couple of things. First, Herbie couldn't tie a knot to save his butt, because Biff was able to move his hands from the arms of the chair with ease. He also learned that a sudden crack on the noggin did not knock you out like it did in the movies. But it did piss you off, not to mention the incredible head blasting pain it caused. It reminded him of the post high school prom hangover he'd had the night he attempted to introduce Betty Jean Armentrout to the wonderful world of teenage love, armed with offerings of Paramount Cherry Vodka and Trojan glow-in-the-dark 'ribbed for her pleasure' condoms. Both of these presentations were declined without possibility of appeal, forcing him to imbibe in self pity, the entire bottle of the rose-colored booze, and a Penthouse magazine until he had relieved himself of some youthful stress. This was followed by an unexpected regurgitation of an earlier consumed Big Mac and fries onto the floor of his '68 powder blue VW.

Brinkley sits and watches as Herbie and Danny work feverishly at the console, apparently in preparation for a broadcast. "You know, your show starts in a couple of hours," he said to their backs. "If you wanted an earlier time slot..."

Neither of them answered or even acknowledged he was in the room. He heard Herbie address Danny. "Okay, that's how we'll do it then. We'll have peckertop back there," he said, pointing at Biff with his thumb, "do a little more talk and then we'll break in with a special bulletin."

"Sounds good," Danny answered. "Until then, we'll play these greatest hits of Tony Orlando."

"Peckertop?" Biff thought to himself. "What the hell was that all about?" He figured Danny and his sidekick were going to do something noble, at least in their minds. But Peckertop? Oh, well. Just another unflattering title in his undistinguished, unsuccessful, but not undisturbed, life.

He looked around the room that now was his world. A small sound booth with cracked glass, peeling paint, and second-hand broadcast equipment previously used by some other ill-fated radio station that had been repossessed by the Juarez Bank and Trust after it had failed to meet its debt obligations. The Juarez financial institution had followed their policy to the letter in the process and recouped their losses by seizing equipment, shutting down the station, and of course, shooting the owner.

"What a life," he moaned.

He thinks back to his younger days when his dreams of fame and fortune were still intact, the day when he finally left his parents' Florida home in search of answers to the mysteries of the universe. Alright, so it wasn't all that complicated. He just wanted to be a musician. So, like any normal young man with similar goals, he formed a band. Not a hard driving rock band or a jazz band or a country band. No, nothing that mundane. He and four associates became "Biff and the Fontanas," a Village People cover band. Hey, you gotta start somewhere.

Ah, those blissful unfettered days of youth and the unwavering search for fame, fortune and of course groupies. Unfortunately, problems with the group started almost immediately. None of the members could really sing, instrument playing was out of the question, and try as they might, they could not find proper attire to mimic the group they planned to exalt. They scoured every second-hand store in Dade county and during one intoxicated evening, they even went door to door in distant Fort Lauderdale asking for donations. Their efforts however, had not produced the needed policeman, cowboy, and Navy uniforms they so badly needed.

Instead, they had collected a butcher shop apron, a nun's habit, a Santa Claus outfit, four pairs of Big and Beautiful tan pantyhose, and a high school band uniform from East Cocoa Beach High School, home of the "Fighting Clams." But the strangest item they had received was a giant white bulldog head they had been given by a University of Georgia graduate, now residing in Florida. The man had even been more inebriated than the beer swilling, trawling costume moochers when they arrived at his dwelling in hopes of securing band attire. The man seemed almost glad to see them and invited them into his home, told them to have a seat and then, without provocation, told the five future stars that he had arrived home that day to discover his wife of twenty years had left him for another man.

The very tall, very skinny, dark haired man dressed in a sports shirt, jockey shorts and black dress shoes, between swigs from a bottle of Three Feathers Whiskey, began reading to them his wife's well written goodbye letter. She had actually written him a goodbye poem of sorts. As the man read the verses, he became more agitated, but the last stanza set him off.

He read aloud:

"Mike, we don't have sex,
Not a single day.
That's why the neighbors,
Think that you're gay.
You turn me off,
My life is a wreck.
So I've left with Fred,
From Georgia Tech."

"Can you believe she said that?!" He nearly yelled.

Biff said, "She's just trying to make you mad by saying you're gay."

"Gay?" The man said, leaning toward the boys. "Gay? Who gives a shit about that. She left with a Georgia Tech guy for Chrissake!"

He then threw the letter down, took one last long swig from the bottle and dashed into the next room, out of sight from his now slightly concerned visitors. When the man returned to the room where the band members were still seated, he was staggering greatly, while periodically crashing into a wall or knocking over pieces of furniture. This was partly due to this drunken state and partly due to the fact that his balance was thrown off by the giant fur covered dog head he was now wearing.

Surprised, but not wanting to be impolite, Biff said to him, "That's a real nice head you've got there."

"Shut up, kid," the man said.

Biff, being all of five foot four and a hundred and forty pounds in full dress heeded the warning.

The man sighed. "Sorry," he said. "I was the mascot at Georgia back in the day. The number one Bulldog. You know, the guy out front, leading the band. Some great times."

His voice from inside the head sounded to Biff like someone speaking in an echo chamber with a sock in their mouth. Suddenly, the man removed the head and thrust it at Vinnie, the closest of the group looking at him. Freckle-faced and red-haired Vinnie had bulging eyes that bulged out even more as he sat within kissing distance of the University of Georgia's claim to fame. He then used his beanpole six foot frame to lean away as far as he could.

With tears streaming down his cheeks, the man said, 'Here, you take it. I can never look at it again."

Still holding the head, the man sat down on the arm of the couch Vinnie was perched on. His voice was soft and melancholy, Biff and the group leaned toward him to hear. Holding the head up and admiring it tearfully, the man said, "I wore this on our first date. She said it made her feel special. Said it even made her feel romantic. She even made me wear it when we made love sometimes."

Vinnie glanced at Biff while raising and lowering his eyebrows.

"Please," the man said, almost whispering. "Take it."

Vinnie said, "You should keep it. You might feel different tomorrow."

"Take it, dammit!" The man screamed, making them all jump to their feet from the couch.

"Okay, okay, okay, got it," Vinnie said. "We'll take it."

Biff reached out and took the head and handed it to Vinnie.

"Yeah sure," Biff said. "We'll take real good care of it."

Everyone looked at each other and Biff made a slight nod towards the door. They all rose and with Vinnie and the head, they went out to the van to depart. The man followed them outside. It was a beautiful, warm Florida evening and many of the local residents were starting to come outside to enjoy the sunset. The band loaded up the van and started to back out of the driveway as Biff rolled down the passenger side window.

"Take care, mister," he said as the man, still in his underwear, waved sullenly back.

Vinnie, seated behind Biff on the back bench seat behind Biff, leaned out the window and yelled, "Thanks for the head, Mister!" Which caused the neighbors to look at the man and the van as it drove out of sight.

The next day, undaunted by their odd experiences, Biff, Vinnie, and the other band members headed out. Skip, a fifty-something Berkeley dropout, complete with beads, peace sign tattoos, and a year's supply of incense. Clifford, a twenty-nine year old would-be airline pilot who was forced into a career change after a bad experience ended his dreams of flying and haunted him to this very day. It seems that, while at the controls during a normal flight maneuver, the altitude loss alarm sounded. He frantically tried to correct it but unable to do so, he lost his nerve, put his hands over his eyes and began screaming, "Oh my God, we're crashing! We're all going to die!" He then jumped up from his pilot's seat and threw himself to the floor whimpering and convulsing. Two things saved the day for Clifford: a calm cool co-pilot, and the fact that he was in a flight simulator at the time.

At the wheel of the official Fontana van was Marco, a totally hairless five foot five inch tall ex-sumo wrestler from Pembroke, New Jersey, who claimed to be a direct descendant of a U.S. President. The good news was that his DNA tests had proved that he was a Presidential descendant. The bad news was the President was Millard Fillmore.

Without a manager, the only gigs they could line up were at small roadside farmer's markets, a few nursing homes, and a bar outside of Myrtle, Missouri called "Shiners." Shiners was located in a dry county, so what they catered to customers was homemade booze in plastic cups, poured from fruit jars that contained a flammable clear liquid that was sometimes infested with numerous insects or an occasional small rodent, all in various forms of intoxication or death.

Finally out of money, out of food, and Skippy – who had finally resorted to smoking his incense – out of his mind, the group decided to give it one last go and play at a senior citizens center near some town in Nebraska called "Sunny Mountain Creek." The name seemed odd to Biff, considering there was no mountain, no creek, and it was raining like hell when they arrived. But, the show must go on.

Set up on a makeshift stage, the guys were introduced by a ninety-year old former magician dressed in a tuxedo much too large for his shrunken frame, carrying a baton-like walking stick with a large ivory colored lion's head on each end. At the conclusion of the introduction, which the old man was obviously very pleased with, he smiled toothlessly at the crow, twirled his baton, and performed a small jig. Everything was fine until the baton's third rotation, when the wooden stick struck him in the testicles, causing him to collapse on the stage where he lay drooling and gasping in a fetal position. Startled, Biff whispered to Marco to do something. Marco, who claimed to have some medical training, reacted immediately. He took his right foot and nudged the old coot off the stage and into the wheel-chair-bound audience below, where a group of former Lawrence Welk groupies wearing t-shirts that said "We slept with Cronkite," kicked at the living carcass until he crawled away.

The rest of the show went pretty much without incident, and most of the crowd even stayed awake. The band was so encouraged that they played an encore number and were rewarded for their efforts by the sound of shaking, half full plastic pill containers and a pair of Depends with a room number inscribed on it with grape jelly being thrown onto the stage.

At the end of their performance, an elderly woman with her shirt on inside out came over to Biff and asked him if he was Walt Disney. When he said, "No," she patted his arm, said, "It's a good thing," handed him a partially used tube of denture adhesive and shuffled away. But overall, things went great. The manager of the place even offered to pay them and told the group he would give them a ten dollar bonus if they mowed the lawn before they left.

Suddenly rejuvenated with this major career spark, Biff and the Fontanas lit out for the great northwest after reading in a three-year-old Guitar World magazine that Portland was the new epicenter of the music world. On the way across the Oregon Trail, and on the road to certain stardom, Biff managed to land them one more date. It turned out to be in front of their largest crowd ever, a group of about thirty drunk, armed, anti-government white supremacists at Carl's Bar and Camouflage Sales Center in Pocatello, Idaho. Unfortunately, their good luck had run its course and little did the Fontanas know that this would be their last performance together. This was precipitated by lead vocalist Skippy, who after drinking two bottles of peppermint schnapps and smoking some Idaho potato plant leaves, managed to misspell YMCA during the opening number. The reaction was predictable, at least for the Idaho panhandle.

Screams of "Kill the gays!" and discharging weapons filled the night air. Fortunately, the boys had the common sense to flee and somehow they made it to their vehicle, unscathed. Well, mostly. Skippy had vomited while running a staggering, weaving pattern through the parking lot and slipped on his own stomach acid and fell, causing some minor injuries. Then there was Vinnie, who had developed some cervical pain issues, probably from wearing the giant dog head during all their performances and this evening's sudden flight. Nonetheless, they made it out of the parking lot and down the road with a sigh of relief, with Vinnie at the wheel.

A few miles later, as they crossed the Washington state border, a state trooper pulled them over for multiple infractions, such as, only one headlight, no tail lights, speeding, expired tags, no muffler, and for riding in a vehicle operated by an unlicensed dog.

The officer then spent several minutes checking ID's and talking into his radio. Subsequently, he arrested Skippy for an old warrant from some county in Alabama, for what the cop called public indecency. Something to do with a department store window, a mannequin, and some Hoover vacuum cleaner attachments, but he didn't elaborate. Skippy just laughed and shook his head and made some indecipherable remarks about LSD, Mike Tyson, and Spotted Owls as he was being hauled away.

One thing was for certain. Biff knew it was time for a change. Still, he wasn't quite ready to give up music just yet, so he decided to give it one more shot. He started a solo career touring the south doing Arlo Guthrie and ZZ Top songs on a harpsichord, Performing mostly in Taco Bell parking lots and small airport lounges. Eventually, he was backed up by a guy who plucked a second hand cello and some Jesse Ventura look-alike who claimed to play the blues harmonica, but mostly just borrowed money, drank beer, and burped. The guy did have one song down. He did a mean honkytonk version of the theme from Mr. Roger's Neighborhood.

After a few weeks, Biff Brinkley was totally broke and completely without prospects. So at the urging of his father, he returned home to follow in his patriarch's footsteps as a radio pitchman. Due to his current financial status, which was zero, he was forced to move back in with his parents while he launched his new career. The living situation was stressful and quickly turned near unbearable after his mother, who had been strapped with another person to care for, was unexpectedly dismissed from her lofty position as head steward of Local Chapter 146 of the Banana Handler Union when it was discovered that she had violated Rule 13, Subsection 6, Paragraph 4 of the fruit/human orifice insertion policy, as stated in the regulatory handbook.

Despite all the everyday home life problems, Biff's career soon took off and the money started pouring in. But after a while, despite the success, he began to feel unfulfilled selling Tanzanian Bibles "Actually autographed by Jesus!" to near destitute Cubans and pension-strapped grandmas in the metro Dade County area. And then a small problem arose when some enterprising South Miami dishwasher found someone able to interpret the religious text, which had been typed, copied and assembled by a company called T.A.D. Turns out T.A.D. stood for "Tanzanian Atheists of Dar Es Salaam". It seemed the Bible contained some editorial issues, such as in the first chapter of Genesis, which was mistitled 'Genitals', the first line, translated to English read: "In the beginning...shit started to happen." It got worse from that point, making some references to a unicorn not being allowed on the Ark due to some improper horn placement involving a yak. Then there was David kicking the living shit out of Goliath instead of slaying him, and a post "water into wine" party that would have made Heidi Fleiss blush. Biff left shortly after the threats of legal actions from the authorities, lawsuits from customers, and a combination crucifixion/castration ceremony from a pissed of Methodist rolled in.

CHAPTER 5

Brian Temple stands in front of a full length mirror in the living room of his two bedroom apartment. His home, which is fairly large by apartment-dweller's standards, is sparsely furnished. An old wooden loveseat, a bean bag chair, a large screen TV, and a dining table. The living room still had the original paint, a color described by the realtor four years earlier as aquamarine covering the walls. Except, the color had changed over time. Mostly due to Temple's daily pot smoking, periodic attempts at cooking that had turned to small kitchen blazes, and continuous incense burning to disguise both odors. Aquamarine now appeared to be brackish backwater.

The sounds outside his three story brick building are alive as an avalanche of engines revving, horns honking, and distant sirens cascade over and through the nighttime experience. Evening in the Capital.

Inside his abode, with windows open slightly, the sounds of the public world mingle with the offerings of the CD playing "Speeches of the U.S. Senate."

Temple, clad in only his black with gold lettered Prison Break Brewery basketball shorts, speaks the words in unison with the recorded speechmaker while he distorts his face as he observes his mirrored reflection in his attempt to impersonate the current office holder.

It's all part of his daily routine. His goal, to completely embody the character of his subject. The senate oratories are just part of his collection of CD's, tapes and records of speeches in the originators' voices that he has accumulated over time, their value to him incalculable. Obama, Clinton, Bush Junior and Senior, vice presidents, senators, congressmen, talk show hosts and, with just enough weed, he could do a sizzling Nancy Pelosi.

Temple had practiced his mimicry lessons so long and in such a dedicated manner that he could now impersonate many of the politically important people of Washington to near perfection. This talent extended well beyond the easily recognizable characters to the present-day Joint Chiefs, cabinet members, and the current White House main resident himself. He possessed a vast library of taped conversations and meetings, utilizing each in his hobby. Some classified, some declassified, some just general bullshit sessions. Through it all, he had gathered enough sensitive material to start several wars, take over any agency or department he wanted to, move the economy in any direction he wished, or blackmail a couple hundred house members and numerous senators that couldn't keep their mouths shut or their flies zipped.

But Brian Temple wasn't like that. At least not yet. For now, he used his talent for the common good. Well, at least he had convinced himself it was for the common good. After all, he did get some things done, didn't he? Yes, he did. Some very crucial situations were handled with his talent. Sensitive issues that needed complete discretion. Issues that could not be left to the elected people or their ill-prepared staff.

Not to mention the fact that people on the telephone gave much more respect to a titleholder than they did an aide. If they believed it was the Secretary of State calling, it was much more pleasant to hear,

"Yes, Mr. Secretary, we'll look into that right away, sir." As opposed to, "listen, pencil-dick, we're a little busy over here, so check it yourself." Both responses meant basically the same thing, but it was the delivery that was important. Hell, sometimes, things even got done.

Temple had even entertained the idea of taking his little act out on the road. Atlantic City perhaps. Maybe even Vegas. After all, State Department and U.S. Capitol jobs don't last forever. Hell, they can end at any moment. Just look at what happened to that dumbness Pulupcheck, the senator's aide from South Carolina last year. He had a great career, a real insider. He had the senator's ear and some serious White House influence as well. Then it all crashed faster than a North Korean missile launch. Fired, just like that. Hard to forget that lesson. The end began when the poor bastard got masterfully drunk at the Senator's home during the annual Gamecock Barbecue and Meet the Columbian Porn Stars Gala put on by the Senator with the assistance of the DEA. But that's not what got him fired. While in this state of third degree inebriation, he managed to stretch a condom to such an extreme that he was able to pull it over his head and dance around the room in front of several legislators, a handful of foreign dignitaries, a couple of supreme court justices, and a major political donor who looked a lot like one of the Koch brothers, not to mention their spouses. But that's not what got him fired. Shortly after he began his strange, musically unaccompanied dance, that looked a lot like a Saturday Night Fever version of the Hokey Pokey, he started to lose what little coherence he had left, due to the fact that the airtight Trojan was not allowing him to breathe. He then passed out, landing face down in the short-skirted lap of the newly elected Speaker of the House's Administrative Secretary, who, at that very moment was seated nearby demonstrating her ability to tie a cherry stem into a knot using only her tongue, to the amazement of a growing crowd of first year congressmen and their aides. But that's not what got him fired. When the crowd gathered around the supine and semi conscious staffer and forcibly removed the prophylactic from his heavily sedated skull, someone inquired as to where he had gotten the pregnancy preventer. In a near saliva-drowned slur, he related how he had acquired the purple colored penis cover from the senator's private stock that the politician kept in a travel case for Campaign trips. The senator's wife, who was standing well within hearing distance, had been treated surgically over a decade earlier to prevent the possibility of conception during boisterous physical liaisons, thus negating the senator's needs for such precautions. Hmm. Yes. That's what got him fired.

When last seen, Pelupcheck was a bedpan orderly in an extended care center for mauled and slightly dismembered bear hunting guides near Frozen Follicle, Montana. It was either that or become the press secretary for the NRA. Not a difficult decision.

So for now, Temple would settle for using his multiple voices to handle delicate government problems and push proper political buttons. Of course, on those long boring Washington evenings at home he would make the occasional prank call, in character, to some unsuspecting and self-important dupe. It's good to have a little fun, he told himself. Relieves stress. Just recently he called the senior house member and told him, in the President's voice, that the White House would drop his party's blocking of a minimum wage hike and would back off his request to cut taxes on the top ten percent of wage earners. In exchange, the President wanted the congressman's support on a new bill for a national holiday commemorating the birth of Jenna Jameson and an endorsement for a one dollar postage stamp honoring Holly Barton, the girl that the President had been deflowered by all those many years ago in the pet cemetery at West Islip, near the tombstone of Melvin the Japanese Goldfish. He also told the lawmaker that he was going to introduce a new tough-oncrime bill which required mandatory helmet use for all children riding in shopping carts, anyone operating a Volvo, and all persons over the age of eighty seated in front porch rocking chairs. Both bills were scheduled to come out of committee and were set to be voted on shortly.

Then there as the THC-laden time he called the special operations section of the Pentagon using the gruff and commanding voice of the Head of the Joint Chiefs and told them that whenever they got the chance, in the next day or so, to slip a couple of long-range bombers over to Tanzania and drop a few tons of blasto on them. No rush, just whenever they had the chance. Oh, and no casualties mind you, if at all possible anyway. No use in getting the U.N. frothing. Maybe just hit some open field, or hell, how about a parking lot near one of the local houses of ill-repute. Shake up the muff-runners, that should do it. When queried as to why and by what authority this was to be done, he responded matter of factly.

"Well, son," he said in General Picken's gravelly tone, "first of all, today is my birthday and the President promised me that I could do a little damage to some third-world country as long as they don't provide us with oil, decent vacation spots, an occasional NBA player, or any women who look like Jennifer Aniston. And don't worry, son, no one will notice. The folks in that little shithole haven't made the news since they discovered that rare blue gorilla back in the nineties. Made National Geographic and everything, as I recall. Of course, right away, we sent a bunch of scientists down there to study 'em. The next thing you know, our beaker heads had studied the rare blue bastards so hard they became even more rare. Rared 'em right into extinction. Of course the intellectual limps blamed it on Du Pont house paint and acid rain caused by the smoke from some brassiere factory in Minneapolis. Couldn't do anything about Du Pont. Too big. And it's not a good idea to piss off Pete. Besides, it was a bullshit claim anyway. But that Vikingland boob-holder shop is gone. Anyway son, I don't really need any authority. I've got more stars on my collar than you've got hairs on your ass. So move on ahead, got it? We need to send them a message, anyway."

"What message would that be, sir?" The Pentagonian asked.

"Hell son, I don't know. We're the military. Our job is to wreck shit. Let them figure out what the message is, I'm sure they'll get it."

A voice in Temple's rooms brings him quickly back to the present.

"Hey B.T. What is it you are doing anyway?"

"Working on my Cory Booker," Temple responded. He turned away from his mirrors and walked over to his large blue bean bag seat that is embossed with a gold FBI logo. He brushes the ashes from an earlier Jamaican jolly maker off the top and flops down on it. He reaches over and plucks a small handful of shelled peanuts from a round crystal container sitting on a nearby empty Shanked Beer twelve pack carton and pops one in his mouth. The lid of the nut holder was custom made in the shape of Jimmy Carter's head. The item was a gift from Temple's predecessor who had kept it on his desk and then passed it on to every Secretary of State's top aide since Carter's administration. The previous aide had told Temple it would make him feel better in bad times. He'd said when things looked their bleakest and the entire country had turned to shit, just take one look at Carter's head and you'll realize that now matter how bad you're doing...it could be worse.

"So," the voice said, "what are you going to do about your little problem?"

"Which little problem? The wall? The North Koreans? Putin?"

"No, the dossier."

"I'm thinking," Temple said. "But I don't see that I have much choice. I'll make the call. I've got some things to do first but, when it's time, I'll do it."

"You're kidding me, right?" The voice resonates from across the room. "You've got a kidnapped messenger boy and a mop slopper, who for some untold reason, have important shit on them. Highly important shit as I understand, and you are going to turn it over to Arnie and his gang of Appalachian asspackers?"

"Who?"

"I don't know their names. But you know who I'm talking about."

Temple stands and walks over to his window, looks out at the night and pops another peanut.

"Well, just what would you do?" He said. "We have to keep this out of the news and the security in our so-called security departments has more cracks in it than Hillary's makeup."

He turns, takes one long exaggerated step and plops down on the beanbag again.

"You don't think any of your government Gumby's can handle this and keep quiet?" Voice asked.

"You're joking, right? Remember the time we tried to cover up that stuff over at HUD? We asked the FBI and Homeland Security for help and the next thing you know The New York Enquirer and The National Times were all over it like stink on shit."

"You mean the New York Times and National Enquirer."

"There's a difference? The point is that there are security breaches all over the place. On the other hand, my people won't let it out. And if they did let it slip, who would believe them? Hell, they couldn't even get on the Jerry Springer show."

Temple heard the voice let out a chuckle.

"Think back B.T. That fat dude of yours got some media coverage, remember? Said he was tied up and sexually molested by alien life forms dressed in green while he was walking through some state forest. I heard it myself."

"Yeah, yeah, I remember," Temple answered. "Turns out, it was just a couple of drunken scout masters that had slipped away from their campsite for a little midnight male bondage."

"You mean bonding."

"Apparently, you've never been a Scout. Besides, it was only broadcast on that late night radio talk show with George whats-his-name."

"So?"

"So? My God, it was sandwiched in between some female kook who claimed her house was haunted by the ghost of Colonel Sander's estranged stepbrother demanding the secret recipe and some guy who had collected over two thousand pounds of feces specimens from Yosemite National Park because he was certain that somewhere in that pile was a hunk of Bigfoot shit. I mean, who listens to that stuff?"

"Pretty much everyone."

He sighs, "Yeah, I know."

CHAPTER 6

"So, you don't have, like, a phone or something in your shoe, do you?" The man asked in the darkness of the room where he and another male were seated on the floor.

"No, I do not have a phone in my shoe," answered the second man.

"I thought you secret agent guys carried stuff like that."

"Listen, I told you. I'm not a secret agent. I don't even know any secret agents, if there is such a thing. I'm a courier. A State Department Courier. So, due to the fact that I'm not a secret agent, I don't have anything that will help. No phone, no bazooka, nothing. I've told you that. How about you? What do you have, Janitor Gadget. Hmm? You have something? How about it?"

Jasper, the courier, hears his companion moving around in the darkness.

"Well, not much really," Wasyl, the first man, said. "Just a comb, some breath mints, that kind with the sweet center, and ..."

Jasper hears a clink as something strikes the floor and rolls to him and touches his hand.

"Hey, what's this? Mace?" He said. "White House janitors carry mace?"

Wasyl opens his mints and pops one in his mouth and puts the rest back in his pants pocket.

"Nice try, but it won't do us any good unless we get real close to someone," Jasper adds.

"No," Wasyl responds. "It's not mace, but it'll come in handy, wait and see."

"Oh yeah? So what is it? A weapon of some kind?" Jasper asked.

"Lemon Pledge mini-spray. Always keep one handy. I like the Evergreen too. Very useful."

"In case you're kidnapped?" Jasper says.

"Actually, I hadn't planned on that. I keep 'em with me because I'm in charge of cleaning the Lincoln bedroom. That's my turf. Use these little devils in the bathroom. Lots of foreigners stay in that room and some of 'em got some strange toileting habits. Could be pretty beneficial here, too."

"Oh yes, could be a vital bargaining chip for our release."

Wasyl feels in the dark for Jarvis' hand, bumps his cheek, says sorry, and finally retrieves the small canister from his companion's grasp.

"You do realize that we're sitting in a shitter," Wasyl said, as he shook the canister then began to spray.

"Really, I hadn't noticed," Jasper grumbled.

"It smells like ass in here," Wasyl added, "Apparently, the flushing handle doesn't work on the pot."

Jarvis feels the dampness of the spray as Wasyl moves his arm back and forth allowing it to cover a wide area.

Wasyl said, "Better in here now, ain't it?"

"Wonderful, now it smells like someone shit a citrus fruit."

Although the two men can't see each other now because of the total absence of light, Jasper was fully aware of Wasyl's appearance. It was part of an earlier scene that was now locked in his mind. His bathroom partner stood just shy of six feet tall with a brown, flattop haircut, light complexion, clad in a dark blue work shirt that struggled to keep an immense belly covered. The probable result of many late-night raids on one of the federal fridges in America's number one home. Despite Wasyl's size, he had only been a blur, as he, along with Jasper, had been shuffled off into a black van parked directly in front of the White House by several hooded men. All the while, the White House security detail was busy detaining some 70-year-old North Dakota woman whose hair was bluer than Wasyl's shirt, because she was taking pictures too close to the White House gate. The woman, at 5-foot-nothing and 200 pounds dressed in a red, white, and blue full-length moo-moo and matching skullcap, was accompanied by an ancient relic of a man who strongly resembled a Precambrian era fossil, wearing patent leather shoes, knee high black socks, a white shirt, round straw hat, and Bermuda shorts pulled up even with his nipples. While the woman was popping her Kodak, the man was busy trying to shake hands with a nearby tree while pointing at a street pole and complaining that he thought the Washington Monument was taller. Obviously terrorists.

Meanwhile, thirty feet way, Jasper, dressed impeccably in his State Department blazer, matching pants and shirt, which was complemented by his professionally coiffured hair, that made the 30-year-old black courier look like Denzel Washington (no one told him this, but he was certain that they thought it) was tossed like so many sacked potatoes into a distinctly suspicious-looking vehicle and driven off by gun-wielding assailants.

The security detail figured it was some sort of political prank, a secret service training session, or a Candid Camera episode being taped. But, unable to locate a camera crew to pose for, they went back to the important task at hand. Tazing the renegade Dakotans.

Meanwhile, Jarvis was blindfolded, gagged with an unlaundered sock, driven a distance, put on a plane, then into another van. He was then put in an old wooden wagon behind a team of horses driven by a man who somehow managed to have a breath odor that rivaled the continued flatulations of the horses that pulled them. Finally, he was dragged down a path, taken to a remote location, shoved through an open door and into a tiny bathroom. No lights. No windows. No seat on an unflushable toilet. No escape...but at least he had a janitor.

CHAPTER 7

“So, Bobby couldn’t come with us because he misplaced his toilet paper. Am I following this correctly?” Skeet inquired of Olga.

Skeet and Paulie were in the front seat of Skeet’s maroon ’98 Lincoln Town Car while Olga was seated directly behind Paulie in the back. Skeet was at the wheel as they were driving out of Gay’s Creek, leaving the Last Dive to fade in the rearview mirror. During their earlier meeting, Boris, or Bobby as he preferred to be called, had greeted them with open arms, hugging each of them repeatedly until they sat down at a round wooden table in the dining room inside the main entry. Once they were all seated, and handshakes and hugs were completed, they waited until the pre-appointed time for a phone call. The call came on Paulie’s cell phone at exactly the moment it was supposed to come. He answered, responded to questions from the caller with a couple of yesses, and okay or two, and then the call ended. He looked from person to person sitting near him. He waited for what seemed like a foolish eternity.

“A little dramatic, don’t you think Blumer?” Skeet said.

“We have a mission. Three of us are supposed to go. I’ve got a location we are supposed to drive to and a contact we are to meet,” Paulie said finally.

Things were going smoothly up to that point. Bobby got excited and announced he would be going with them. Then, just as they got to the front door to leave, Bobby stopped his two American companions. He moved his arms as if he were introducing a famous entertainer to an audience and announced that now that they were all comrades and he could trust them as brothers, he had something he wanted to show them. Paulie and Skeet looked at each other and then back at their host. With his introductory flare continuing, Bobby reached inside his gray coat pocket to retrieve something, but the something wasn't there. He checked in his gray pants pockets, left then right. No something. The duo watched in a state of something a tad less than amazement but more than curiosity as Bobby repeated the search process at a rapidly increasing pace. Paulie and Skeet's attitudes switch into full frontal amazement when Bobby's self-examination turned to disrobing and twisting each piece of clothing in his now frantic search for the something. Frantic turned to mildly berserk as Bobby now realized that his body and previous body coverings did not hold the something. He raised both fists above his head towards the sky and let go a thunderous "nyeeet!" Then chest-heaving and eyes-bulging, he made a quick side to side observation of the room and, dressed only in his grayish pink skin, started flipping furniture.

Answering Skeet's original question, Olga said "Who?"

"Uh, Bobby, you know, your husband."

"Oh yes, husband. That is right as you say. He cannot come because of lost toilet paper," Olga confirmed. "He is very close to it."

"Obviously so," Paulie said. "Looking under the table and chairs I guess is understandable, but he did seem a little out of control."

Skeet laughed. "A little out of control? We're talking about toilet paper. The man was ripping apart his house. Then he tried to give us both a frisking session."

"Frisking?" Olga said. "What is frisking?"

"Grab, grope, put your hands all over someone," Skeet explained.

Olga looked out the car's side window. "He never frisking me," she sighed.

"Maybe you should dress up in some four-ply."

Paulie punched Skeet lightly on the arm and gave him a stern look. Skeet shrugged.

Paulie felt he should at least try to soothe the plainly distressed woman over her situation. Well, actually, he realized, she didn't seem distressed at all, plainly or otherwise. What she did appear to be was genuinely relieved. This was despite the fact that as they were leaving her home, her naked husband was pulling up the living room carpet with his bare hands while yelling obscenities, at least what sounded like obscenities in a foreign language to the background noise of ejected carpet tacks snapping the walls like small caliber bullets. Well, Paulie figured, she must keep her consternation deep.

"You know, people do get attached to some strange things," he said. "My cousin Virgil carried a freeze-dried gopher foot in his shirt pocket for years. Claimed it warded off illness, viruses, and various deadly infections."

"Did it work?" Skeet inquired.

"Don't know for sure. He got run over by a cab carrying doctors to the CDC convention."

"Do tell."

"But the coroner said he was in perfect health right before the impact."

"That's good."

"Yes, very encouraging," Paulie said. "And my wife's sister refused to part with a photo she kept on her nightstand of Wolf Blitzer on a beach showing off his swim trunk tan line."

"Wolf Blitzer?" Skeet asked.

"CNN guy," Pualie answered.

"I know who it is. But, Wolf Blitzer? On the nightstand?"

"Yeah," Paulie answered.

"What did her husband think of that?" Skeet asked.

"Nothing, she'd kicked him out months before. Came home one day and found him stark naked wearing a Darth Vader helmet, trying to get one of those life-size blowup dolls out of the ceiling fan in the bedroom."

"How did it...?"

"Helium. He had some inter galactic fantasy or something."

They stopped at a stop sign at the intersection of the main blacktopped road entering and exiting Gay's Creek.

"Left, right, or straight," Skeet said.

"Left," Paulie said.

Skeet waited for a passing semi tractor with a Dekalb Corn emblem on the side that was reflected from their headlights to go by, then turned left, accelerated to the speed limit plus 5 miles an hour more, set the cruise and popped in a Buck Owens tape.

"Do we have to?" Paulie said, referring to the music.

"Yep."

Buck had just started singing about being "Together Again" with someone about in about the trip's tenth mile when Skeet broke the conversation gap.

"So, what exactly did the man tell you on the phone?"

"The mouse has a blue tambourine."

"Of course. Makes perfect sense," Skeet said. "What the hell does that mean?"

"Obviously, it's code," Paulie stated.

"Uh-huh, so what does it mean, Blume?" Skeet asked.

"I'm looking, hold on," Paulie said as he searched through the hardcover gold bordered blue book in his lap. He used a small flashlight to light the pages as he flipped through them.

Skeet said, “So they actually gave you a code book? With secret code and everything? Just like a big boy, huh?”

“Yep,” Paulie says proudly, “got it by special courier.”

“Official-looking, isn’t it,” Skeet said. “Special courier too?”

“UPS,” Paulie said, holding it up. “Says right in the front, Secret Codes of the United States of America’s State Department.”

“Very impressive. And you’re sure the mouse and the tangerine are in there?”

“Tambourine.”

“Yes, tambourine.

Paulie flips a couple of pages in the front of the book.

“It’s in here. See the table of contents? I’ll bet there’s a whole section on mice.”

Paulie runs his fingers down the M section of the table of contents, mumbling the headings, Mettle, mew, mezzo, micro, milkmaid. Hmm, no mice. Oh wait, that’s plural it says, I need to look at mouse. Let’s see...More pages flipping “Okay, here it is, mouse. Must be an old issue. All the photos in it are of the previous administration.”

“Budget cutbacks. Probably out of print or something.”

“Hey look, there’s a picture of President Obama and Lady Gaga inside the cover.”

“Awesome,” Skeet said sarcastically. “So what does the top secret code book with Gag’s picture in it...”

“Here’s another one with Snoop Dog.”

“...say.”

“It’s directions to our meeting. Take a right on the Coast Road. I’ll tell you when to turn. Boy, you got to get each word and letter just right in this code stuff. One wrong word can really mess up the translation. They say that’s how the Cold War started, ya know.”

"Not to mention Reality TV."

"Uh, yeah," Paulie said just as his cell phone alerts him to an incoming call. He grabs it and looks down at the flickering caller I.D. and sees that it's his home telephone calling. A familiar sensation of dread creeps through his abdomen and travels up to his brain, he lets it continue its bird-chirping ringtone.

"Are you going to respond to telephone?" Olga said, her tone relaxed but very Russian.

"I'm not sure I should," Paulie said as he reluctantly pressed the answer button and raised it to his ear.

"Hello," he said.

"Hey, Captain Corpulent," his sister's voice answered.

"What is it, Ruth?" He replied.

"Where are you? Doesn't make a difference. You need to get your abundancy back here."

"Ruth, I'm a little busy right now," Paulie said, glancing over a Skeet.

"Yeah, right. I'm sure your schedule is just bursting at the seams in overflowing void. Meanwhile, my dear centerfold for Blimp Builder Magazine, back here the feces has struck the bladed cooling device."

"Huh?"

"Shit has hit the fan."

"Now what?"

"That mother-in-law of yours just drank my last two bottles of Nyquil."

"Nyquil? She drank Nyquil?"

"Yes."

"Why?"

"Probably due to the fact that due to her due diligence, the wet bar is due for a refill because it is no longer wet."

"We just restocked that."

"Exactamundo."

"Well, put her to bed."

"Can't."

"Why not?" Paulie asked. "That much booze, and all the cough suppressant would put anyone out."

"Most people, yes," Ruth said. "But not the Queen of the Silver Doll Hair. It sent her into some kind of libidinous orbit. Told me she's got a date with Frank Sinatra. Put on a pair of Junior's swim trunks, that cowboy hat you bought at the Alan Jackson concert last summer, slapped some Ajax Cleanser under her arms, mumbled something about the poor quality of talcum powder today, then headed out to meet her date."

"But Frank Sinatra's dead," Paulie said.

"No shit, Professor Portly. It's that reincarnation crap again. She says old Frank came back as Burton Klemper's twin."

"Burton Klemper?"

"The meter reader from the water department."

"But he doesn't have a twin."

"Not according to Mama Mania," Ruth quipped. "You know Burton's big hairy dog?"

"The St. Bernard?"

"That would be the one, Bacon Belly. She claims that's old Blue Eyes himself disguised as a canine."

"Disguised?"

"To avoid groupies."

"Oh, Lord."

"Exactly."

Paulie sighed, "Where is she now?"

"Drove off to meet furry, four-footed Frank."

"But there's no car there."

“True, Jiggle Jowls, but your John Deere riding mower is…or, should I say…was. She burnt off, shorts falling, skin sagging, sombrero flopping, popping wheelies in fifth gear and singing ‘Strangers in the Night.’ It was quite a sight.”

“Driving down the street?”

“No, fortunately, she didn’t take the street.”

“Whew! Thank God”

“Yes, very fortunate.”

“Fortunate is good.”

“Unfortunately, she must have accidentally put the blade down because she took out Luann Winter’s rose bed, that small maple tree by the Miller’s front porch, and there’s a pile of something that looks like fur in the Beamer’s back yard that could very well be the remnants of Carl and Jolene’s pet orangutan, Jerome.”

“This isn’t good.”

“Nothing gets by you, does it Dr. Galactic Girth? Anyway, I gotta go. My ride’s here. We’re going to the annual Flea Free Forever Dance down at the warehouse on Sixth. Wendell and the GutThrobs are playing. We’re raising money for a new LMT free clinic.”

“LMT?”

“Louse, Mite and Tick.”

Paulie hears a car horn in the background.

“Just a damn minute, Jimmy!” Ruth yelled as she hung up.

He puts his phone slightly back into his shirt pocket.

“Problems, Blummie?” Skeet asks.

“No more than usual,” he sighs.

“You know it could always be worse.”

“I’m sure it will be.”

CHAPTER 8

Biff Brinkley had somehow talked the disturbed duo ransacking his place of employment into taking him along when they left. He wasn't sure why he had, but he had, and here he was. Of course, before they left they had to complete their task. That task, apparently, was to take over the Juarez radio station, lock themselves in the sound booth, and spend the next several hours broadcasting their "save the whatever the hell it was they wanted to save" message to the dozen or so people that were listening at that hour.

In the process, they interrupted Brinkley's radio show. It was no big deal, he figured, after all, it was his last broadcast. His most recent attempt at an airwave career had spiraled into the ground as usual. Career hell, all he was now doing was spending the bleak hours before dawn playing classic hits by Zeppelin, Chicago, and Peter Frampton. Not originals of course. These were covers, sung and played by a Mexican band called The Tijuana Toe Tappers. Their lead singer, Jose Manual Rafael Miguel Garcia, had recently changed his name to Jose Jones in order to appeal more to American audiences. Unfortunately, Jose's voice sounded very much like Curley from the Three Stooges, and the band's screeching off-key efforts at rock and roll were horrifying. On the other hand, Biff had to admit he hadn't noticed any difference in the Frampton songs.

The latest dip in the Brinkley job juggle had come on the heels of one of his periodic, but ever brief, peaks. During one three week period, Biff had basked in the limelight as the star of a 30-minute infomercial for Dr. Pellagra's Permerect, a new sexual aide for the elderly gentlemen, made from a secret hormone found only in the testacles of South Texas ferrets.

The wonder drug, that came in pill or lotion form, was guaranteed to make any man shudder with desire, put him long in the lust department, and make his physical abilities physically able, thus providing for him a session of pride that would last and last and last. Guaranteed. And it worked. Very well. Very, very well. So well in fact, that it caused one El Paso man a trip to the local emergency room after a pride session lasting approximately 72 hours. The man, after the third day of prolonged prolongness, had found himself in a state of ready and able, but no longer willing. His wife, now in a similar non-active mood had shut and locked the bedroom door on him while screaming "enough is enough!" The woman even went so far as threatening to dial 911 for police assistance if he didn't leave her alone. She ended the barrier-imposed conversation by telling him he needed to get a grip on himself. Something else he found now was also not as enjoyable as it had been earlier.

So, unable to deflate himself, and finding it impossible to get a change of wardrobe from his barricaded bedroom closet, off the short chubby bald-headed man went to the hospital, clad only in a pair of pink flannel pajama bottoms and cowboy boots in hopes of acquiring some desperately needed medical assistance.

Unfortunately for him, three days of redirected blood flow brought about by Permerect had drained his brain of needed oxygen, causing him to faint at the wheel of his slightly rusted out yellow Ford Pinto.

He steered into a fire hydrant, ricocheted off the man-made obstacle, slammed into one of mother nature's car stoppers, an oak tree, slid sideways into a 6-inch curb which caused his vehicle to flip in midair and land upside down in the parking lot of a Freezy Cone Ice Cream stand. He then self-ejected and staggered about 20 feet and passed out, flat on his back, near a row of benches and small round tables where customers were spooning sundaes, gulping malts, and watching the action. Soon the group of sweetened, cow sap slurpers' mood changed from amazed silent stares, to boisterous laughter at the sight of the now-snoring man in their midst with the onerous problem that was currently protruding from his dark pink pajamas and pointing skyward.

One elderly, slightly stooped lady in a gray rabbit fur coat and a white flower decorated head scarf, apparently did not see the humor in the situation. She threw down her half-eaten chocolate and vanilla swirl cone, walked over to the unconscious prostrate figure, where she uttered a few epithets including, but not limited to, pervert, deviant, and chicken choker. She then executed with a perfect form, a Tiger Woods' tee shot to the man's affected area with the hook end of a wooden handled umbrella she was carrying to the cheers and groans of the gathering crowd. When last seen, she was wandering down the street mumbling something about how the world had become an unsafe place for defenseless women like her, ever since Janet Jackson had showed her boob during that damn football game.

At least those were the facts as stated in the one hundred twenty-seven page damage suit brought against the station, the doctor, and all the participants in the infomercial by the painfully swollen Texan. He was suing for physical pain, mental anguish, costs of cosmetic repair, surgical procedures, and a lifetime supply of anti-inflammatory drugs he was going to require just to pee regularly.

Pellagra had fled during the night, immediately following the court's ruling in the injured party's favor. The next day, authorities seized his leftover assets. A '69 purple Dodge Dart, about 3 dollars' worth of Mexican currency, and a barn on a half acre lot in Anthony, Texas, that was home to about three thousand recently neutered and very pissed off tube-shaped rodents.

When Biff arrived home that same evening, he found a note from the newly AWOL fake practitioner that said Pellagra was going to travel deep into the uncharted jungles of West Virginia in hopes of finding a cure for the male baldness and parakeet molt from the various herbs and animal secretions located there. To raise capital for the excursion, the good doctor wrote he was taking a job with his cousin Rudy's carnival for a few weeks as it traveled the Midwest. He said thanks to the ferrets, he had become quite adept at weasel-juggling. He closed the letter by saying they wouldn't be seeing each other again but the good news was the missing quack had left full payment for Biff's radio services in lockbox 6 at the Juarez Bank, Bar and Over-the-Counter Automatic Weapons Store. And as luck would have it, his former employer had left a key.

Biff located the bank, which was not located in a better part of Juarez, as if there is such a thing, and then spent the next several hours belly-crawling behind dumpsters over-flowing with overflow and sprinting in a crouched position past bullet-riddled walls spray painted with various gang signs and anti-anti drug slogans. Positively not a better part of town. Finally, he made it to the front door of an old brick building, opened it and entered.

Inside the front lobby, about fifteen feet from the front door, was an old wooden counter with a heavy glass top. Standing behind the counter in the partially fake wood-paneled room was the banker, bartender, and weapon salesman. Mr. Three-in-One was a large man. About six foot two and pushing two hundred fifty pounds wearing a Smith & Wesson T-shirt and sporting a Mohawk haircut..sort of. His hair was cut in the style one would identify as a Mohawk with one very distinct difference. Instead of having one line of hair from forehead to the back with baldness on both sides, this man's hair grew in a bushy line from ear to ear with the shaved areas in the front and back. Biff thought it made the man's head look like a peacock's ass in full bloom. He approached the man, told him why he was there and paid four dollars and sixty-eight cents for the cover charge to go back to the lockbox area. This was the standard fee. It was also every last cent Biff had in his possession. As it turned out, the standard fee was every last cent you had in your possession as the large man explained. And the man was large enough to make Biff agree the price was reasonable. Policy is policy.

After paying, Biff walked down a dimly-lit hallway that smelled something akin to moldy baby diapers dipped in fermented butter. As he felt his way along, his foot bumped into something, causing him to nearly fall over whatever it was. The whatever it was, let out a muffled moan and Biff, his eyes now adjusting to the lack of light, was notified by his brain that the mystery object was a slender drunk man rolled up in a multicolored blanket jelly roll fashion. He stepped over the intoxicated human obstruction onto some broken glass and found himself face to face with the wall containing the lockboxes. Actually, lockbox. Box number 6 was the only one present. He reached into his pocket and retrieved the key, put it into the corresponding key hole and opened the bounty holder. He pulled out a small drawer, lifted the cracked, dusty Plexiglass lid and there it was. His reward for his dedicated service to the doctor and the previously erectionless male populace. An empty Corona bottle, a homemade pot pipe (pot not included), the dried carcass of a long-deceased scorpion, and an autographed picture of Freddie Fender, circa 1975, wearing swimming trunks. Freddie was standing near a pool with a fat pale woman who was donning a sun hat and a blue one piece bathing suit that was struggling so hard to maintain her massively abundant figure that it had developed stretch marks of its own.

Most people would be discouraged at such a find. Not Biff. No sir. Biff rationalized that Freddie's photo with Freddie's signature attached must be worth something. Must be. That's when Biff made another discovery. Upon closer examination of the photo, he realized that the photo was not signed by Freddie Fender. It was signed by William Blitch. Bill Blitch, for some ungodly reason, had signed his name right across the front of Freddie's semi-hairy chest. Freaking William Blitch.

Biff stood in lost silence, staring into Fender's worthless photo wondering who the hell Bill Biltch was and what else could possibly happen to screw up his already screwed up life. He was brought back to consciousness by a sudden gaseous production from the body of the inert inebriant behind him on the floor, strong enough to cause what little paint was left on the walls to curl. He turned, crushing glass again under his foot, stepped over the odor source and strode into the lobby. The man behind the counter was attempting to dig an item out of his teeth with a nail while looking at this reflection in the glass countertop. Biff walked numbly past him out through the front door and into the street where he was immediately approached by two large men carrying handguns and wearing ski masks demanding his money. He sighed, handed one of them Freddie's photo and the rapidly disintegrating scorpion cadaver, patted the second man on the shoulder, and walked off down the street wondering if he was going to be shot, but not really caring.

The van struck a bump in the road, snapping Biff's attention back to his current situation. He looked at his two companions seated in the front, separated by a small storage compartment between the seats. They seemed to be as diverse physically as they were in attitude and wardrobe. Herbie, the one on the passenger side was short, five-foot-five at best, in his cheap sandals. He was also as wide as he was tall, stretching to near button-popping extremes, the material in his Hawaiian-style pink, blue, and yellow shirt covered with pineapple and flower designs.

"Are you sure this is a good idea?" Herbie asked the driver.

Danny was tapping the steering wheel with his fingers in time to a Bon Jovi song on the radio. He's dressed in a white T-shirt without sleeves, stonewashed blue jeans and New Balance cross-trainers. His jet black hair is perfectly cut and combed. He is laid back and lean. Danny is the epitome of cool. Herbie is the epitome of not.

"Yeah, it's good," Danny responded after a moment, "Wanda wouldn't have called us otherwise."

"Don't sound good to me," Herbie said. "Bad voodoo can happen, especially when you stick my neck out. Never stick anything out. Bad voodoo." , "You're kidding me, right?"

"No, I'm not kidding," Herbie said.

"Herbie," Danny started, "we just took over a radio station, after we broke and entered, a totally lawless act, you do realize. Then we got shot at by everyone in Juarez that has a gun, no small number I might add, had our car blown up by that military machine that looks like Godzilla with a cannon, stole this van and got chased all the way to the border by a bunch of hyped-up Federales who think you look like Escobar's cousin. And all that just so you could yak over the late night AM sound waves about the near-extinction status of the Flat Nose Wardrober."

"That's a Black Rose Warbler," Heabie replied. "It's a bird."

"Uh-huh. My mistake," Danny stated. "Well, I have to tell you. I wish you'd never seen one, old pal."

Herbie looked away from his friend and coughed slightly.

"What?" Danny asked pointedly.

"Well, actually I ain't really seen one...exactly."

Danny turns his head away from the windshield view to look at Herbie, raising his eyebrows as he speaks, "National Geographic again?"

"No."

"Some PBS special, perhaps?"

"No."

"What then?

"The Greenpeace Endangered Species Top Ten alert. Comes out once a month in the El Paso Shopper," Herbie said.

"Herbie, are you nuts? It could be a fake."

"What? You don't think it's real?"

"Not from them," Danny said. "Anyone who believes all that propaganda would believe that Tom Cruise was a good pick to play Jack Reacher. Do you even know if there is such a thing as a Stub Toed Hobbler?"

"Black Rose Warbler. I think so, I mean there's no picture 'cause they're so rare."

"Instead of the Half Wit Gobbler, why don't you try to save the Frip, Herbie?"

"It's Black Rose Warbler. Frip?"

"Yeah. Frip. How about that? They're really endangered. Why don't you start a Save the Frip campaign? We could write a song about 'em. Get on the airwaves. Get shot at."

"They're endangered?"

"Are they ever."

"What is it? A Frip, I mean."

"It's a small brown furry rodent that's notorious for sucking farts out of dead chickens."

Herbie's eyes widened.

"It's fake, Herbie," Danny said. "That's my point. It's something made up and I could tell you just now that you were ready to launch."

"Fake?" Herbie said, almost sadly.

"Yep, fake," Danny said. "But I'll bet it's as real as the Sack Cloth Groveler."

"Black Rose...whatever."

"Exactly."

CHAPTER 9

"So, what do you think they'll do to us?"

"I don't know. Maybe kill us. Maybe just torture us for a while. Then kill us. I don't even know who they are," Jasper groaned.

He rearranged his sitting position.

"Can you flush that thing?" He asked.

"If'n you're trying to ease my concerns, it ain't takin'," Wasyl answered. "And I told you

the handle's broke."

"Listen Whistle."

"Wasyl."

"What?"

"Wasyl. The name is Wasyl."

"Of course it is. Well, Wattle, all I know for sure is, they, whoever they are, cannot get their hands on these documents," Jasper said. "You still have them hidden where we put them, right?"

Wasyl exhales, "I ain't real perked on this hidin' spot we're using either, I gotta tell ya."

Wasyl feels Jasper pat his arm from across the top of the toilet.

"Don't worry," Jasper said. "It's going to be fine."

"Don't worry?" Wasyl said. "Are you kidding? What if they decide to look up there? Embarrassing enough just thinking about it. Can't believe you secret agents don't have better ideas than that."

Jasper said, "I told you. I'm not a secret agent and stop fretting, they won't look. Think about it, when's the last time anyone looked in that spot?"

The room momentarily filled with quiet darkness as Wasyl searched his memory.

"Been a spell," he said. "Only happened twice that I can recall. First time when I joined the army. Of course, everybody got cheek-peaked that time. Then they sent us all off to Afghanistan. Jesus, what a trip. Second time was on a blind date with some third shift truck stop waitress from Little Rock named Lorna. Nothing much good came out of either of those two excursions," Wasyl sighed, "I still have flashbacks and night sweats to this very day."

"I'll bet. I heard Afghanistan was tough."

"I ain't talking about Afghanistan."

CHAPTER 10

"Did you just call the White House? Was I hearing right?"

"Yes."

"And that was the First Lady you were talking to? In the President's voice?"

"Uh-huh."

"You have the number one couple's private number?"

"Of course," Temple answered.

"I guess I won't ask how you got that," Voice said.

"Yes, it's best that you don't," Temple added, then inhaled deeply from the special

blend marijuana cigarette he held in his hand. He held the joint up about 12 inches from his face and appeared to be studying it as he exhaled a plume of smoke. A warm evening breeze flowed through the open window near his beanbag chair. It flowed past the green and white cloth curtains causing a slight ripple effect in the fabric as the air pushed the burning tobacco vapors, forming distorted drifting patterns in the dark blue light of his living room.

"I wasn't eavesdropping or anything," Voice said, "but I couldn't help but overhear you tell the High Priestess of Pennsylvania avenue that you would like to do a few strange bedroom acrobatics later. Did you really say that?"

"Yes I did, and yes, you were."

"Guilty as charged. So, what did the Empress say, or should I say scream, before she hung up?"

Temple placed the joint on top of an empty Harlan's Hemp Rubbing Jell jar he was using for an ashtray. He reached up on a wall behind his seat and pushed a switch to an upward position causing the rapid flicker of a strobe light to kick in.

"Well, what did she say?" Voice asked.

"Nothing much."

"Nothing much?"

"Not really."

"Hmm. So you've done this before, I take it. Call and imitate the Prez. You don't go over there, do you?

Temple laughs slightly. "No, of course not. I've heard that they like a little kink, the He and She, so, I just like playing a little."

"You heard this? About the kinky stuff?" Voice said.

"NSA boys and girls told me. Caught it on some phone conversations when the boss man is out of town and gets lonely. Got the dialogue on tape even."

"The NSA is tapping the first Lord and Lordess' phone?"

"Job security. Budget time is coming."

Voice's laugh fills the room. He said, "What, they suspect them of terrorism?"

"No, but nobody is above the law. Except Wells Fargo executives, of course."

The conversation is disrupted by the sound of Brian Temple's cell phone, belting out the theme song from the Beverly Hillbillies. He picks it up from its resting place on the dark carpeted floor. His movements are comically exaggerated by the operating stroboscope as he raises the phone to eye level.

"Let me guess," Voice says. "It's old S.O.S. right?"

"You got it," Temple said, then commenced the conversation. "Yes, Mr. Secretary, how are you, sir?"

"Temple," the Secretary of State responds, "What the hell is wrong with your voice?

You been smoking that Bahamian Brain Burner again? For the love of Pat Sajak, you need to be on your toes boy! You got that? On your toes!"

"Yes sir, on my toes."

"24 hours a day, you got that?"

"Absolutely. 24 hours a day, on my toes."

"What if the Russians were coming?"

"Yes sir, Russians coming, on my toes, twenty-four hours a day."

"Good," Harberts said. "Anyway, I need a status report, right away."

"On the mission, sir?"

"Mission? What mission?"

Temple said, "Missing courier carrying classified documents, sir."

"Oh, yeah. I'm sure it's going fine. No, listen, the Secretary of Education told me at lunch today that Wink Martindale's real name is not Wink Martindale."

"Who sir?"

"Wink Martindale. The game show host. Where have you been Temple?"

"Deep in meditation, sir. Mr. Martindale's first name is not Wink, sir."

"You heard that too?"

"Yes. You just told me that, sir."

"Oh, yeah. It's John or Conrad or something."

"Hard to believe any parent would name their son Conrad when Wink is available."

"Truly spoken, son."

"So what do you want me to do about it sir? Do you want me to acquire a copy of Mr. Martindale's birth certificate?"

"What? No, no. Pay attention boy," Harberts said.

"Of course, sir."

"Chief of Staff called. Wants to know who's in charge of cleaning the Lincoln bedroom. We've got a little issue here. It seems some 90-year-old human skeleton of a Tanzanian Ambassador stayed there last night. Apparently got a hold of one of them D.C. after dark newspaper ads, some place called Big Booty Alaskan Goddesses. Somehow he smuggled in a twin set of 250's, and they brought along a five gallon bucket of pudding, at the old beanpole's request of course. So, apparently, during his tapioca bath they decided to give him a back walking session. Well, with 500 lbs. of fake Alaskan Eskimo-lovin' tap dancing on his spine, shit went south in a hurry. Hell of a mess. He ended up with some broken ribs, a dislocated hip, a missing wallet, and there's some stuff on those walls I can't even identify. So they need the janitor, pronto."

"He's been kidnapped sir," Temple says, deep drag.

"Kidnapped? Who in the hell kidnaps a janitor!"

"Remember? The State Department courier, sir?" Temple said, exhaling a purple plume.

"A State Department courier kidnapped the janitor? What in the hell is wrong with these people? Don't we do background checks on anyone?"

"No and no, sir"

"No and no, what?"

"The courier did not kidnap the janitor, and no, we do not do background checks on government employees, just regular citizens."

"Well, offer the kidnappers some money, or guns, or a free tank or something and get him back."

"We're on the case, sir."

CHAPTER 11

After several hours on the road, Skeet was massively bored from driving, but not willing to let either of his passengers take the wheel of his Lincoln. He pulled from his black and gold Iowa Hawkeye CD case the only disc he had not yet played on the trip and shoved it into the dashboard player.

"Why do you still have a CD player in here?" Paulie asked him.

"Old fashioned. I just got over 8-tracks and vinyl and used to miniature plastic tape cases and they pull that streaming shit. I'm gonna bypass streaming and wait for the next new thing."

Paulie listened to the music for a few minutes then looked over at his friend. "I had no idea you were a Simon and Garfunkel fan."

"I'm not. Just this song."

"Cecilia?"

"Yep. Don't really care for the rest of their stuff. This is the only CD that I've got that's just a single. Sentimental reasons, I guess."

"Cecilia, huh? Lost love or something?"

"Kinda, but not really. There was a gal I met back in Iowa, from a little town by Des Moines. Cecilia from LeGrande."

"Pretty?"

"Yeah, LeGrande's okay."

"I mean Cecilia," Paulie said.

"Oh yeah, petite blonde, blue eyes, you know what I mean."

"So? It didn't work out or what?" Paulie asked.

"Naw. She had some odd little kinks about her."

"Kinks? Like what?"

"Well, she wouldn't eat meat. Vegetarian to the max. That was bad enough, especially in Iowa, but she had these strange little ideas of foreplay. Pasted up nipples, high-heeled black shoes, those crotchless pantyhose, and dancing around solo to Barry White love songs."

"Wow, it actually sounds kind of hot to me," Paulie said.

"Well, it's obvious you've never seen me dance in heels before."

"Oh, well if you feel the relationship was not good..."

"Horrifying."

"...then why do you keep playing the song?"

Skeet looked out the side window, then at Paulie, then back out the window shield.

"Because, I'm trying to figure out one thing. I just need to know. Kind of like one of those mysteries of the ages."

"I bet I know what it is," Paulie said, nodding. "Often wondered myself."

"What the hell was Garfunkel's job?" They said in unison.

Suddenly, Paulie pointed ahead. "Right there, pull into that parking lot."

Skeet turns into the lot and stops the car facing a pink and white painted building with a large billboard. Sitting almost directly under the sign, he and Paulie both lean forward and up from the windshield. Olga opens her side window and sticks her head out the opening to look as well. Skeet looks at the sign, then at Paulie.

"Wanda's School of Passionate Discipline and Leather Craft Emporium?"

"Yep," Paulie said. "This is the place."

Olga smiled.

CHAPTER 12

"You guys have any idea what kind of vehicle we have here?"

Herbie turned in his seat to glare at the passenger sitting in the dark back of the van.

"Hey blowhole, who asked you anything," he said.

"Now that you mention it," Biff said, sitting near the back double doors, "nobody, but I just thought I should maybe point out something before we travel too far."

"What would that be?" Danny asked.

"Who the hell cares," Herbie blurted. "That piss ant wants to talk about what kind of wheels we got, like we don't know."

Biff said, "I don't think you do know."

"Shut up barf breath, it's a goddamn van, a blue one. Is that good enough for you?" Herbie said.

Biff, still sitting as far back in the van as possible, moved forward slightly, pushing aside some cloth curtains hanging from the vehicle roof.

"Does the dome light work?" He asked Danny.

Danny turned the headlight switch in a circular motion on the dash in an attempt to light the interior.

"Nope," he said, "I noticed when we jumped in, the light didn't come on, and it was already running while the driver ran inside that tobacco shop, but no light came on."

"What's wrong buttwipe, you scared of the dark?" Herbie asked.

"That's not the issue. By the way, are you always such a dickhead?"

Before Herbie could respond, Biff said "Hey, I found some matches. There's something I need to look at on the floor."

After the sound of the match struck on a rough surface and a light glow appeared, Biff said, "Holy crap, here's a candle."

He lit the candle and a wavering light from the active flicker of the candle brightened the interior. Silence followed for a moment.

"What is it?" Danny asked.

"Lorenzo Amaya."

"Huh?"

Biff now leaned back against the passenger side wall of the van and slid down to a squat.

"The it," he said, "is Lorenzo Amaya."

Another silent moment.

"Dead guy," Biff said, "on the floor."

"What? What do you mean?" Herbie squealed.

"Dead...guy...on...floor." Biff responded.

"Jesus H," said Herbie, slightly panicked. "A freaking dead guy! What the hell is he doing back there?"

"What most dead guys do...nothing," Biff answered as he blew out the candle.

CHAPTER 13

"Where do you suppose this here bathroom is located? Town or state wise, anyway? We traveled a far spell after they loaded us up."

"No idea," Jasper said. "But I'm guessing some foreign country or some place where no sane or sober person would ever go."

Wasyl nodded, "You mean like San Francisco?"

They sat for a few minutes in the dark. Jasper listened to the rhythmic finger tapping noise his roommate was making on the toilet seat.

"Is there something bothering you?" He asked.

"Well actually, yes," Wasyl answered as he ceased tapping.

"What is it?"

"Listen, I don't mind helping out and all, but is there any way you can carry these here papers on you?"

"No."

"Why not?"

"Because," Jasper said, "they would expect me to have important documents on my person. I'm a State Department Courier, an important cog in the government wheel, a handler of top secret information. Information entrusted only to someone with top level security clearance and of important stature."

"Uh-huh, so what is it?"

"What is what?"

"What is so important that you're...I mean, I'm carrying."

"I don't know."

"Uh-huh. Well Mr. Important Stature, I don't see how you're such a bigshot. After all, right now you're sitting here with me on the floor of this bowel bomb storage facility. Kind of makes us even."

Jasper said, "I am a State Department employee and you are, well, you are...you."

Wasyl squirmed and repositioned himself and leaned back against the wall next to the toilet."Feels like I've got the rear axle of a Peterbilt stuck up my ass."

"My God," Jasper said, "could you possibly be any more vulgar?
"Probably."

"Wait, think about it. You'll be a hero," Jasper said. "You'll be able to tell your children all about this adventure someday. A true Hero."

"Does kinda give a whole new meaning to putting your ass on the line."

"Well, rest assured, as I said earlier, no one has ever thought of checking the rectal area of a janitor for anything," Jasper said in a confident tone.

"I'm not so sure about that," Wasyl said. "Just a couple of months ago, my cousin Arlin of the Murfreesboro Wasyls, he's the custodian of the courthouse there, was driving down the South Hill blacktop when he was stopped by some aliens, stripped naked, and ...well, you know, they eyeballed him and such."

"Really."

"Poked him with a stick too. Least he's hoping it was a stick."

"He was anally probed."

"What he says."

"By aliens."

"Yes, sir."

"From another planet."

"Kentucky."

"Kentuckians are not aliens."

"They are in Tennessee."

A slight creaking noise halted their conversation. Suddenly, their attention was drawn to an increasing amount of light as the bathroom door slowly opened and a figure began to appear.

CHAPTER 14

Olga, Paulie, and Skeet prepared to enter the establishment after sitting for several moments staring at the front of Wanda's School of Passionate Discipline and Leather Craft Emporium. The building had a large billboard on its front, lit by two miniature searchlights that moved slowly over the face of the exterior advertisement, similar to a 20th Century Fox movie opening. It was bright enough in the evening darkness to allow passersby to get a clear view of the panorama featuring a large, full-breasted, full-bellied woman and an acutely thin single-toothed man sporting a somewhat disturbing and particularly overstretched smile. Both of the painted subjects were pointing down at a sign that said "OPEN 24 HOURS ", while the female sat on a saddled sawhorse, whip in hand. The boney male, clad only in a fringed loincloth, was holding a bottle that was labeled "Passion Pumice."

Paulie noticed on the bottom of the sign was a legal disclaimer of sorts with some weather-worn fine print that was difficult to read except for a few words such as scars, rashes, and various skin discolorations.

As the three travelers entered, they heard a bell attached to the door tinkle followed by a musical device playing the first seventeen notes of Aerosmith's "Walk This Way' three times in succession to announce their presence on what sounded like a carnival keyboard.

Directly in front of them, was a slim, pretty young woman with shoulder length red hair sitting at a horseshoe-shaped reception desk in the center of the room. The room was covered in red wallpaper that had a velvet texture to it. The carpet on the floor was red as well, just like the dress on the receptionist, the desk she was sitting at, and the telephone she was speaking on when the trio entered. She looked to be in her late twenties and was demonstrating her ability to multitask as she shuffled papers, spoke on the phone, and held up an index finger pointing toward the ceiling in Paulie, Olga, and Skeet's direction to signal she would be with them in a moment. Just as she hung the phone up from the first call, a second one rang in. She mouthed "Sorry" to her guests, punched a button and spoke into the telephone mouthpiece attached to her collar.

"Wanda's School of Passionate Discipline and Leather Craft Emporium. No matter the weather, it's love and leather. May I help you?" After nodding and saying a yes or two, and one uh-huh, she said "I think we still have those in stock but our sizes will be limited. We've had a real run on those attachments ever since the President announced upcoming tariffs on Chinese made sex toys. I'll forward you to our warehouse."

She looked up at her visitors, smiled a quick semi-sincere smile and without missing a beat started a well-rehearsed monologue while pushing several forms across her desk to them.

"Here are your registration forms. Personal info on the top of the first page including a phone number and next of kin in case of an emergency. Any health problems or medications are to be listed on page two. Class titles are on page three. Check the box by the class you intend to enroll in, sign each form on the three spaces marked X. We accept most major credit cards, debit cards, cash, or local checks."

Olga couldn't help but read the class names, even though she wasn't there for that purpose. But then again, she wasn't really sure why the hell she was there. All she knew for sure was she was taking her husband's place and she wasn't going to waste all the time she had taken learning to speak and read the American language. Her eyes scrolled down the class list:

Beginner's Whipcord

Joys of Sympathy Pain

Advanced Bondage (must have signed a medical waiver).

Paulie pulled the paper from Olga and slid it back toward the receptionist. Olga pulled it back just as quickly.

"Uh, Miss," Paulie said, "we're not actually here for a class."

"Oh, okay" she said, almost absentmindedly as she retrieved a booklet from her left side and placed it on the desktop. "Here's a catalog and order forms, and if you would like to view our seasonal line, you're welcome to go back to our showroom." She points toward the back of the building without looking in that direction.

"You have showroom?" Olga asked

"Certainly. Showroom, theme rooms, sample testing..."

"Theme rooms?"

"Yes. Caveman, Spiderman, Show White and the Seven Dwarfs for groups, and more next door at our Pander Pavilion." The receptionist points to the right with one hand while she hands Olga a brochure with her left.

Paulie tries to intercept the brochure but Olga snatches it and walks away from the desk area, reading as she goes.

"Miss uh...?" Paulie says.

"Popeloski," the young lady answers.

"Yes, Miss Popeloski. We're not here as customers, you see..."

"What? Oh my mistake," she said, "you are here for the job fair! Well, it starts tomorrow, but there is still time to register." She hands more forms to a staring Paulie and a smiling Skeet. She continues, "At the bottom you'll see a list of career opportunities with The Potent Parrot, that's our parent company. We're a franchise, you know. Just to give you a little insight, there are going to be a lot of openings in our pelvic waxing department because of the new federal regulations."

Skeet said "Pelvic waxing? That's a job?"

"Yes," she said smiling. "And we've set new training standards for our professionals to provide our clients with the very best in pelvic polishing procedures since we had that unfortunate incident a while back."

Skeet, being unable to resist, asked her about the incident while touching Paulie's forearm to keep him from stopping her description.

"Oh yes," she said, now showing an exaggerated frown. "Mr. Bulger, a client from Utah...he's a mole man."

"You mean, Mormon?" Skeet asked.

"Something like that. Anyway, he was meeting for his regular session with one of our wax application specialists, Louise, who had misplaced her glasses and set the special micro-wax-wave oven timer for three minutes instead of 30 seconds. So, when she removed the spill-proof waxtainer, it somehow malfunctioned and dripped screamingly hot wax and oil into Mr. Bulger's rather deep posterior crevasse while he was lying on his stomach, having already assumed the protuberant pubic purge position. And the rest, as they say, is blistery."

"You mean history?" Skeet asked.

"What?"

"Never mind."

Paulie gave Skeet an elbow nudge to take the discussion back to their intended subject.

"Miss Popeloski, please, what we need to do..."

"Do you provide caveman?" Olga said across the room with the theme room brochure still in hand.

The young lady, smiling back, answered "No, sorry, no caveman. You have to bring your own. But if you like the Gettysburg Room, we do have a couple of Civil War reenactors that serve as Southern Belle ravagers."

"Gettysburg room?"

"On page sixty-four."

"Thank you," Olga said and turned away to peruse further.

Paulie rolled his eyes up towards the ceiling in frustration, took a deep breath, and prepared to speak again. Before he could exhale, the girl behind the desk pointed at Skeet's basketball shorts.

"Hey! Are you that guy from the TV show?" She asked excitedly.

"TV show?" Skeet answered.

"Yeah, that war doctor show. You know. The Korean War dude," she said, "I thought you'd look older now. That show went on forever."

"Do you mean Hawkeye from Mash?" Skeet answered politely, "No, Hawkeye is a team name. I'm from Iowa."

"Oooh," she said, "Iowa, of course. That's where they grow all the potatoes."

"No," Skeet said. "That would be Idaho."

"What would be Idaho?"

"Where they grow all the potatoes."

"Then why did you say you're from Iowa?"

"I have no idea."

The girl shrugged. "So, what was it you wanted?"

Paulie feigns a smile at the sudden attention.

"I'll take this class," Olga interrupted, reappearing between Skeet and Paulie with a completed class registration form in her hand.

The receptionist took the paper as Paulie groaned in exasperation.

"Okay. The Exxon Sexon. Excellent choice. That's a nine week, hands-on course on the proper allocation of oils, both scented and unscented. It's $199.00 for the class and supplies."

"Supplies?" Olga asked.

"Our new oil product," the girl said, "Mood-Lube. In Tub or Tube."

Suddenly, from seemingly nowhere, the girl was holding up next to her smiling face, what looked like a toothpaste tube and rectangular jar, very similar to a petroleum jelly container, nodding her head slightly towards each item, in full TV-commercial mode.

"I bet your name is Vanna," Skeet said jokingly.

"Now Miss.." Paulie started.

The girl's eyes widened in shock. "You must be psychic!" she said to Skeet in an amazed tone.

"Miss!! Please!!" Paulie screeched, having reached even his mild-mannered breaking point. Everyone stopped and looked at him.

"I'm sorry," he said, feeling a little embarrassed, "it's just that I, uh, we need some assistance here."

"Certainly," she said, "anything you need."

"Thank you," he said.

"No problem. Whatever you need, I'll handle it. Name your wish, your desire, or want and it's yours, instantly."

"It's extremely important."

"I understand, and I will stop at nothing to get whatever, and I mean whatever, you ask for."

"Oh great," Paulie sighed. "I need to speak to Wanda."

"No."

CHAPTER 15

"He seemed pretty nice," Wasyl said.

Jasper looked through the dark in the direction of Wasyl's voice with a look of total incredulity on his face.

"Pretty nice? Pretty nice?! He threatened to remove our testicles with a sharp object and he didn't elaborate as to why. Where does pretty nice come in?"

"Okay, in an evil sort of way," Wasyl said. "Seemed very professional though."

Both men were still seated on the floor of the tiny unlit bathroom. Wasyl put both hands on the side of the toilet and pushed himself up slowly.

"Man, I need to stand up," he said.

Once erect, he stretched his arms out from his sides to release tension in his back. Then his right hand with an open palm went to his chin and pushed his head to the left in a quick, jerking motion, causing several popping noises to emit from his neck and back.

"Do you have to do that?" Jasper asked.

"Hey, did you notice anything weird about that guy?" Wasyl asked, ignoring his companion's complaint.

"Like what? Other than the fact that he is apparently a testicle collector, not a thing," Jasper answered.

"Nope," Wasyl said. "Not that. I'm talking about the way he looked."

"What, now you have cat eyes? It's darker than hell in here. I can't see a thing, so how would I, or you for that matter, know how he looked?"

"I mean, you could tell he was a fella and not a gal, right off, couldn't ya?"

Jasper grumbled to himself, "I'm stranded with a living brain donor." Then he turned to Wasyl.

"Listen you hillbilly. He had a man's voice. That's a dead giveaway. I don't believe any woman in the world could sound like that."

"That's not what I meant," Wasyl said. "And actually, he sounded a lot like my date at the Baldy Baldwin Memorial Dance, Goat Gropin' and Cow Chip Tossin' Gala at Parker's Crossing a few years ago, Buela Bonzer. Big old gal. Weighted about 20 pounds less than Grandpa Wasyl's Massey Ferguson Tractor. Hell of a dancer, though. She must have danced with old Baldy twenty times that night."

"Well...what? Your date talked like a man and danced with a dead guy?"

"Dead guy? Baldy ain't dead."

"You said Baldy whatever memorial dance and..."

"Anyway," Wasyl said, "it wasn't his voice I'm talking about. It's when we had the door open and the moonlight or whatever was shining a bit behind him."

"What ARE you talking about?" Jasper said. "The guy wants to knife us and you want to talk about his silhouette in the moonlight?!"

"I wasn't worried about no knifing," Wasyl said.

"Oh yeah. Okay, Fearless Floor Foreman. Why not?"

"Because he didn't have nothing to stab or slice with in his hand, and when he turned around in the background light, it was pretty plain he didn't have no pockets to keep a stabber or slicer in. That's why."

Jasper was quiet for a moment as he replayed the stranger's visit a few minutes earlier. Suddenly, he said "Oh. Oh. Oh, Holy Pope. He was naked."

"As a newborn beagle pup."

"Man, we have got to get out of here," Jasper hissed as he leaned back against the wall, striking his head slightly. "Ouch. Lord knows what's next."

"I got that," Wasyl answered.

"But how?" Jasper moaned, rubbing the back of his head. "There's no window to break. No tools to pry open the door. No way out. We're doomed. We're going to be killed and cut up by some crazed nude dude who sounds like a woman that dances with dead people."

"Baldy ain't dead."

"Maybe not, but we will be."

"There is one thing."

"We've had it. I can just hear the police notifying my parents, 'yes, we're sorry about your son', How did it happen? My mother will ask. Well, it seems he and a janitor were sitting around the old toilet bowl one night when they were whittled to pieces by a naked terrorist who happens to sound a lot like the star of Dancing with the Deceased."

"Baldy ain't dead, and there is a way."

"I'm going to die right here in this shitter. All those years of study, making my way through college. Up all night working on papers and studying for exams while everyone else was partying, playing, and probably having sex. Not me. No, not me. I studied until I was blue in the face."

"You're black."

"Don't interrupt," Jasper said. "I never cut class, never missed a lecture, always asked for extra credit assignments, graduated with every honor that can be bestowed upon a student. I worked so hard I never even made any friends."

"Well, I kinda like ya," Wasyl interjected. "Despite what you are and all."

"What? Oh great. I'm going to die with a racist. So, you like me despite the fact that I'm black. How nice."

"Uh, no," Wasyl answered. "Being black has got nothin' to do with it. I think you're kind of an asshole. But a likable one all the same. Besides..."

Jasper cut him off. "You don't get it, do you? After all my sacrifice and preparation for greatness, to end it all like this and...Oh my God! I just thought of something else!"

"Now what?"

"Autopsies!"

"Autopsies?"

"Yes, autopsies! When they find our carved up carcasses molding away in this malignant mens room, they'll do autopsies!"

"Getting' a bit overbaked, ain't ya?

"Don't you see? They'll autopsy both of us and, if by any chance during the carnage about to be unleashed upon us by that horde of maniacal sword-wielding dismemberers, they don't find those documents, during the post-mortem, they will find them. And they will be hidden in your custodial butt locker, making you an immediate hero of epic stature, posthumously of course. And I, well, I will be empty-assed and forever forgotten and probably buried in the tomb of the unknown courier. I can see it now, your funeral services on cable news, attended by senators, congressmen, and dignitaries from all over the world. You'll be honored and eulogized by the most prominent people to enter the White House during the previous and current administrations.

"The Presidents?"

"Jay-Z and Kim Hardashian."

"Oh."

"And while your flags are flying and the bands are playing, they'll just roll me into an old piece of carpet and toss me in a drainage ditch. Hell, no one will show up except maybe that fat girl from congressional steno pool and some old Sunday School teacher singing the old ragged cross..."

"Rugged Cross."

"Not at my funeral. Then they'll look down at me and someone will say how natural I look and the Sunday School teacher will say, "Yes, and you know they cut off his nuts," and they'll nod and say it's too bad he didn't hide anything in his ass. His life would have been so much more meaningful."

"If'n you wait a minute," Wasyl said.

"Then, as a final insult, they'll send some former vice president to speak."

"Whoa! I think you're mashing down on the old panic knob a little hard there, don't you?"

"Oh, really?

"Yes. First off, probably ain't gonna be no autopsies, 'cause there ain't no horde and there ain't no swords. Just a bare-assed boy spouting off at us. Second of all, you said yourself, we don't even know what's on these papers, and third, if'n you want to be the hero, I'll gladly dig 'em out right now and hand 'em to you."

"No...thank you."

"And last thing," Wasyl continued, "if you shut up for just a minute, I'll tell ya something."

"What?" Jasper said, folding his arms.

"There is one chance."

"One chance of what?"

"One chance to get out of this poop palace."

"Oh really. One chance. You mean one chance to get out. Well, okay, king of the dustpan, what is it?"

"Well..."

"Does this brilliant plan involve mathematical calculations, repelling down walls, some telepathic messaging, or maybe just some magical hocus-pocus? Please, I can hardly wait. Lay it on me, oh janitorial genius."

"We could walk out the door."

"That's it? Just walk out the door? What an ingenious plan."

"Well, it ain't locked."

CHAPTER 16

Olga stood near the desk reading her class syllabus, while nearby, her associates Skeet and Paulie were staring at the door that was the exit used by the receptionist after she had declined to honor Paulie's request.

"Wow," Skeet said. "Women always react to you like that?"

"Pretty much," Paulie said.

Skeet reached over and put his hand on Paulie's shoulder.

"Don't worry, she'll come back and when she does she'll be putty in your hands," he said.

"Or granite."

"More than likely."

Paulie looked around the room.

"There's got to be some way to get a hold of Wanda. We can't just stand here," he said.

"I'm with you," Skeet said as he was sitting down on the red sofa. He was still bemused at the girl's behavior when Paulie had asked for Wando. She just said "No" and took off. Very odd.

Just as Paulie looked back at Skeet, who had crossed his legs to relax while reading some material he had found by the couch, the phone signaled an incoming call.

"She's not even coming back to answer that," Paulie said.

"You answer it," Skeet said.

"Why would I answer it?"

"Simple. You answer it, talk to whatever weirdo is calling in, yell to the receptionist that it's an emergency, and blammo! She comes back."

"Emergency? At a sex store?"

"You got a better plan?"

Paulie looked down at the red flashing desktop telephone. Instead of a business phone, it looked more like a communication device the President would use to call in the end of the world.

"What'll I say?" He asked Skeet.

"Who cares? Just answer it."

Paulie picked up the receiver. "Hello? Uh, Wanda's...uh, leather place."

"Who is this?" A female voice asked.

"This is a person at Wanda's. A work person. At Wanda's," he stammered.

"A work person?" The female said. "Paulie? Is that you?" she asked.

"Oh, God. Yes, Ruth, it's me," he answered his sister in disbelief.

She laughed and coughed then started to cackle, "What are you doing down at the heavy petting zoo, my biological blimp?"

"It's a lot to get into right now," he said.

"Did you get a job there?"

"No, I did not get a job here."

"Too bad. Might've helped you in the old push-ups with partners league."

"Listen Ruth, I have to go. I've got an issue to resolve."

"Do you ever," she started. "In fact, you've got a couple of items back here that could use your massive misguidance."

"Well, they'll have to..."

“First off, Junior called. Wedding’s canceled. Seems old half-ass...”

“Semi-colon?”

“Yeah, him. Seems old Elvis Palsy and Junior had a disagreement on how to handle post-nuptial consummation proceedings and Junior jetted on the old lad lover.”

“I guess that’s some good news,” Paulie said. “Is Junior there right now?”

“Nope.”

“Where is he?”

“Headed out to seek employment, start a new life. Says he’s quitting college.”

“What? Quit school?”

“That’s what the chip off the old chitlin said.”

“What kind of job is he going to get?”

“I have no idea. Maybe he’ll go down to the grocery store. Get a job picking fly shit out of the pepper. Listen Corporal Corpulent, there’s more.”

“Isn’t there always.”

“Guess who’s back? Old Granny grab ass.”

“Hmm. Okay. Is that good or bad?” He asked.

“Depends on how you look at it, my porcine pal.”

“Meaning?”

“Meaning at this very moment, she’s tucked safely away in her room upstairs,” Ruth said.

“Safely in her room,” Paulie said. “This is good.”

“Yes, it is.”

“Okay.”

“And she’s taken a hostage.”

Paulie says nothing momentarily. He moves the phone away from his head and looks at it as if he were making sure it was really a phone and not an alien being. He slowly put it back to his ear.

"Hostage?" He asked.

"Wow. Did I stutter Ample Ass? Yes, she kidnapped old Blue Eyes."

"Who?"

"Frank."

"Frank?"

"Frank the dog. And she won't let him off her bed and he's afraid to leave because she's armed."

"My god! She has a weapon?"

"One of those big crochet sticks. You might say she's holding him at needlepoint."

"Jesus. What's next?" He moaned.

"Well, how about a list of demands, because she's got 'em."

"List of demands? Is she crazy?"

"Nuttier than squirrel shit. I wrote them down for you. So, here we go. First, she wants transportation, supplies, and absolutely no more cops."

"Cops?" Paulie chirped. "Holy Mother of Jesus. The police haven't been there, have they Ruth?"

"Just long enough to look in the bedroom and see the canine and the fossilized felon."

"So, uh, what did the police say to do?"

"Put it out of its misery and bury it out back."

"My God. Kill the dog? Why?"

"They didn't mention the dog," Ruth said. "Now, as I was saying, she wants transportation and travel supplies."

"And what would that be? A helicopter and cash, I suppose," Paulie said.

"Nope. A greyhound bus ticket to Joplin and 2 bottles of Johnny Walker Red."

"Is that it?"

"No, there's two more. One of them I already took care of for you. She wanted her lost dentures returned. I found them jammed into the business end of a plumber's helper, stuck to a picture of Mel Gibson with a piece of Bazooka Bubble Gum."

"What the..."

"Don't ask. Oh, and the last demand is Old Frank upstairs has to sing one of his greatest hits to her while they dance."

"She wants the dog to sing to her."

"Preferably Moon River."

"Moon River? That's Andy Williams."

"Does it make a difference? By the way, what are you doing down at the sex supply shop anyway, Mr. Mantits?"

Paulie sighed loudly. Oh what the hell, he figured. He might as well tell her, so he did.

"Really?" Rush said. "So, you need to talk to Wanda? That's it? No problem, O bloated brother of mine. Who's working the desk there anyway?

"Ms. Popeloski," Paulie answered. "But she went into the back room and won't come out."

"What did you do, give her a little flab flash?"

"No."

"Just tell her Ruth is on the phone. Yell it if you have to."

"Okay. I'll try it."

Paulie held the phone against his chest, looked at Skeet, shrugged and yelled towards the back door, "Ruth is on the phone!"

No sooner than he had said Ruth, the door opened and the young red-haired receptionist appeared. She walked over to Paulie and took the phone from him.

"Hi Ruth!" the girl said, smiling.

The telephone conversation lasted a couple of minutes, then the girl picked up some paper and started writing on it.

"Okay," she said. "How many? Ten. Okay. Uh-huh, we still have those. I'll throw a couple extras in. Charge it to who?" The girl looked over at Paulie. "Sure. What's that?" The girl looked at Paulie again, giggled, and turned her head. "Really? That is so bizarre. Okay, here he is. She wants to talk to you again." She handed Paulie the phone.

"Yes?" Paulie said.

"Well, it's all set," Ruth said. "She's gonna call Wanda for you."

"Thanks Ruth," Paulie said. "Life is strange sometimes. I mean, I can't imagine anything stranger than me answering the phone and it being you. What could be weirder than that?"

"You want weird, just have her read back my supply order."

CHAPTER 17

After a few moments of reflective silence in the dark, Danny asked "How do you know the guy's name anyway?"

"Toe tag," Biff said.

He then pulled out another match, struck it and relit the candle.

Biff said, "I think this must be some kind of hearse or something. Curtains, candles, and this dude's in some kind of container. It's not a coffin. Just a big ziplock bag or something."

He leaned over and pulled an official looking paper from the front of the deceased man's carrying case.

"Death certificate," he said. "Says the cause of death is heart failure."

"Heart attack, huh," Herbie said.

"Yep, heart attack," Biff continued. "Probably brought on by the fifty or sixty puncture marks and bullet holes in him."

Herbie said, "Well, at least it ain't something contagious."

"In Juarez it is."

They drove on in silence for a few miles.

With the van interior lit by the flickering flame coming from the large, round funeral candle sitting on a box between the front seats and the cargo area. Danny couldn't help but notice his friend's attire. He'd seen it earlier but he hadn't said anything to him about it.

"Hey Herbie, I've been meaning to ask you something," he said.

"What is it?" Herbie asked.

Danny said, "What's the deal with your clothes? You never dress like that. Swim trunks, sandals, and that shirt's loud enough to cure the deaf."

"My new girlfriend," he said. "She wants me to wear more revealing stuff. Flashier, beach-like stuff. Says it turns her on."

"Do tell. Who is the new woman anyway?"

"Tina Ortiz," Herbie said in a low tone as if he was trying to say something he didn't want anyone to hear.

"Big Tina? From the tattoo shop?"

"Yeah, yeah, yeah, that's her," Herbie said, "and for your information, she is a tattooist, a true artist. She's even taking an advanced ink class online from InkSkinU!"

"Oh, Yeah?"

"Yeah, it's the world's most respected tattoo college."

"Tattoo college, huh? There is such a thing?"

"Yeah, lots of famous tattooists have graduated from there."

"What famous tattooists?"

"Just some famous ones."

"Who?"

"Well, Slick Needle Jones, and Remmie the Inkster Brandt. Oh yeah, and of course Billy Blue Skin," Herbie said.

"Never heard of them," Danny said.

"Pretty elite crowd. Tight circle. You know how artists are."

"I bet. Where is this Tattoo U at?" Danny inquired.

"Someplace in New Jersey. She turned down an offer from that school in Massachusetts...MIT."

"Uh, MIT? MIT offered Tina a scholarship? THE MIT?"

"Yeah, THE MIT. Manny's Ink Temple. What do you think I been talking about?"

"Right," Danny said, looking Herbie up and down. "So how come you don't have any body art?"

"Actually," Herbie said, "Tina is using me for her graduation project." He smiled, folded his arms in front of him and turned his grinning face towards Danny.

Danny looked him over again. "I see a lot of skin, but no inkblots. Hasn't she started yet?"

"Well yeah, she started. She did one," he mumbled.

"Let me see it."

"No."

"Why?" Danny said. "Oh, so she screwed it up, didn't she?"

"No, it's perfect, but ....no."

"Oh, I see, bad placement huh?"

Herbie slumps down, "A Damn barber pole on my ... I didn't think there was enough Tequila in all of Mexico to get me that drunk."

"Ouch," Danny said.

"You don't know the half of it."

"I hate to break in on your discussion of the current epidermal art trends, but how much longer will this trip take?" Biff asked from his position by the side wall.

"Long time," Danny said. "Probably most of the night."

Biff moved to the area just behind and between the front seats. He took the candle, blew out the flame and perched himself in the box formerly holding the flame.

"How's the air conditioner in here? It's getting pretty warm," he said.

"Holy shit," Herbie said. "Now what's wrong with you buttbrain? You afraid you're gonna sweat a little?"

Biff leaned forward slightly. “No, perspiration is not what I’m concerned about. We’re all sweating already. I’m more concerned about the one of us that’s not perspiring.”

He nodded his head back towards the rear of the van before continuing. “It appears to me that our late passenger has been late for a while now, and according to this form I have here...” he held up with the thumb and index finger of his right hand,” ...he was on his way to be embalmed when we intercepted him. Therefore, the pre-burial bloat prevention process has not been properly administered...I think you get my drift, and if not, soon we will all get his.”

Herbie grabbed the paper from Biff’s hand and held it in front of the dim light of the console radio face.

“Great,” he said, “a whiner and a stinker.”

“You know,” Biff said, “when I was a young boy, I knew a kid just like you, Herbie. We used to invite him over whenever we had a party so we could play pin the tail on the asshole.”

“Oh yeah!” Herbie yelled. “How would you like...”

“Hold up there, Tonto,” Biff interrupted, holding his hands up, palms facing towards Herbie, “I’m just trying to make a point here about our cargo.”

“He’s right,” Danny said. “We’ve got to get rid of the dead guy, or the van, or both, and soon.”

Herbie shakes his head, “Damn it Danny, how in the hell did you manage to pick a funeral van to steal? You should have looked inside first to make sure there wasn’t any decaying meat before you yelled to jump in.”

“I had no idea that’s what it was,” Danny said. “I mean, what are the chances that out of an entire parking lot of cars, there’d be a dead body in the one we took?”

“Are you shittin’ me? Herbie said. “We’re talking about Juarez here. It’s the freakin murder capital of the world. Christ, I think the last AAA Traveler's Guide said one in three motor vehicles and fifty percent of the parking garages contained at least one stiff, not to mention unrented hotel rooms and some laundry chutes."

Danny shrugged, "Didn't cross my mind. Besides, it's not a big van. You'd think they'd want something bigger to haul bodies around in."

"Hell, it don't take much room down in the Casualty Capitol," Herbie said. "They found one guy stuffed in a gym bag outside the library, and don't forget Simmy the Lop."

"Simmy the Lop?"

"Yeah. Stole some pot from one of the local distributors. Found him stuffed in a Clorox Bleach bottle."

"No way. How?"

"Don't ask me, but he was all in there. All except his shoes of course. Even put Rosary beads in with him."

"Very considerate of them."

"Yeah, they're like that."

CHAPTER 18

Vanna looked at Paulie and Skeet, shook her head, sighed deeply, and sat down in the red chair behind her red desk.

"I don't know why this can't wait," she said. "Wanda is very busy and she hates to be bothered when she's doing research with Dr. Grinspoon. But, Ruth said to call her."

"She does research?" Skeet inquired.

"New product designs. Dr. Grinspoon is world famous for his health and safety product line for active older people with health issues," she said, glancing at Paulie.

"Did you say Grinspoon?" Skeet responded.

"Obviously you've heard of him," she said.

"Uh, well, I'm not sure."

"Well, surely you've heard of some of his inventions. The Skinny Minnie Late in Life Tubular Bra, or the one hundred percent life-like Ben Matlock Love Masks. His most famous product is the All Leather Testicular Sag Stopper, now with Koala Bear fur cup lining, guaranteed to put a smile on your face while it keeps you in place."

Paulie just stared blankly at the young human advertisement. She shook her head slightly.

"Okay, I'll call Wanda. Who should I say wants to talk to her?"

"Our names won't mean anything to her," Paulie said.

"Great," she said.

"So just tell her this," he said, and handed the young woman a piece of paper with the code he had copied from the code book.

She looked at the paper, then looked up at Paulie and then at Skeet. Paulie stared back. Skeet shrugged. The girl looked back at the paper.

"How much are Peppermint Panties?" Olga yelled from across the room.

"$9.95," Vanna responded, still looking at the paper then addressed Paulie. "So, is this for real?"

"Yes, it's for real."

"Okay," she said and began pushing numbers on her phone. Someone eventually answered and she made her request, then said, "Yes Raymond, I'm sure she is busy, but I do need to talk to her."

Paulie and Skeet had moved two red folding chairs to the front of the red desk. Olga was coming in and out of the room, asking opinions on different clothing items she had apparently located in the back of the building in the showroom area. Skeet found her activities strangely cute. Paulie found them strangely strange.

The receptionist was lightly twirling a red pen in her right hand as she continued the conversation with the guy who had answered the call.

"Yes, I do understand Raymond. I know she's tied up right now but...Oh, I see, she actually is tied up. Okay." She looks imploringly at Paulie. He whispers, "Just have that guy give Wanda the code. Exactly as it's written."

Skeet said, "You sure you should do that? Just tell some sex lariat looper the code?"

"It'll be okay," Paulie said. "He won't understand it."

"That's a pretty safe bet," Vanna said.

"Do it," Paulie said. "Please."

The receptionist smiled at Skeet, raised and lowered her eyebrows in an "Oh well" gesture and said into the phone, "Raymond, get a pen and paper." She then reached over and slid the piece of paper Paulie had written on closer to her on the desktop.

"Okay, you ready Raymond? Good. Tell Wanda this, exactly," she cleared her throat slightly, "To you my dear, my love is following. Canyon yodeling and echo swallowing."

There was a short moment of silence as if she was waiting for Raymond to respond.

"Did you get that Raymond?" She asked. "Read it back to me. Yes, that's it...Uh huh."

Paulie said, "Well?"

She holds her index finger up to signal to wait.

"Yes Raymond. I know, Raymond. Tell Wanda please, and now would be a good time."

She starts to address Paulie when she quickly stops and speaks back into the phone again. "Hello? Wanda? Wow, that was fast. Yes, there are three of them..a little fat dude, a good looking guy in shorts, and around here somewhere is a short dark-haired woman who talks funny. I think she's from Minnesota or Pakistan or something.. uh-huh...okay, let me write that down...say it again...okay, yep got it. What's that?"

Paulie tries to grab the paper that Vanna has written on, but she quickly pulls it back and gives him a stern look. "Just wait a minute," she said. "Huh? Oh no, not you Wanda. What was it you asked? No, not much is going on. Mr. Manwhither was in. He loves the gerbil-fur slip-on toe warmers, and Mrs. Lapklinger called also. She's out of the hospital and recovering nicely. The doctor told her not to attempt that position again, especially while hanging upside down...something to do with her weight and her thyroid medication...no, that's all...yes, I'll give them the message. Word for word. Okay," she said and hung up.

"Well?" Paulie said again, almost breathlessly.

"Well, I believe you people have all lost your freaking thinking knobs," she said.

"Can I see the message?" He asked.

"Calm down," Skeet said.

"I'll read it to you," the receptionist said. "Are you ready?"

"Yes! Yes! Let's hear it!"

"Okay. Here it is. The skates are real. That's what I feel. The doctor said banana peel."

Paulie quickly started looking through his blue code book, flipping the pages with his right while holding the book on his lap.

"A little spastic, isn't he?" Vanna said to Skeet, who just smiled back.

Paulie finally stopped at a page and mumbled some words to himself. Suddenly he bolts to a standing position in front of his chair.

"Oh my God. Oh my God!" He screeched.

"What?!" Skeet and Vanna yelped.

"It's right here in the code book!"

"What?" Skeet said. "What's in the code book?"

"Drunken Presbyterians disguised as Lithuanian radicals are going to attack the cantaloupe fields near Cuba City, Missouri with nuclear warheads."

Skeet raised his eyebrows. "What the hell are you talking about?

Paulie held the book out in front of his friend. "It's all right here in the code book. The message. The skates are real. That's what I feel. The doctor said bandana peel."

"Bandana peel?" Skeet said. "How do you peel a bandana?"

Vanna shook her head, "It's not a bandana peel, it's banana peel."

"Huh? Oh," Paulies said, sitting back down slowly and looking at his back again.

"Hopefully that makes a difference. Every letter in every word is important." He looks up at Skeet and Vanna, "Whew. Here it is. It means she'll be here in an hour."

"Man," Skeet said, "you gotta brush up on your code reading, Blumer."

"Bandana peel," Vanna said giggling.

CHAPTER 19

Both men were standing by the door in the dark bathroom looking down at the area where the door handle should be located, but neither moved or attempted to touch it.

"So, uh, let's go ahead and look outside," Jasper said with obvious hesitation.

"Okay," Wasyl answered. "Let's."

There was still no movement.

"Rock, paper, scissors," Wasyl said.

"What?"

"Rock, paper, scissors. Loser takes a look outside."

"Don't be stupid. That's a idiotic way to decide."

"Okay, so how?"

"Well," Jasper said, "we'll do it the only fair way I can think of right off hand. I'll think of a number between one and ten. You tell me what it is."

"I'll just look," Wasyl said.

Wasyl felt for the doorknob. It made a slight metallic rattling noise when his hand came in contact with it. He grasped it firmly and slowly started to turn it. As he did, the door opened slightly and a thin ray of white light began to shine through the opening into the room. He stopped.

"Well," Jasper whispered, "look outside."

Without answering, Wasyl put his face against the narrow door opening and peered out into the night with his left eye.

"Oh, gawd almighty!" He gasped.

"What is it?" Jasper asked.

"Must be a hundred of 'em."

"A hundred?"

"Mebbe two hundred."

"Two hundred?" Jasper said, grasping Wasyl's shoulder with his hand. "Two Hundred? Two hundred kidnappers?!"

"Naked people."

"Naked people?"

"I said that already."

"But..but..but..."

"Exactly."

"I don't get it," Jasper said, stepping back from the doorway.

"I do," Wasyl said. "Nudies. And they got us surrounded."

CHAPTER 20

When the cell phone in the van rang, Danny answered, knowing who it was on the dedicated line before the caller spoke.

"Location?" The woman's voice said before any greeting transpired.

"Ten miles from the compound," he answered.

"You realize you're late."

"Yeah. We had a delay. We ended up with a corpse in our vehicle and had to dispose of him."

"Corpse?"

"It's a long story."

"Save it…Wait, is this someone you killed?"

"No, just a dead guy. Amaya or something. Anyway, we got rid of him so we're good now."

"What did you say?"

"I said we got rid of him"

"No, not that. What was the dead man's name?"

"Amaya. Something like that," he said, glancing back at Biff seated behind him to his right.

"First name?" The woman asked.

"Hell, I don't know. Just a minute," Danny said then turned back to Biff. "What was the stiff's first name?"

"Miguel."

"It was.."

"I heard," the woman said. "How did he die? Could you tell?"

"Yeah, He died from an overdose of holes as far as we could tell. He sure had a lot of them."

"Describe the man to me."

"What? Who is this guy anyway? I thought we were supposed to get our fannies to this compound."

"Describe him to me," she said.

Danny handed the phone to Herbie. "Here," he said, "describe the dead guy to her." Herbie pushed the phone away.

"What?" He said, "I'm not describing the guy. I have no idea what he looked like. Tell Biff the ballerina to do it."

Danny held the phone back towards Biff. Biff shrugged and took it.

"Hello," he said.

"Who is this?" The woman asked.

"My name is Biff and I'm supposed to describe some dead guy in a ziplock bag to you."

"You're kidding, right?"

"Really, the guy was in a big plastic bag."

"No, I mean your name's really Biff?"

"Yes," he said.

"Sorry," she said, "I've just never talked to a Biff before. Is that short for something?"

"Lady, what in the world would Biff be short for?"

"Okay, a description please."

"Well, I'm about six foot..."

"Not yours. The deceased man's description."

He then gave her a description and handed the phone back to Danny as she instructed him to.

"She wants to talk to you," he said.

"Yes?" Danny said into the phone.

"What did you do with the body?"

"Dropped him off at the service delivery door at a funeral home."

"Go back and get him and bring him back with you. I will call again to verify a new meeting place."

"Uh, get him? Is he important?"

"He could be useful."

"Hey, I don't want to complain, but this dead guy hasn't been treated yet, if you get my meaning. You know that maturing process dead stuff goes through? Well, he's going through it. If he was an apple, they'd use him for cider soon."

"I get the picture."

"Good."

"Pack him in ice. Get him now," the voice on the phone hung up.

CHAPTER 21

Jasper was sitting on the edge of the toilet seat. Wasyl was sitting on the floor to his right, leaning back against the wall. They were both staring off into the bathroom darkness, immersed in their own thoughts.

"I've never seen so many nude people at one time," Jasper said in amazement. "It's like a giant, outdoor locker room."

"Hard to figure," Wasyl said. "Even harder to figure why a bunch of naked nellies would want to put us in a bathroom, and it can't be a nudist colony, I didn't see nobody playing volleyball."

"All I know is, we're stuck," Jasper said, putting his face into his hands.

"Not really," Wasyl said.

"Not really? What's that mean?"

"We just walk out through the crowd and leave," Wasyl said as he stood up.

"Are you kidding?" Jasper said, raising his head up. "Two fully clothed men just walk unnoticed through a naked crowd...Just like that?"

"Well, we'll have to take off..." Wasyl answered.

"Ooh noo," Jasper said. "That's not happening. Not on a bet."

Wasyl gave a slight shake of his head. "Listen, I'm thirsty, I'm tired, and I damn sure don't want to wait for some of them boys to come in here and jerk off my grapes to make a necklace for their homecoming dates. So let's go."

"No way."

"And, I might add, pretty soon I'm gonna have to take a squat on this here unflushable piece of porcelain. And, due to the fact I had double bean breakfast burritos with extra refried, not to mention the Super Slammin Salsa, we are not gonna want to hang out here much longer. Specially considering I'm about out of Lemon Pledge."

"That would mean disclosing the whereabouts of the documents."

"In a most unfortunate way."

"Okay, let's go," Jasper said after a moment.

"Better undress for the part."

"Oh, Lord."

CHAPTER 22

Brian Temple steps from an early morning shower while simultaneously reaching for a ringing wall phone. The landline in Temple's house was registered under a number only one person aside from himself knew.

"Good morning Mr. Secretary," he said after picking up the receiver while scrubbing his hair with the towel in his opposite hand.

"Temple?" His boss answered. "Give me a status report."

"Currently stark naked, sir"

"What? Stark naked? What the hell is wrong with them?"

"Them? Them, who sir?"

"Who the hell do you think I'm talking about?"

"No idea, sir."

"That glorified mailman and the maid."

"Janitor."

"Janitor, maid, what's the difference?"

"They've left the bathroom, sir."

"I guess that's good news, whatever the hell it means. And how do you know this?"

"Contacts on the compound," Temple said, reaching into his medicine cabinet and retrieving a black hairbrush and combing through his dark wet hair.

“Well, Holy Ed McMahon boy, then have the contacts get them out.”

“How sir?”

“Pull some guns out and start blastin’. Haven’t you ever seen one of those Ken Eastwood training films?”

“Clint, sir.”

“Clint what?”

“It’s Clint Eastwood, sir.”

“No shit?”

“Absolutely none sir.”

“Who the hell is Ken?”

“No idea, sir.”

“Anyway, Eastwood makes great training films.”

“They’re not actually training films, sir.”

“Kills a lot of people. Great stuff. So, have those contacts of yours draw down on them assholes and get Jasper out.”

“No can do, sir,”

“Why the hell not?”

“No weapons, sir.”

“Explain, Temple.”

“No place to carry weapons, sir. They’re undercover at a nudist compound.”

“How in the hell can they be undercover if everyone is naked?”

“You could call it undercoverless, sir.”

“They’re all naked? I thought this place was some kind of church.”

“It is. It happens to be a nude church gathering.”

“Christ. Bare-assed Baptist. Has the world gone AWO loose?”

“Apparently, sir.”

“Well, if you can’t get them out, then take out the whole damn compound. Ramp it up. God, I always liked the sound of that. Ramp it up. That’s real military shit.”

“How much time do we have, sir?”

"I don't know, but not much. Hey, remember the good old days where we had stuff like Napalm?"

"No sir, but I've heard."

"Boy, that crap did the job. Wipe out a whole area. Fried shit right down to the nub. Couldn't grow mold for a decade after you smacked it with Napalm. Well, I guess we can't always get what we want."

"Guess not, sir."

"By the way, Temple, what the hell is the 10:30 appointment I'm supposed to have with the legal department?"

"Paternity suit, sir."

"Paternity suit? Whose?"

"Yours, sir."

"Paternity?"

"Establishing parenthood, sir."

"Christ, I know who my parents are, Temple."

"Not your parents, sir. Miss Maplehandle from the Capitol Club is suing to prove you are the father of her as-yet unborn child."

"Maplehandle, huh? Do I know her? Hey, does she have a tiny scar on her...?"

"Wouldn't know, sir. She's short, chubby, very irate, and wants to file a paternity suit to prove you are the father."

"Oh, yeah? Well, we'll countersue. See how she likes that."

"Countersue? How sir?"

"It's obvious. She wants to file a paternity suit to prove I'm the father. Well, we'll file a maternity suit to prove she's not the mother."

"That should work, sir."

CHAPTER 23

Wanda was seated behind her dark-stained, wooden desk wearing a conservative navy blue business pantsuit and lady's sport coat. She was a professional looking woman from top to bottom. She was dark, her hair was dark, straight, and shoulder-length. Her face was pretty but serious and her almond complexion was highlighted with just a touch of make-up and lipstick. A pair of brown eyes looked out from dark round framed eyeglasses.

"So," she said in a very business-like tone, "you're the ones that are going to retrieve our lost dossier."

Skeet shrugged. Paulie nodded. Olga read another brochure. Wanda's office, unlike the rest of the building' interior, was not red. Two of the walls were paneled in a dark wood grain style while the others were painted or papered in a lighter brown motif. Each wall sported photographs or paintings of important looking women, dressed formally, staring out at the room's occupants. Paulie and Skeet were seated in expensive brown leather, thick-cushioned office chairs directly in front of Wanda's desk, while Olga sat on an office sofa along a paneled wall directly beneath a painting of Tina Turner smiling out at the world like only Tina Turner could.

"What do you know about this mission?" Wanda asked.

"Very little," Paulie answered.

"How much is very little?" She inquired.

"A grand total of what you've said so far," Skeet chimed in.

Wanda reached down with her left hand and retrieved a black file folder from a desk drawer and laid it on her desktop. The folder was marked "Mission Docs-Sensitive/Classified" in large bold letters on the top with a round seal directly beneath it. She then rested both of her forearms on her desk and nodded at the folder.

"Open it up," she said. "Take a look."

"Is more class and toy stuff?" Olga asked from across the room.

"No dear," Wanda responded. "Mission details, risk analysis, top secret info."

"No, thank you," Olga said and went back to her reading.

Paulie flipped open the file as Skeet leaned toward him so they could both read the documents together. After a moment, Skeet and Paulie looked at each other and leaned back in their chairs.

Skeet said, "Says here that a United States State Department Courier was kidnapped by a home health care delivery service company posing as a drug cartel."

Wanda nods.

"Seems a little backward," he said.

"How so?" She asked.

Paulie interrupted, "I think what he means is, why would a legitimate business like a medical supply service pretend to be a drug cartel?" He gives her a smile. She doesn't return it.

"Tax reasons," she answered.

"Oh," Paulie said, glancing at Skeet.

"Tax reasons," she repeated. "Government needs to have drug cartels. They're a must. Drug war. Drug czar. Agents kicking in doors, prosecutors and judges protecting us, the poor everyday working souls. Very newsworthy. Makes for wonderful re-election platforms as well. Not to mention the drug trafficking schools the arrested people are sent to by the feds."

"Drug trafficking schools?" Paulie asked.

"Certainly." She continued. "Just put a bunch of small-time potheads into the Federal Prison system with established dealers. None of them have any skills, so except for their new druggie relationships, they have nothing when they get out. Feds have taken everything they own, so back they go, doing what they did before, but even bigger now. Recycling is not just for paper and plastic, boys."

"Uh...okay...but..." Paulie stammered.

"The real war has been on small business," she continued. "There's no shooting. Mostly anyway. They just regulate and tax them into oblivion. And, if and when they go under, no big deal. There's always some other person with a dream worth crushing coming along."

Skeet tapped the black folder lying on the desk, with his right index finger. "It says W.A.S.T.E. on it, what's that stand for?"

"War Against Small Time Entrepreneurs. Anyway, the smart ones pose as drug cartels, most of them don't sell drugs, at least not yet. Of course, they can't let the feds know that or there's hell to pay. So they'd better be dealing."

"So, no taxes?" Skeet asked.

"Have you ever heard of gangs and drug cartels paying taxes?"

"Nope."

Paulie asked, "So, how do the feds operate if they don't get tax money from all this?"

Wanda leaned back in her chair and folded her arms across her stomach.

"When they get done siphoning away from the businesses, they hit Johnny and Joan Lunchbucket."

"Who?" Paulie asked.

"Working class people. Tax the crap out of them and scream, 'It's for the children! Terrorists are coming! Must stop China!" She said waving her arms above her head in a mock attention getting motion. She then put her arms back to a resting spot in her lap. "Can't argue with any of that. It would be un-American."

"But what if everyone can't pay?" Paulie asked, furrowing his brows.

"The government has their two magic words to fall back on."

"Magic words? What magic words?"

"Deficit... Spending."

Paulie stood up slowly, "I'm not sure I want anything to do with helping out in this deal."

"Me either," Skeet said, still seated. "Sounds as messed up as a bad Vin Diesel movie."

"Has there ever been a good one?" She said, then taps her desk with a red-nailed fingertip. "Sit down."

Staring momentarily at Paulie as he retook his seat, she took off her glasses and placed them on her desk.

"Changes are coming. They're happening right now. The person you are working for is on the white hat side. That person agrees with you. So, uncramp your colons."

CHAPTER 24

"You always get me into shit like this," Herbie said, still seated in the passenger side of the van.

After Danny's phone conversation had ended, he had turned their vehicle around and started heading back to the location where they left their deceased cargo.

"It's not a big deal," Danny said. "We pick the guy up and take him where they want us to take him. Then we drop him off and we're done. Simple."

"Yeah, sure. Everything will be just dandy. He's probably got stuff starting to ooze out all over him, or worse yet, he'll raise up from the dead and when we least suspect it, he'll jump us and suck the cartilage out of our bones."

"Christ, Herbie, where do you get this stuff? Nobody is gonna suck the bone cartilage out of us."

"It happens."

"No...it...doesn't."

"Oh yeah. Well stiffs do rise from the dead."

"Really? When?"

"How about Godfrey? Huh, Mr. Smart Guy? Explain that."

"He didn't rise from the dead."

"Sure he did. Got up from that coffin and walked around like God Almighty Frankenstein himself, all moaning and groaning. Jesus, what a sight that was."

"Herbie, he was drunk. He overdosed on Tequila Sunrises and party snacks and then fell on Marcello Greenwood's couch and broke it when he passed out. It wasn't a coffin. The groaning came right before he barfed on the rose bushes. It was a party. Think about it. When did you ever see a Frankenstein movie when the scary part was the monster puking up meatballs and pickle relish into some flowers."

"You are just not a believer. So, never mind about Godfrey. But no matter what you say, I have this feeling we're headed for a serious foreskin stomping."

"What are you complaining about, Herbie? I ask you to help me with one simple thing and you complain. Just think for a minute... Look at all the things I've done for you."

Herbie said, "Like what? Name one thing."

"Hey old pal, lots of things. Think about it. How about that dancer from Austin I hooked you up with? Lorna or Lena or..."

"Leona."

"Yeah, that's it, Leona. Did you forget about that?" Danny asked.

"Hard to forget Leona," Herbie said sarcastically.

"Now, she was hot."

"She had a face like Ozzy Osbourne."

"She didn't believe in chemical based make-up."

"She had sex with the mailman on my couch."

"Some basic boundary issues."

"She emptied out my bank account."

"Fiscally challenged."

"Then she burnt down my trailer."

"Some misperceived renovation work."

“That happened while I was in the hospital having my stomach pumped from the rat poison she had put in my bean soup.”

“Just not a student of the culinary arts. But the point is, you never would have met her if it wasn’t for me. Did you ever think of that?”

“More often than you know.”

From behind them in the van compartment between the seats, Biff pointed ahead through the windshield, “There it is,” he said.

The sign on the building said, ‘Three Feathers Funeral Home.’ The building was actually a three-story house that was illuminated by large lights and painted a bluish gray with white trim around the windows. The roof was shingled a dark reddish brown and the sidewalk to the front entrance was bordered by well-kept shrubbery which was surrounded by a perfectly manicured yard. Next door to the building was an open lot with a sign that said “Coming Soon-Three Feathers Casino.” Danny drove around to the back entrance where they had left the remains of Mr. Amaya earlier. As the headlights brightened the backdoor and service entrance, it became obvious that Mr. Amaya was not present. He was missing.

“Shit,” Herbie said. “Somebody stole him.”

Danny looked at Herbie. “Stole him? Who would steal a dead body?”

“Oh, okay, nobody took him. That means he rose up and took off. Oh wait, that’s right, dead people don’t rise up. At least that’s what I’ve been told,” Herbie said.

Biff said, “Someone probably took him inside. It is a funeral home, after all.”

“Well,” Danny said looking at the building’s back door, “we need to go in and get him.”

“We need a plan,” Biff added. “After all, we left a body here and now we want to get it back. Probably gonna be questions. A good plan would be in order.”

"Okay," Herbie said, "I got it. Danny, rev up the motor. Me and Peter Packer back there, will jump out. When you get it to maximum RPM, launch and crash it through the back wall and we'll follow you in. I'll take this tire iron with me in case I need to crack some heads. We'll toss the stiff in the van and go. Got it?"

"Or we could just knock," Biff said.

Danny said, "Good idea, Biff."

"Pussies."

CHAPTER 25

Temple pours a cup of coffee from the small hotel-style coffee maker he keeps in his bathroom. It's 5:20 a.m. and his phone call from the Secretary of State now completed, he walked into his living room, clad only in dark maroon boxers emblazoned with "Escapa Cervasa" in white letters that run parallel to the bottom hem on his left thigh. He sits on his beanbag chair and stretches his legs full length in front of him.

"Well?" Voice said.

"You're up early," Temple responds, then sips from his Roy Rogers coffee mug as he holds it with both hands.

"Don't be ignorant. Sleep is for dead people. Tell me, what did old Foghorn Blowhorn want? I clearly heard the phone of insipidity ring in the john."

"Insipidity? Is that a word?"

"It is now. I have some juice with Mr. Webster."

"Uh-huh."

"You might say I'm very wordly."

"Cute."

"Thank you. Back on topic. What did the bishop of bloviation want?"

Temple takes another sip from his cup, picks up an inch-long joint leftover from the previous night from the floor near his seat and lights it with a small butane lighter and takes a deep, eyes-closed inhale.

"He wants me to level the compound if the captives are not decaptived," he said, exhaling a smooth expanding stream of smoke.

"Decaptived?"

"I have words too."

"I salute you. When do you expect this event to take place?"

"Soon."

"Soon?"

"Almost immediately."

"Ah, I see."

Temple takes another long inhale then places the still smoldering pot cigarette on a small white saucer and exhales slowly.

"I take it he's not bloviating this time," Voice said.

"I detected no blove," Temple answered.

"Doesn't sound like you're going to be able to wait for Hillbilly Bob and Buttbandits to arrive in time to save the day."

"No. And they're not butt bandits."

"You have proof?"

"None."

"I stand uncorrected."

Temple rises and walks into his bedroom. When he returns, he is carrying a white sport shirt, black socks, and a pair of black dress pants. He sits on his beanbag and pulls on his socks, then stands as he puts on his pants.

Voice said, "So, if you don't get them out, and out very soon, you are to declare war on Montana, correct?"

"Just the western part."

Temple began to tuck his shirt into his pants he had just put on and buttoned it. He picked up his cell phone and took his seat again.

“I’ve got some calls to make,” he said. “We’ll need some distractions.”

“A little wag the dog?”

“Yes.”

“Sounds like you might want to shake the whole kennel.”

CHAPTER 26

Wasyl and Jasper stood just inside the door, staring out through the partial opening into the night. They were both completely nude.

"I cannot believe this," Jasper said.

"Are you okay?" Wasyl asked him while moving slightly to get a better view of the outside.

"Am I okay? Really?! Am I okay?"

"Just checking."

"I mean, what could be wrong? After all, I'm about to run through a crowd of naked people in hopes of securing my escape from some maniac who has threatened my life. A maniac, I might add, that was also naked at the time he leveled his threat. And, of course, just to make sure the trouser-less triangle is complete, I am going to attempt to slide through this skin circus totally unattired."

"I'll be with you," Wasyl said.

Jasper looked at his portly companion. "How encouraging."

"So, you're okay then?"

Jasper glared at him without answering.

"Alright then, let's get on our horse and ride," Wasyl said.

"What horse?"

"Manner of speaking."

Wasyl opened the bathroom door slowly, allowing light from the outside to fill their chamber. It was a moonlit evening with a warm and pleasant breeze flowing through what appeared to be an expansive yard. The modest movement of the air pushed and mingled odors of marijuana smoke and a whiff of something that smelled of burning fuel. The latter, the product of fumes expelled by camp-style lanterns hanging from several trees and parked upon the tops of numerous wooden picnic tables scattered about. The yard was flat, grassy, and well-tended featuring an almost golf course quality. The area's occupants were walking and talking or seated at one of the green tables like any outdoor gathering. Most of them were drinking something that had the foamy appearance of beer in plastic cups. The contents were confirmed when Jasper and Wasyl observed several kegs situated along the only wall in the area. It was more of a barrier than a wall, made from see-through criss cross wire that formed a fence tall enough to serve as a backstop for a neighboring tennis court. The tennis area was fully lit by several overhead lights mounted on utility poles. Currently, the courts were inhabited by several clearly intoxicated naked amateurs chasing yellow balls they had miss-hit, while giggling senselessly.

The two men had taken leave of the bathroom and now stood outside the door on a small square cement landing a short distance from the nearest group of people.

"Well, now what?" Jasper said. "Do we just stand here naked, gawking around? That's probably going to draw some attention, don't you think?"

Wasyl was slowly moving his eyes from side to side taking everything in.

"I don't believe the naked part will," he said, "but the gawking might. No one else seems to notice all the nakedity 'cept us."

"Okay, so what do we do?"

"Time to move on. So let's dance."

"Dance?"

"Manner of speakin'."

They stepped down onto the grass and began a gradual move towards the partygoers.

"I really don't want to hang out here," Jasper said out of the corner of his mouth.

Wasyl said, "Hangin' out ain't the plan. The plan is to cruise around a little, maybe find a way out. Hopefully a parking area. Then find a car or pickup or tractor or something. Wouldn't hurt neither if we found some shorts or something for the trip outta here, too.``

"I told you we should've at least brought our underwear along. We could have just carried them."

"Yeah," Wasyl said. "Nobody would have noticed a couple of strangers toting their boxers along at a nudist party."

Wasyl and Jasper had moved into the inhabited area of the yard and found themselves fully illuminated by the moon and lantern light combination. Wasyl glanced over at his obviously stressed partner and chuckled.

"What do you feel is so funny?" Jasper asked.

"Well," Wasyl said, still smiling, "I heard all those stories about fellas of your persuasion being uh...you know. Well-proportioned."

Jasper looked down at himself then back at Wasyl.

"What's that supposed to mean? Are you some kind of penis profiler or something?"

"Didn't mean to offend ya. Apparently it's just a rumor. Maybe you had a Chinese uncle or something."

"Whenever you're through."

"I'm through."

"Which way should we go?" Jasper asked.

They looked around the yard. It was nearly the size of a football field and was surrounded by a thick, tall line of trees. They stood silently, making a mental assessment of the area.

"Amazin' ain't it," Wasyl finally said.

"Amazing?" Jasper answered. "I wouldn't say that. I've seen trees that tall before."

"I don't mean the trees. Look around ya. All these people, not a stitch on 'em and not one of these gals would make a photo you'd want to hang in your shower on a lonely night."

Jasper stared at Wasyl momentarily. "Alright," he said, "now that we've established that we're stranded on the land of ugly dumplings, let's find a way out of here."

Nodding in the direction of the beer kegs, Wasyl said, "Let's head that way. Must be some kind of an opening there for them to bring those kegs in."

They started at a slow pace, cautiously walking towards the large silver beer containers that sat fifty yards away.

"I wonder what kind of party this is?" Wasyl said. "And don't ya think it's odd that after all the trouble they went to just to get us here, they didn't tie us up, or even bother to lock the door?"

"Probably part of their diabolical plan," Jasper said. "Don't you see? They want us to walk away so they can follow us."

"No, I guess I don't see. Follow us? Where? Hell, we don't know where we are, let alone where we're going. Why didn't they just follow us back in Washington? I had someplace to go there. Dollar Store had Handy Wipes for a buck and then McDonalds afterward. Of course, that was all before I got stuck bodyguarding."

"Fine job you did, too."

"Oh well, at least we got us an adventure."

They continued on, maintaining a leisurely pace in hopes of remaining unnoticed, at least as much as possible. As soon as they came within twenty feet of the keg area, their path was abruptly blocked. The obstruction was in the form of a heavyset woman in her late forties. The blockage had partially black and partially gray hair that had an oddly haphazard look to it, as if the woman had attempted to color it by tossing a bucketful of dye into the air and standing under the resulting downpour. She was four feet ten inches tall in high heels, if she'd been wearing heels, which she wasn't , and her face was covered with thick layers of makeup that ended in a distinct line at the midpoint of her neck. This caused her head to look detached and appear to move independently from the rest of her body.

She was accompanied by a male who was at least a foot and a half taller. He had jet black hair that appeared to be quite long but grew only from the back side of his head and had been combed over the front in an attempt to cover a vast area of hairless territory between his ears. The hairmat project failed miserably due to the fact that the evening breeze had pushed the man's one-sided follicular growth straight up in the air, leaving his barren brain shield without cover, allowing the bright evening moonlight to reflect from his noggin and back into space. Wasyl thought it looked like a combination of a New England lighthouse and his Uncle Garlin's 1960 Studebaker with the hood open. Although the man was much taller than the woman, he was demonstrably thinner. His kneecaps were the widest part of his legs and his ribcage looked like rows of xylophone keys.

"Hello boys," the woman said to the neo-nudists. "I don't recognize you. Are you new?"

"Yep. We're new," Wasyl answered. "Real new."

"Oh, good. Well, let me guess. I'll bet you're in receiving. Most people begin in receiving."

"Uh, yeah, that's where we're at. Yes, ma'am, receiving," Wasyl said.

"I started in receiving myself," she said.

Jasper stood mute, still staring at the two intruders.

"There was just so much paperwork for me," she said. "We never had enough file space for all the paperwork, so we started stuffing papers anywhere we could."

"That hasn't changed," Wasyl said, looking at Jasper.

"I don't know how you do it."

"You're probably better off that way," Wasyl said.

"Oh, how rude of me," she said, "I'm Simone Walandra. I head up the public relations department." She nodded toward her companion. "This is my fiancée, Dr. Leon Longnecker."

"You're a doctor?" Wasyl asked.

"A Carbonatologist," the man responded.

"Carbono...what?"

"Carbonatologist. I am involved in a multi-year study of carbonated beverages."

"Huh. You mean like soda pop?"

"Exactly."

"Oh, so you study how it affects, like our insides and all."

"How positively amusing. No, my area of research is much more scientifically in depth than that."

Simone said, "He wrote a book, didn't you, dear?"

The man bowed slightly, "The Anatomy of Fizz."

"Did you say fizz?" Wasyl asked.

"Certainly. In fact, currently I am deeply engrossed in the study of the erosion effect on plastic soda bottles from rising fizz bubbles."

"Uh-huh."

"Another scientific paper and book will follow."

"A book on fizz," Wasyl said again.

"Textbook. For college and post graduate study. Three to four hundred pages."

"On bubbles."

"The life span and journey of fizz."

"There's a journey?"

"From the bottom of the plastic container to the cap itself."

"All that way."

"Yes, an incredible journey."

"You get paid for this?"

"Of course. Grant money. The federal government funds the entire study."

"I thought the government was broke," Wasyl said.

"No matter," Dr. Longnecker said, "They're still able to pull money from social security for whatever they want."

"By the way," Simone interrupted, "what are your names?"

Jasper stood open-mouthed but made no sound.

"I'm Fernando, and this is Mr. Gout," Wasyl blurted, pointing at Jasper.

But before there was any acknowledgement of the introduction, Simone's attention was suddenly drawn to an area directly behind Wasyl and Jasper. She let out a high-pitched squeal of surprise, "Oh look! Saggers!"

The two men turned around to see two very naked and very old women standing about thirty feet away, both obviously afflicted with the infirmities of elderly female gravitational yank.

"Can't argue that," Wasyl said, flinching at the sight.

"Oh, you know them too?" Simone asked.

"Uh, no," Wasyl answered.

"It's Evelyn and Lucinda. The Sagger sisters. There have been Saggers in our organization for generations," Simone said in a final statement as she marched away with the fizz doctor trailing to meet the ladies.

As they were walking away, Jasper turned to Wasyl.

"Fernando and Mr. Gout?" He said.

Wasyl shrugged.

"That's the best you could do? Fernando and Mr. Gout? And I had to be Mr. Gout?"

"Well, I sure didn't hear you say anything, Mr. P.I.V."

"That's VIP."

"What is?"

"Never mind."

CHAPTER 27

The trio's meeting with Wanda had been interrupted by the appearance of Vanna walking unannounced into the room. She strode directly to Wanda, leaving the door open and handed her a note. Without speaking, she turned to leave. As she walked away she looked down at Skeet in his chair, giving him a flirty smile and wink, followed that with a scrunched up nose and a stuck out tongue for Paulie, who was also still seated.

Vanna passed by the sofa where the diligently reading Olga was seated.

"Here, Olga," Vanna said. "These are the brochures you wanted on body buffing."

"Oh, thank you many times," Olga said as she took the papers and went immediately to reading. Vanna smiled, looked back at Skeet quickly and left, closing the door to the office.

Wanda looked at Paulie, "Is your phone turned off?"

"Well no, it's in the van. I figured we didn't want any interruptions. Why?"

"Call home," Wanda said.

"Right now?" Paulie asked.

"Yes."

"But it can probably wait, you see..."

"Your sister is Ruth, correct?"

"Well, yes, but...wait, how did you know that?"

"How I know is not important. What is important is that Ruth is a long time associate of mine."

"You mean customer."

"No, not just a customer. It's much, let's say, deeper than that. She's a cog."

"A what?"

"Cog. It's a big wheel and she's a cog."

"But, she's always said she was a dancer."

"Sometimes we all claim to be something we're not."

"I don't," Paulie said, folding his arms in front of him in defiance.

"Maybe you should."

"But, Ruth, my sister, a cog? Really?"

"Yes, really. And not only that, but others find Ruth very important. And when I say "others", capitalize the 'O'. Make the call."

"Okay," Paulie said with some disbelief, "I'll get the phone."

"You can just call from this phone," Wanda said.

"No, I don't know the number to the landline of my house. It's coded into my phone."

"You don't know the phone number to your own home?"

"Some things are just better forgotten."

"You don't have her cell number?"

"She won't give it to me."

Paulie rose and headed out the door.

Wanda addressed Skeet, "You don't happen to smoke do you? I could use a cigarette."

"No, never touch them," he said.

"I quit a while back," she said, "but at certain times, I just crave one."

Olga had walked over from the sofa and taken Paulie's seat. She never looked up from her reading during the trip across the room. Wanda was looking through her desk but having no luck locating something to smoke.

"Oh well," she finally said. "No big deal. Actually, the only two times I feel the urge is during meetings like this and right after sex." She looked at Olga. "You know what I mean? Don't you like a cigarette after sex?"

Olga looked up at her, "Never." Then looked back down at her reading.

"Oh, non-smoker huh?"

"No, non-sexer."

Paulie walked back into the room, phone in hand.

"I can't seem to get a strong signal in the other room," he said, and seeing his seat occupied, sat down on the sofa. Holding the phone to his ear, he said, "There, it's ringing okay now."

"Quit jammin' that stuff into the blender! It's flying all over the place!" Ruth was yelling to someone as she answered the phone call.

"Ruth?" Paulie said.

"Well, well, well, if it isn't Billy Blubberbump."

"So, you were calling, what's wrong?" Paulie asked.

"What's wrong?" Ruth said in a mocking tone. "What makes you think something is wrong?"

"Well, it's just normally..."

"Normally? Listen Baron Von Big Butt, there is no normally here at the House of Unholy Histeria. In fact, at this very moment, we are planning a wedding."

"Uh, you said wedding?"

"Did my needle skip Tommy Top-Heavy? Yes, a wedding."

"Ruth," Paulie implored, "please don't tell me that Junior has decided to marry that palsied old man after all."

"I won't and he's not."

"Thank the heavens."

"Besides, old half ass has gone back to his prior wife, the one of the female persuasion. Apparently, she found some use for his muscle tremors when properly placed."

"Okay."

"And Junior's way too busy. New career and all."

"He's not quitting school for real, is he?"

"Already quit. Said he found a new star to follow, discovered his destiny or some moronic shit like that."

"Doing what?"

"Down at the grocery store, picking fly shit out of the pepper, "she said sarcastically," How the hell do I know?"

"But..."

"Later! First things first. How many bodies will fit into the demented den here?"

"Uh, probably a hundred or so. Is it you?"

"Is it me, what?"

"Are you getting married, Ruth?"

"I don't think so, Jelly John. You should be well aware of my feelings about marriage by now. And if you ever ask me that again, I may be forced to puncture your paternal pelican pouch and stuff your leg through it."

"Then, if it's not Junior or you, then...holy..."

"Got it in three, mammoth man mammaries. The old Mesozoic madame is about to become a matrimonial matriarch."

"She's marrying Frank? He's a dog!"

"Where do you come up with these things, Dimple Duster? No, she is not hitching up with the dog."

"Some good news, I guess," Paulie exhaled. "Isn't it? It is good news right, Ruth?"

"Yes, excellent news."

"Okay."

"She's marrying Buffalohead Johansson."

"Did you say Buffalohead? Is that, is that a human?"

"Yes, yes of course. Well, mostly. He used to work at that top secret Club 54 down in New Mexico."

"You mean Area 51? Club 54 was in New York."

"I've been to both, very little difference. Anyway, Buffalohead's okay, but he does have a few side effects from his employment time at the government laser light show."

"What do you mean, side effects?"

"Missing a few anatomical appendates, his eyes have an odd glow, and of course, he's got that big old head."

"Big?"

"Very considerable."

"Well, how big is it? You make it sound like, real big."

"It's huge. And his body is like a beanpole. He looks like a broom handle with the state of Arkansas stuck on top."

"That big?"

"For God's sake, the man's name is Buffalohead! He's got a big old melon. He wears a parachute for a hat. He was voted most popular cartoon character float at the Macy's Thanksgiving Day Parade. They say that when the last space shuttle crew looked back at earth, they could see the Great Wall of China, the lights of New York City, and Buffalohead."

"So, why is she marrying this...person?"

"He's the reincarnation of Bruce Springsteen."

"Uh, Springsteen is not dead."

"Technicality. Anyway, Hairless Helen's brother has agreed to perform the ceremony."

"Hairless Helen's brother. Let me guess, his name is Hairless Harry."

"Great, that saves on the introductions. And old Harry is an ordained man of the cloth, as luck would have it."

"An ordained man of the cloth named Hairless Harry."

"Absolutely. Of course, the cloth is an old Van Halen T-shirt that Eddie V wiped his nose on one night after a concert in Salt Lake, but he is ordained."

"Are you sure he's ordained?"

"Graduated from Oral Bob College just one year ago."

"You mean Oral Roberts University."

"No, I mean Oral Bob's, and let's not get into that right now. Anyway, Paunch O'Plenty, we're having the ceremony at this new church, The Immaculate Misconception, followed by a reception here at the hopeless shelter and then down to the...let's see, it's written down here on this bar napkin...yeah, here it is. Seven p.m. at the Salvation Army Supperclub, everyone is invited for live music and boil lancing."

"Boil lancing?"

"No, wait, it might say balloon shaving, there's something spilled on it. Maybe it says ballroom dancing or brassiere flanging. Not to worry, it won't make any difference by then with this group."

"Is this wedding thing really a good idea, Ruth?"

"Personally, I think she'd be better off with Frank. At least he's house-broken."

"But..."

"Hey! Whose leotards are in the damn toaster!?" Ruth yelled away from the phone to someone as she hung up.

CHAPTER 28

Brian Temple stood next to his boss, Secretary of State Harberts, in the latter's office as they met with two diplomats from the African country of Botswana. It was a typical meeting in the practice of international diplomacy fraught with hand squeezing, back patting, and bullshitting.

One of the visitors was a special envoy to the United States on a state visit. He was a diminutive black man dressed in traditional Botswanian garb consisting of a bright robe of varied colors made from some type of thick woven material, sandals, and a headdress adorned with several feathers stuck into a leather band.

The second man was taller and heavier but still not over six feet in height and much less than two hundred pounds. Unlike the smaller man, he was dressed in an American business suit of light brown with matching shoes. This man was the bilingual ambassador who was acting as an interpreter for Harberts and the smaller man, who spoke only the Tswana language. The tribal guest would speak. The ambassador would interpret. The Secretary would speak. The ambassador would interpret in reverse.

"So far, so good," Temple thought to himself.

Of course, so far, they had only discussed the Washington weather, American baseball, the price of a Big Mac, and the possibility of the Bostwanian representative getting his photo taken with Elvis, John Wayne, O.J. Simpson, or Bruce Jenner. It was during the time in which he was being informed that his requests would be difficult to fill as two were dead, one was in prison, and one was having some ongoing identity issues, that things began to get a bit shaky.

While the smaller man was carrying on a lengthy dialogue with his intently listening interpreter, Harberts gave Temple an attention-getting elbow in the ribs.

“Say, did I ever tell you that I spent some time over in Africa?”

“Yes, sir.”

“Did a week or two in this little fella’s country too.”

“Very good, sir.”

“Even learned the language from a couple of late night hostesses over there.”

“Remarkable, sir.”

“So, I don’t really need this guy in the used car salesman outfit here telling me how to handle this tit-da-tit we’re having here.”

“Tete-a-tete, sir.”

Temple, who had been feeling atypically comfortable with the meeting up to this point, suddenly felt that very same good feeling open an escape window.

“Sir, I believe the interpreter is doing an exceptional job. He is, after all, an ambassador. We shouldn’t try anything experimental at this juncture.”

“Watch this,” Harberts said.

Temple’s good feeling jumped out the window to its death as the Secretary rambled what sounded like several incoherent sentences to his two man audience. It was quickly apparent that not all of the sentences were garbled gibberish, because there was a reaction. A rather emphatic one. The smaller man let out a strange, high-pitched scream while withdrawing from somewhere inside his brightly decorated outfit, a weapon that looked very similar to a giant nail. The interpreter stepped out of the man's way, also yelling something that did not sound remotely congenial, while pointing at the American office holder in a declaration of support for his attacking comrade. Meanwhile, Harberts just stood there, arms folded and smiling, as if he had just pulled off a major victory and winking at Temple to say I told you so.

Temple, however, not sensing the same celebratory event his boss did, knew he needed to react quickly to diffuse the problem. He figured if he could find out what Harbert's had said, he may be able to explain that the issue was in the translation error, or just a misspoken word, and all would be well.

"What did he say?" Temple shouted to the interpreter over the smaller man's loud challenges.

The interpreter responds, "The Secretary said the chief's mother has a braided pubic scalp."

So much for the translation error.

The Secretary, in his usual state of disconnect, thus not understanding the present threat, snatched the large nail from the feeble grasp of the African, thanked him in English while patting him on the back with sufficient force to knock off his ceremonial bonnet. Harberts then physically guided both of the visitors to the exit area of his office, where he forcefully enough to stagger but not to tip over, moved them out into the outer office. As he was closing the door he gave one final Tswani verbal salute, which, deciphered correctly, meant, "Hug the winds of the dead gecko," and closed the door on the confused duo.

Harberts turned to Temple, "Do you think the President realizes all the damned political fence mending I do for him?"

"Probably not, sir."

Harberts looked at the oversized nail-like object in his hand, and tossed it near the exited diplomat's feather hat on the floor. He picked up the remote control from his desk and turned on his wall-mounted television as he sat down in his desk chair. The TV screen comes alive with the image of the U.S. President speaking from a seal-fronted podium to an unidentified crowd.

"Doesn't he ever quit talking?" Harberts grumbled to himself.

"Sir, about the assault on the compound we discussed earlier."

"Uh-huh," Harberts answered absentmindedly as he flipped through the TV channels until he finally settled on a back-and-forth channel change between ancient episodes of Bonanza and Gunsmoke.

"Sir, I was thinking that..."

"You know what?" Harberts interrupted, pointing at the TV with the remote. "The world is a lot like Gunsmoke and Bonanza."

"Okay sir. Anyway..."

"See," Harberts continued as if Temple had never spoken, "Bonanza is kinda like the peace-loving countries of the world. Pacifists, you know what I mean? See, ya got old Ben Cartwright and them boys of his living out there in wherever the hell it is they live."

"Nevada, sir."

"Really? Never seen one casino on the show. Just saloons. Anyway, there they are out in the middle of nothing, and yet, every week some problem comes along. Rustlers, bank robbers, rancher disputes and what not, but no matter how serious it is, Ben tries to keep his boys from popping the top on a fresh can of whoop-ass. The way he wants to settle all the problems is with reason. Talk it out. Be sensitive. Compromise. And, about every week, he weasels his way into a peaceful ending. Every damn week. Might be a little shooting, but Ben will put a stop to it. Ben, my boy, is a pacifist."

"Yes sir."

"On Gunsmoke, it's a whole lot different. Matt Dillon will haul your ass to the shed. Dodge City ain't the pussified pacifist Ponderosa. No siree. You screw the pooch in Dodge, at the very least, you're getting an ass-kicking."

Temple, realizing he must absorb another rambling monologue, takes a seat in front of the desk.

"But Matt's fair about it," Harberts said. "He's got three levels of butt-busting he hands out, depending of course on what you did. Let's say you were to mess with Festus. Well, Dillon's gonna punch the hell out of you. I've seen him do it. Standard beating. Fists only, nothing fancy, usually quick. Now, you pluck a hair from old Doc's head and you're getting your ass pistol-whipped into oblivion. He can do it too, ever see that long-barreled handgun he carries? Damn thing looks like an oak tree with a handle on it. He strokes that across your gourd and you'll know it." Harberts then pointed the remote at Temple to emphasize his next point. "But you be foolish enough to even think about Miss Kitty the wrong way, just once...you're gut shot. No trial. No jail...Gut shot."

"Yes, sir."

"Do you know what I'm getting at, son?"

"No possible way of knowing, sir."

"Well, we can be reasonable like old Ben Cartwright and settle our differences and learn a moral lesson along the way. You know, peaceful-like. The Ponderosa way. But, just look at the results. Little Joe's girlfriends all go blind or die, Hoss is a chronic overeater that couldn't get a woman if he had a diamond headed dick, and Adam left home in a pissy mood and never has come back. Not to mention that damned little oriental..."

"Hop Sing, sir."

"Yeah, Hop Sing, creeping around that back room all night and day doing Lord knows what. But, on Gunsmoke, Dillon keeps the peace just by throwing lead at violators with that dogleg..."

"It's hog let, sir."

"...of his. No talking. Just blasting. Hell, just look at the intros. Cartwrights come riding up in this beautiful field, smiling and giggly looking like they just got done having a group hug with old Hip Song.."

"Hop Sing, sir."

"...in the middle. A bunch of gay gauchos. Not Dillon. No,sir. Dillon starts right off on some dusty street blastin' the belly button out of some no account, probably just for stiffing Kitty for a drink."

Harberts sits back in his chair and puts his feet up on his desk. "Do you know what I'm saying now, son?"

"You want to move ahead with the assault on the compound."

"What compound?"

The moment is cut short by the sound of a phone on the secretary's desk buzzing two times in rapid succession while flashing red, then repeating.

"It's the National Security line, sir," Temple said.

"Christ. Do you think it's important?"

"It's flashing security level two, sir. Security level three is nuclear war, so, I would assume it's important."

"Oh, alright," Harberts said, picking up the phone.

"Harbert's here. Huh? Yeah. What? Well, threaten 'em or something. Whatever, I'll get back to you."

They sat for a moment before Temple said, "Well, Mr. Secretary, what's the problem?"

"You know those people over at the Defense Department are a real pain in the postern sometimes."

"It's posterior, and what do they want, sir?

"Somebody is threatening to declare war on us."

"Who would that be, sir?"

"Hell, I don't know."

"Well, you did talk to the Defense Department on the telephone. I'm sure they indicated someone, sir."

"Let's see, it was some weird ass country. Strange name, sounded like Boat Mommas or something. Boat mamas? Sounds like a bunch of goddamned surfers. Surfers are declaring war on us? What the hell is wrong with these people?"

"Boat Mamas, sir? Could it have been Botswana, sir?"

"Yeah, I think that's it. Who the hell is that?"

"The two people that just left here, sir."

"Huh. Wonder what got their tampon twisted?"

"No idea, sir."

CHAPTER 29

They stood at the back door of the Three Feathers Funeral Home. Biff, Danny, and Herbie.

"This ain't much of a plan," Herbie complained.

"It's a good plan, just follow along," Danny said.

"It'll work," Biff added, "hopefully."

"A gambling joint next door to a salon for stiffs? Must be an Indian place," Herbie said looking at the empty lot advertising the future site of the Three Feathers Casino on a large sign.

"Cool it, will ya?" Biff said. "And so what if it is?"

"You're gonna wish we had busted the door in when this is over. Wait and see."

Biff pushed a buzzer on the service entry back door and then stood back with his companions in the twilight.

A light came on above the door as it opened. Standing in the doorway was a man with black hair. From the light coming from the room behind him, you could tell he was of dark skin and well proportioned, standing at 6 foot and an inch or so, weighing about 200 pounds. He was wearing after hours attire which consisted of gray sweatpants and a white short sleeve t-shirt that said "Lock in Sock Lager Beer" across the front.

"Told you," Herbie whispered.

Before anyone could tell Herbie to be quiet, the man spoke, "Good evening," he said in a deep melodic tone. "My name is Michael Davis. Is there something I can help you with?"

Biff said, "Well sir, this is going to sound a tad bit strange."

"Alright," the man responded.

"I'm Biff, this is Danny, and that's Herbie."

"Yes, that's a little strange, but I've heard stranger things."

"Huh? Oh, that's not it. You see, we're here to pick up our uncle so we can give him a ride home."

"Your uncle?"

"Yeah, uncle," Herbie said, "comprende?"

The man's dark eyes flashed at Herbie, then settled back on Biff.

"What makes you think your uncle is here? And let me assure you, there is no one here in need of a ride. At least not anywhere but there," he said pointing into the distance behind them where dim lights showed the front gate of a cemetery. All three of them turned to look and then turned back in unison.

"Gentlemen," Davis said, "at present, there are only two people here. They are both deceased. One elderly female from the reservation and one male that I found out back here, right about where you are standing."

"That would be Uncle," Biff said, adding a smile.

"I see."

"So if..."

"Why was uncle lying out back here?"

Herbie chimed in, "Michael? Let me explain something to you, by the way, Mike sure don't sound like no Indian name to me."

"And," the man said, "Herbie doesn't sound like the name of a potbellied piss-ant, but here you are."

“Shut up Herbie,” Danny said.

Mike Davis said, “This man you spoke of is your blood relative? I shouldn’t release him to anyone but a blood relative. If I release him.”

“Yes, he is,” Biff said.

“Which one of you cotton skins is Hispanic?”

Biff glanced at both of his companions. “Well, as you can see, none of us, actually.”

“But he is your blood uncle.”

“On our aunt’s side,” Herbie quipped.

“Uh-huh. There is one other issue,” Davis said, folding his hands in front of him.

“Which is?”

“Holes.”

“Holes?”

“Yes, he seems to have a lot of holes in him. I was contemplating contacting the authorities about the ...holes.”

“I can explain those,” Biff said.

“I’ll bet.”

“Here we go,” Herbie mumbled.

“You see, Uncle was attending one of those hypnosis things, you know, where they get you to quit smoking and make you bark like a dog and stuff. And anyway, after he was put under, the hypnotist decided he wanted to have a little joke, so he had uncle lie on this bed of nails. It was all in good fun, and it was fine until Uncle somehow woke up and, splish, down he went in the nails. Crazy, huh?”

“Yes, crazy would be the word.”

“We’re thinking that maybe we have a possible civil action against the hypnotist, you know, for bringing him back wrong, or something.”

“Hypnopompic.”

“What?”

“That is what you are referring to. Hypnopompic. Returning from a hypnotic state.”

"Oh, yeah, well thanks, I'll remember that," Biff said. "So anyway, what do you think, Mr. Davis? Can you help us out?"

"I don't really want to have to deal with this tonight," Michael Davis said. Then stepping back, he motioned them in. "There he is." Along the wall on a flat platform was their dead man.

"We can take him?"

"Yes. I don't know what the deal is. I don't want to know what the deal is. But I know these things. If he stays, I'll have to bury him. No one will pay for it. Then the cops might eventually show up, and you, for some reason, want him. So, he's yours."

"Okay, let's go," Herbie said. "Give us a hand will ya?"

"No," Davis said, "I carried him in. You carry him out."

The three struggled, twisted and turned, grunting and swearing as they took the body out the back door to the van. Balancing the carrying board the man was on, Danny reached back and opened the doors of the van and they slid him in.

"Keep the wood platform he's on," Davis said.

Huffing wind, Herbie said, "Is that your lot next door where they're going to build the casino?"

"Belongs to my people," Davis said.

"Another casino? How much do you people want, anyway?"

"Same question we asked your relatives a couple hundred years ago."

"How do you guys keep getting these things anyway?"

"Feds. And it will continue until you people get smart enough to start playing cowboy and congressman."

"I'd like to get in on that casino stuff," Herbie said, still puffing.

"No problem. Stop back after it's built. I can probably get you a job as a throw rug."

"Let's go Herbie," Danny said.

Biff walked over to the funeral home proprietor.

"Thanks for the help. I'd like to tell you the whole story, at least as much of it as I know, but I can't."

"But, we're not doing anything wrong. I'm pretty sure anyway," Brian said.

Davis looked at the fat Herbie in his Hawaiian clothes, the van with the Mexican registration plates, and the hole covered corpse as Danny was closing the rear doors and said,"Yeah. Looks legit to me."

Biff walked to the van, opened the front door to get in, looked in the back, then turned and called out, "One last thing."

Davis said, "You want some ice?"

CHAPTER 30

Sometimes when the unexpected happens, it's good. Or at least it looks good. As soon as Wasyl and Jasper had their immediate area vacated by Simone and the fizz doctor, that particular sometimes appeared in a female form. Both their heads turned when they saw her. Immediately their eyes fixed into an intent gaze. She was the perfect embodiment of feminine beauty. The kind of woman that other women hate as they desperately try to find fault with but are never able to do. She had a model-like sashay as she glided on a collision course with the two men.

Short, neatly cut auburn hair just touching her eyebrows, and expertly applied makeup that highlighted a flawlessly tanned face. She had dark eyes that seemed to be locked on her target, accentuated by a slow blinking of her eyelids, and a bright but seductive smile that one would expect to see only in the movies. Her body, though small-breasted, was synonymous with wow as she moved silently through the human forest of the less fortunate.

"Look at that, will ya," Wasyl said.

"Yeah, I see her," Jasper answered. "Well, at least there's one looker in the crowd. I wonder what she's doing here in the cellulite sea?"

"Well, it appears she's coming over here. Looks like she's got some purpose 'cause she aint lookin' at nobody else. You think she knows about us?"

"Jesus, I'll bet she does. We're dead. Let's run for it!" Jasper said, starting to move away from the approaching female.

Wasyl grabbed his arm. "Hold up. Where would we go? We're kinda stuck here in this big old yard. I've got no idea where we could even run to."

Jasper hissed, "Let's do something. We can't just stand here. She obviously knows something is up...Let's just run for it!"

"Okay. And in case a couple of salt and pepper nude dudes runnin' in a circle don't draw enough attention, let's scream first and maybe wave our arms around or somethin'. That oughta help."

But before they could have moved away, she was standing directly in front of them. She smiled and nodded at a nervously staring Jasper, then side stepped to stand toe to toe with Wasyl.

"Hi Wassie," she said.

The two men froze in place.

"Well? Hello," she said.

"Wassie?" Jasper said in a confused tone. He peered over at Wasyl for a brief moment before returning his gaze to the mystery woman.

"It's his nickname," she said to Jasper. She then turned her attention back to the befuddled janitor. "How have you been?"

"Uh...who?" Wasyl stammered.

"You, Wassie. How have you been?"

"Uh, okay, I think."

Her voice had a sultry, somewhat husky, but not unpleasant tone to it. She gave her head a sympathetic shake.

"It's me," she said.

"Me?" he responded.

"Carla."

"Carla?"

"My God," Jasper interjected. Are you just going to keep repeating everything she says?"

"Carla Harvey," she said. "Skunk Holler? Remember? Skunk Holler Harveys?"

Jasper's head swiveled from the woman to Wasyl.

"Skunk Holler? What in the world is that? A rodent disease?" He asked.

"It's a place," Wasyl answered. "A place back home."

Jasper said, "Well, do you know her?"

"Uh, well no, maybe yes."

"Great," Jasper groaned, "now it's all coming together."

Wasyl turned to face his male companion. "I mean, I know the Harveys from Skunk Holler. Everybody in those parts know the Harveys. I hung with the boys for years, Clayton, Clifford, Clinton, Carl..."

"That's me," the woman said.

"What's you?" Wasyl said, looking back at her.

"Carl. I'm Carl. At least at one time I was Carl. And now I'm Carla."

"You sure don't look like Carl, especially the neck down," Wasyl said.

"I hope not," she said. She tipped her head slightly to one side, "I changed, Wassie."

She waited for her old friend to respond. Wasyl waited for his brain's memory banks to kick in. Jasper waited for a troll to jump out of the bushes screaming, "Candid Camera!"

Suddenly, Wasyl's eyes opened wide and he slapped his forehead, as if the meaning of life had suddenly dawned on him.

"Oh Lord!" He said. "I get it."

"You do?" Jasper said.

Wasyl ignored him. "I'm so sorry. No one told me. I've been gone so many years, I should have been there for you. Was it a sickness or an accident? Did that damn bull of Dick Waller's kick you in the head?"

The woman raised her eyebrows in a look of slightly bewildered amusement. Jasper just stared at Wasyl.

"That Psycho at the county fair said these things happen," Wasyl said.

"Psycho at the county..." Jasper said.

"Psychic," Carla said.

"Oh, psychic, of course," Jasper said. "What the hell are you talking about, Wasyl?"

Wasyl said, "Well, don't be so damned closed-headed Mr. Sum Cum Louder, it's as plain as the feathers on an owl's ass."

"Summa Cum Laude, and what is so plain is the fact that no one has any idea what you are talking about."

"What happened to Carl is what I'm talking about. Must have been while I was away getting my BCS degree."

"Your BCS degree. And that is...?"

"Bachelor of Custodial Sciences."

"Good lord."

"That's when it must've happened. Poor Carl."

"You said that. So what happened?"

"He passed on, of course. Then he reincarnated. Came back as a woman. Right fine one, too," Wasyl said, nodding.

"No Wassie," Carla said, holding up her hands in front of her to stop the conversation. "I didn't reincarnate, because I didn't pass on."

"You didn't?" Wasyl answered, now re-taking his confused status.

"No. I told you. I changed. I took hormones, had surgery. I am completely changed."

"You can do that?"

"Yes, Wassie, you can do that."

"Well, I guess you can," he said. "I'd heard that you could, I just never believed it because I'd never seen it."

"Well, you can believe it now," she said.

Wasyl looked her up and down like he was examining a possible auto purchase.

"You sure don't look nothin' like a fella now. Little boobies, no chest hair, nice legs, and I'm afraid to even ask what happened to one-eyed Willie."

Carla leaned forward and whispered into his ear for a few seconds, during which time his eyes narrowed and then widened again.

"Oh, sweet Sunday preachin'," ' Wasyl nearly gasped, turning his head to face Jasper. "Do you know what they did to Carl's , I mean Carla's, you know, uh, man part? Do you?"

"Yes, I'm fully aware of what they do in that surgical procedure," Jasper said.

"You are?"

"Yes! For Christ's sake, what about this don't you get?"

"Pretty much none of it."

"It's okay, Wassie," Carla said. "It'll take awhile to get used to it. But you will, you'll see."

Wasyl just looked at the ground.

"I hate to interrupt this...whatever it is, but we should be moving along," Jasper said, intent on leaving, but Wasyl would not abandon his inquiring line of thought.

"Wow, so how did your family take the uh...news?"

Carla laughed. "You know how they are. They're all a little backward. My brothers asked me if I could still pee standing up. Pa said if God intended for a man's tallywhacker to be cut off, we'd all have been born with a Bowie knife in our boxers, and Ma just told me that from now on I'd have to help with the dishes."

"That's not too bad, I guess."

"No," she said. "They were a lot more surprised by Uncle Ebert and his episode. You remember that, don't you?"

"I remember that," Wasyl said. "It was a bit unsettling."

Jasper cut in. "Okay, I have to ask. What did your Uncle..."

"Ebert," Wasyl said.

"Yeah, Uncle Ebert. What could he have possibly done to surpass your sex change operation? Fly to the moon? I mean, really?"

Wasyl said, "Well sir, it was disturbing. One day, he and Milton came out of the closet."

"Uh-huh," Jasper grunted.

"And then he announced his eternal and undying love in both spirit and flesh, for Milton."

"And?"

"That's it. Real shocker it was."

"Really?" Jasper said. "Your people are shook up because your Uncle came out of the closet and told them he was in love with this Milton?

"Yes," Carla said.

"So, big deal. It happens all the time."

Wasyl said, "Ya see, he and Milton actually did come out of a closet."

"Uh, okay," Jasper said. "So, that's a little odd, I admit. But it's out in the open now."

"Sure is," Wasyl said.

Jasper held his arms out in a pose of pastoral understanding. "Don't you two see?"

"See what?" Wasyl asked.

"This is a new world. A world of acceptance and understanding."

"But..."

"A world of choices and freedoms."

"Yeah, but..."

"A time for spiritual and physical love to be shown without jealousies and biases."

"Yeah, I get that, but..."

"Uncle Ebert should be embraced and commended for publicly declaring his emotional and yes, sexual love for Milton."

"Milton is his goat."

CHAPTER 31

"Washington," Danny said, breaking the phone connection and putting it on the van seat by his leg.

"Washington? We're going to Washington with a dead guy?" Biff asked.

"Yep."

"Are you freaking kidding me?" Herbie said. "All the way to Washington from, from, wherever the hell we're at?"

"We're in..." Biff began.

"It don't make a dog's ass difference where we are! Taking the dead dude to Washington? How important is this guy? I sure don't recognize him and he's gonna get a bit more unrecognizable as we travel on this asswipe trip!"

"Keep the ice on him while you're back there," Danny said.

"That's another thing. Why am I stuck back here with fermenting Freddie anyway?"

"I have to say, as hard as it is to believe, I have to agree with our Hawaiian shirted fat boy. It seems a little strange to be hauling a dead guy all the way to Washington," Biff said to Danny. "I mean, are there any instructions for us when we get there?"

Danny said, "Instructions are to go to Washington and drive directly to the White House."

"With a dead guy in a stolen van," Biff said.

"Yup."

"There has to be some logical reason behind all this, right?"

"My God, I think he moved!" Herbie hollered from the back of the van.

"Herbie, he didn't move," Danny said.

"Oh yeah, Mr. I don't believe in zombies. You wait until he jumps and starts slinging these ice cubes around and does a Michael Jackson Thriller dance all over our foreheads. Won't be so funny then."

Ignoring the backseat excitement, Biff asked, "Is someone going to be waiting for us?"

"We are part of a detailed plan," Danny answered.

"Which is?"

"She only told me there is a plan. She didn't give any details."

"Liver eater," Herbie said.

"What?" Danny and Biff asked simultaneously.

"Liver eater. That's what his guy is. I've seen his kind before. Come back to life, throw some ice, dance on your forehead, then eat your liver."

"I guess we'll see what happens when we get there," Biff said to Danny.

"Damn liver-eating zombies," Herbie mumbled.

CHAPTER 32

The meeting with Wanda had been informative and inspiring. Well, somewhat. At the very least, they had received a bit more information than they had started with. As a bonus, they all had some things to take with them. Paulie left with an official-looking pad of coded instructions to go along with his prized code book. Skeet possessed Vanna's phone number, a copy of a class term paper she had written on the world of Tibetan massage therapy, and a photo of her in a rather odd looking yoga position on a bearskin rug completely body painted to look like Spiderman's twin sister. And Olga, well, Olga had hit the libidinal jackpot. She toted two boxes of material including, but not limited to brochures, DVD's, numerous books, instruction manuals and two complimentary tickets to the opening night of a play called "How the West Was Fun," performed by a cast wearing life-like rubberized Halloween masks with some rather odd attachments, cowboy boots, and ...well, that's all. She had been advised by Vanna that the final round-up scene was something to behold.

The cost of Olga's purchases had been added on to Ruth's earlier order with the purchaser, Paulie, in reluctant agreement. The arrangement had been arrived at only after Wanda had convinced

Paulie that the government would gladly reimburse him through one of their vast and unaudited expense accounts. It wouldn't be a problem. After all, she had told him, the same people funded secret service agents for Clinton's daughter and Bush's horse and an analyst for the entire Obama White House staff. Not to worry.

While attempting to load up Olga's bulky product containers, Paulie tipped one over in the parking lot, spilling out the contents in every direction. He told her he was sorry and he and Skeet jumped into the task of clean up because they couldn't resist doing a little investigative inventory. As they assisted Olga in placing her treasure back into their original cardboard containers, they gave each other a raised eyebrow look, accompanied by Skeet's smile and Paulie's gentle head shakes.

There were glossy, professional-looking brochures entitled, "Penetrating the Pregnant Portal Problem with Path Finder Positions" and "101 Honeymoon Uses for Raspberry Jam." There were books with names like "Female Masculinity-Discovering Your Inner Arnold," and "No Pain, No Gain-The Manual of Leather Straps and Humiliation." These were accompanied by DVD's with such identifiers as "Toe Fetishes and You, A Digital Journey of Love," and a concert video of the greatest hits of a group called "The Mattress Thrashers."

They finally loaded and closed the trunk and Olga hopped into the backseat of the Lincoln with a book and a couple of brochures in hand. Paulie returned to the front passenger seat and Skeet to the driver side. He started the car and backed out into the dark street and headed for their new destination.

At their meeting earlier, Wanda had told them that they would be receiving more messages in code, and hopefully soon, but for now they were to drive east until they reached a small town with an abandoned schoolyard near it. When Skeet asked if there was a particular road they should use, she reiterated to just drive east. Upon arrival at the mystery school, they would be met by some individuals that would be giving them instructions they were to follow to an as yet undisclosed location. She also told them that there existed a fairly strong possibility that, at some point during this mission, they would be set upon by violent human elements of a foreign or domestic origin, behaving openly as enemies or posing as friends. These people would attempt to capture, torture, or kill the trio given even the slightest opportunity.

To ensure that nothing they had been told would intentionally or inadvertently be passed on to the enemy conspirators, they were each given a piece of licorice containing a combination of Strychnine and Cyanide in ample amounts to kill each of them, the entire Ugandan Army, and every mammal, reptile, and marsupial on the island of Madagascar. But at least they were given a choice of flavors. Olga chose strawberry.

"So, Paulie," Skeet said as they cruised down the road, "we're heading to a town that we don't know the name of, or the location of, to a schoolyard that nobody uses, to meet with some people that we won't know, to get more instructions, and then go somewhere else."

"That's correct," Paulie said.

"And we may be captured, tortured, or killed by mean or nice people, who may be locals or foreigners, so we need to kill ourselves if they show up, even though we have no way of knowing who they are, and we have to commit to mass suicide to ensure that they can't find out about all this stuff that we don't know."

"Absolutely, Skeet. Can you imagine what they might do with this information if it fell into the wrong hands?"

"Actually...no...Just tell me when to eat the licorice."

CHAPTER 33

"What is this place anyway?" Wasyl asked as he, Carla, and Jasper stood near a line of large trees at the edge of the yard.

Carla responded, "It belongs to Mr. Reyes."

"Who is Mr.Reyes?" Jasper asked.

"He's the CEO of a home health care delivery company. The Happy Hemoglobin."

"Nice name," Jasper said.

"These folks all work at the Hemogoblin?" Wasyl asked.

"Hemoglobin. Well mostly," Carla said. "But all of them belong to his church."

"He has a naked church?" Wasyl asked.

"Church of the Holy Tryst."

"Tryst?" Jasper asked. "As in..."

"Yes, as in exactly what you're thinking. Everyone here believes in Mary, Joseph, and the Baby with one minor editorial aside."

"Which is?"

"The conception wasn't immaculate. Mary actually had a fling with someone. If it wasn't Joseph, and it wasn't some Roman soldier, that leaves just one candidate."

"Are you saying what I think you're saying?"

"Yep. A one-nighter with the one and only star of the heavens."

"Willie Nelson?" Wasyl said.

"Never mind all that," Jasper said. "Listen, Carla, we need help, we were kidnapped by a dozen Mideast terrorists armed with automatic weapons in a convoy of Humvees, then flown to this country. We're lucky to be alive. If we don't get out of here right now, I'm certain they'll tie us down next to some fire ant hills and cover us in honey. And there we'll stay until the last particle of flesh has been picked from our bleached-out skeletons."

"Dramatic, isn't he?" Carla said to Wasyl.

"Slight character flaw," Wasyl said.

Carla then smiled at Jasper. "It wasn't a dozen terrorists or a Humvee caravan. It was three medical equipment service techs and a prosthetic leg salesman, and the only thing they would have been armed with was some Penthouse magazines, a repair manual, and a tool kit."

"Well, it was dark."

"It was noon, And, rest assured, there are no fire ants or fire ant hills to tie you down to. Besides, if Mr. Reyes wanted to do you in, he would have put you through an anatomical change quite similar to the one I went through."

"That was mentioned."

"I'm sure it was."

"What about this place? Africa? Brazil?"

"Montana."

"See?" Wasyl said, looking at Jasper. "No fire ants. That's good."

"Yeah, great," Jasper said. "But we're still stuck...Hey! How do you know all this stuff anyway? Are you one of them?"

"Depends on who 'them' is," she answered. "Let's say for now that I am in the employ of someone in the government that wants to help you."

"Uh-oh," Wasyl said.

Jasper said, "We both work for the government. We, or at least I, am very aware of the impending doom of the 'government is here' to help statements."

Carla turned and slowly began to walk away. The two men looked at each other, Wasyl shrugged, and they followed her steps. As she walked, she spoke.

"Well gentlemen, here are your choices. I can escort you from this impoundment and together we can hopefully, and again, I say hopefully, return you and your cargo to Washington or you may remain here until Mr. Reyes returns with associates for another visit. A surgical one."

"We have another choice," Jasper said.

"Which is?"

"We make a run for it through the woods. Find a phone, call the cops, and presto chango, we're freed."

Carla stopped and turned to face the two men and folded her arms over her breasts.

"The woods are filled with razor wire. There are no phones, land lines or cells, except for the security detail, and although this is Montana, you would be hard pressed to find this place on a map, so cops are nonexistent. Oh, and if the razor wire doesn't cut you into tiny, bite-sized coyote treats, the bees that Mr. Reyes has transplanted here by the millions will sting you to death. Some type of African/ South American hybrid. Particularly nasty."

"So there is honey, huh?" Wasyl said. "But no fire ants."

"Shut up," Jasper cut him off. "Then how did all these people get here? There must be three hundred at least."

"By helicopter mostly. Ten to twelve at a time."

"No chopper right now?"

"Nope, none. And we shouldn't wait."

Wasyl and Jasper surveyed the landscape in the evening darkness.

"So, there is a way out?" Jasper said.

"Yes," Carla answered, nodding her head slightly to the right. "There is one path. It goes through there. But it's not marked and one wrong step and you become instantly toeless."

"You know the way? Even in the dark?" Jasper asked.

"I think so," she said.

"Very inspiring."

Wasyl slapped Jasper lightly on the back and said, "There you go buddy. What do we have to lose?"

"Just body parts, and please don't touch me while I'm naked. It's creepy. For all I know it's some backwoods petting technique." Then, addressing Carla, "So how do we do this?"

"Follow me," she said and walked towards the beer kegs.

Wasyl glanced at Jasper. "Well, let's burn rubber."

"Burn rubber?"

"Manner of speaking."

They followed their guide as she nodded and smiled at a few people they passed by, then stopped at a picnic table and picked up two plastic cups of beer, handing one to each of her companions, then retrieving a third for herself.

"So, this is the plan? Jasper asked. "Just hang out and drink beer?"

"No. The idea is to look natural," Carla answered.

She then casually looked around the bordering trees as if admiring the view. Her gaze seemed to halt momentarily at one particular area, then she took a sip from her cup and sat it down on the table. Carla stepped to the next picnic table where a heavyset, cigar-smoking man was seated and asked if he had a lighter. He did, and she asked if she could use it. The man, who was obviously intoxicated, picked up a lighter from the bench he was seated on and, with a wobbly arm motion, handed it to Carla.

"Here, honey baby," he slurred.

"Thanks," Carla said, taking the lighter as the fat man lost his balance and fell over backward onto the ground landing on his back with his pudgy fat legs propped up on the bench he had been previously seated on. For a moment, everyone in the immediate area glanced over at the spectacle, then looked away.

Wasyl looked down at the very chubby, now unconscious and snoring man with his arms and legs spread. "There's a picture I bet his mom doesn't have on the mantle."

Carla's attention had been drawn away from the scene and back to the nighttime forest. She stepped away from the table, and holding the lighter in front of her abdomen, blocking most of the view of the people behind her, lit the lighter once, twice, three times for about one or two seconds. She completed her task, then remained at the spot watching the distant darkness, now joined by the two men. Then, they saw it. A short flicker of light. Twice.

"Okay, let's go," she said and tossed the lighter onto the belly of the passed-out man who had given it to her.

"Where are we going exactly?" Jasper queried.

"To meet up with Myron and hopefully get out of this place."

"Our savior's name is...Myron?"

Wasyl said, "Had a dog named Myron once, or was it a teacher?"

"Christ. Myron," Jasper said. "I'm entrusting my life to someone named Myron? I don't believe I've ever seen or met anyone named Myron."

Carla smiled. "Oh, you've met Myron."

CHAPTER 34

The wagon bounced and bucked, jolting the skeletal structures of its four occupants as it made its way along the very old, very unpaved road. Their travel route was actually not much more than a path that had been severely muddied by the pelting of spring rains, and now, the more recent summer heat had dried it into a rut-covered obstacle course.

The timeworn wagon was a flat wooden farm model. Currently, it was being pulled by two large brown workhorses who dealt with their chore in an uncaring but unwavering march cadence in low gear.

The driver was about five foot plus a couple of inches tall with a minimal amount of flesh that was supported by a bony frame and held together with the leathery skin of a heavily-sunned seventy year-old man. He wore stained blue coveralls and black work boots. He had a pointed gray beard and his head was partially bald, mostly on the front and top but it did have fairly long grayish hair on the back and sides that was tied in a ten inch, tightly twisted ponytail. He was an odd creature to say the least, but his most remarkable features undoubtedly were an empty left eye socket completely uncovered by any form of a patch and three missing fingers on his corresponding hand. The only surviving digits being his thumb and pinky.

It was an all-too-familiar situation to Jasper from his earlier blindfolded trip. Same wagon. Same driver. Same horses, with the same gastrointestinal issues. Everything was the same, except now they were going out, instead of going in.

Jasper was seated in the front next to Carla, who was seated next to the driver on an old west style buckboard seat. Wasyl sat directly behind them on the bed of the wagon as they traveled through the early evening wooded area. Without being introduced, Jasper knew. The captain of this ship of stench was the mysterious Myron.

"What is that smell?" Jasper asked after several moments of indulgence.

"Horse farts," Myron answered like he'd been asked the time of day.

"No, besides the obvious. It's something else. Something right here in this wagon. Something very close and putrid. It's almost like ammonia."

"Oh that. That would be cat piss, son."

"Cat...piss?"

"Yeah, I'm used to it, and of course my old smeller don't work so good anymore, didn't notice it."

"Cat urine? I don't see any cats. Do they live or sleep in this wagon or something? My God, it's horrifying!"

Myron pulled the reins of the wagon to the left to steer the horses around a particularly deep rut.

"No," he said, "I don't let the cats live in the wagon or sleep in it."

"Then where is that...odor coming from?"

"My clothes."

"You have cat urine on your clothes?"

"Certainly."

"Okay. You said certainly. Does that mean this is something you do intentionally?"

"Absolutely. Always be prepared."

"Uh-huh. And this state of preparation is for what in particular? And before you answer, I will say openly that I am certain I will be completely and entirely sorry for asking."

"Simple. To keep the chiggers, mo-skeeters, and June Bugs off, and of course to keep the Red-Eyed Moss Dodgers away. They haunt these particular woods here about."

"Red-eyed Moss Dodgers?" Wasyl asked from behind the seat.

"Yeah," Myron answered. "Ugly little bastards. Never know when one might pop up. So every morning I slap on a little feline bladder discharge and out I go."

Jasper shook his head, "You actually keep this stuff on hand?"

"Keep a supply in the cupboard at home. Want to know how I gather it?"

"Absolutely not!" Jasper barked.

Carla finally interrupted, "Myron, how long will it take us to get to some type of civilization?"

"Well, right now we're about 50 miles from being a hundred miles from anywhere."

"Okay," Carla said. "What about communication?"

"We'll have a phone in your hand shortly," he answered, to which Carla nodded.

Jasper said, "Do we ride the entire way in this wagon? I mean, those horses have been blasting away..."

His question is interrupted by a loud gurgling sound emitting from somewhere in the body of one of the large hoofed mammals pulling the human cargo carrier.

"Look out!" Myron yipped. "Could be a bad one!"

Everyone leaned back in a goggle-eyed stare as Jasper squealed, "Oh my God!"

"Live one! Live one!" Myron shouted just as the horse directly in front of the passenger side of the bench seat launched a feculent projectile of impressive proportion toward the hauling vessel and its helpless occupants. Fortunately, due to the weight of the discharged item and the earth's gravitational pull, the massive bowel ejection landed harmlessly between horse and wagon with an unceremonial 'splat'.

"This can be dangerous work," Myron said calmly.

CHAPTER 35

Entering his small personal office adjacent to the Secretary of State's expansive domain, Temple closes the door, flips on the lights and walks over to a small white apartment-size refrigerator. He retrieves a container of chocolate milk and opens it as he crosses the windowless room and sits down in a wooden office chair. The chair is situated directly behind a desk that is all natural wood, although what type of tree gave its life to become a piece of furniture is uncertain. The desktop has been stained and varnished numerous times, evidenced by the color of the copious engravings of the previous owners on the handed-down drawer holder. The desk had obviously been used through multiple changes in the White House as the wood carvings were directed at politicians of various eras. Temple liked to admire each engraving as he sat and imagined the person sitting here with a penknife or some other sharp object working out their frustrations on the assembled pieces of wood. He ran his finger across some of them as he sipped his milk.

He looked at each and said, "I feel your pissed offedness."

"Pissed offedness?" Voice asked.

"I didn't know you were here," Temple said.

"Stealth."

"I see."

Temple opens the top left drawer of the desk and peers in. Within, he sees a few scattered nickels, dimes, and pennies, a couple of ink pens, a book of matches with a cover that says "Club Hemp" in green lettering on a white background and a blue harmonica case with the name "Blues Traveler" signed on the top in black. He picks up the instrument holder and places it on his desk, pops it open with his left hand while sipping milk with his right. Once the lid is open, he plucks a newly twisted joint from beside the silver harmonica.

"Even here?" Asked Voice.

Temple lights a match from the matchbook and inhales.

"So, what brings you to my humble commode?" He asked, exhaling.

"I think you mean abode."

"Perspectives my friend. Perspectives."

The odor of marijuana from the cigarette now glowing in full bloom, drifts through the room like confused miniature clouds.

"An odd place to partake in the holy leaf isn't it?"

"I sometimes require a change of scenery," Temple said.

"Understood. But aren't you concerned B.T.? What would happen if you were to have a surprise visitor? Possibly an official one?"

"That's the only kind we have here. And no, I am not concerned."

"You seem rather roguish today."

"Ah, the ever expanding vernacular. Yes, that would be the correct term. Roguish. I came for the relaxation opportunity. You have come to view the four Jimmies, have you not?" Temple said, making an introductory wave of his hand to all four bland walls of his office. Each painted faded gold and decorated in separate shrine-like caricatures of his favorite Jimmies. Page, Brown, Jones, and Cricket.

"Not exactly the four horsemen," Voice said.

Temple takes a shallow drag and releases it. "Oh, but they are. Artistry, strength, evil, and cartoons. Washington encapsulated."

Temple tilts his head back far enough to look at the ceiling in a thoughtful pose.

"How long have you been following me?" He asked.

"An ample amount of time."

"And what have you heard?"

"I heard you tell, or should I say, General Pickens tell the military to strike fear into the hearts of those defenseless fellows across the ocean."

"Don't be critical. No one will be hurt. It's just a show."

"A show. Is it necessary?"

"They did declare war on us. And they directed some very foreboding epithets toward our Secretary of State."

"Which he deserved."

"Undoubtedly."

"Seems a little inequitable to me."

"It's world politics. As I have said before, just a little wag," Temple said, lowering his eyes from the ceiling to the room's lower interior. "So, other than the Jimmies and Botswanian injustice, why are you here?"

"I'm not welcome?"

"Don't bruise so easily. Being welcome or otherwise has never bothered you."

"True. I am here for an update."

"Of which update do you speak?"

"Your minions. Have they secured the papers? Are they free from the bondage of evil doers? Is the world again safe from the ravages of demonic superpowers? Basic stuff."

Temple took a few moments and recited the events as they had happened to date. He gently crushed out the joint in a nearby cup to not damage the remnants from further use. He tossed the milk container across the room into a small garbage can that had been manufactured to look like a basketball hoop and folded his arms across his stomach.

"Any comments?" he asked.

"Well, to summarize, the Montana beachhead has been abandoned. You are prepared to attack a small African country for daring to defend the honor of a diplomat's mother. Two completely untrained..."

"Agents."

"Yes, agents, along with an unknown Russian woman armed with sex brochures are on their way to a secret and as yet undetermined location. There, they will rendezvous with the courier and his bodyguard janitor who are being transported by a one-eyed semi-mutilated demolition expert and a transsexual who are currently traveling in a horse-drawn wagon through a vast area inhabited by an inordinately large clan of dangerous, perverted, and inbred people who are in the employ of a major enemy of the government."

"Correct."

"Oh, and a stolen van with some DJ's and a Greenpeace Advocate are on the way to help. And to make sure everything goes well; they are bringing a dead body."

"Yes, I believe that covers it."

"You seem to have it under control."

CHAPTER 36

"So," Wasyl said to Myron between intermittent road rut bounces, "you don't belong to that church group back there behind us?"

"No. Got no reason. Don't believe in God. Leastwise not like theirs. Besides, too many fat people back there. Some of them folks ought to have their butts up on Mt. Assmore. Too much for me. They just hire Edmond and Darnell..."

"Who?"

"Edmond and Darnell. Them horses pullin' us. Anywise, they just hire us to do stuff."

"Like kidnap us," Jasper snapped.

Carla interrupted, "If it wasn't for Myron, we'd all be stuck back there. Nobody would bother me, but by now you'd be wishing for the smell of cat urine."

Wasyl said, "I guess what I'm wondering is, I've never seen much beer drinkin' and pot smokin' at church. That place back there reminded me more of a bar back home called 'The Last Straw' than it did a place of worshippin'."

Myron let go another tobacco spit. "Yeah, it ain't the usual gospel-spewing that a churchgoer would be used to. But religion is so twisted it can be any old thing you want it to be. Hell son, you could worship a scalded ass cat and people would follow ya. Probably give ya money and build ya a fine lookin' worshippin' place.

"I suppose so."

"Take for example the fella that formed that birthday suit band of religious revelers back there. He claims he was a devout atheist until one night on a beach over on the Gulf coast in Florida, one of the disciples appeared before him from a pile of dried kelp."

"Do tell, which disciple?" Wasyl asked.

"Leon."

"Leon? I don't believe there was a disciple named Leon."

"I don't believe there was any disciples at all, but this fella claims Leon came to him and told him the real story behind the birth and all. Seems according to old Leon, it was a bit more bawdy than what was publicized in their book. So, them folks figure the holy kid the Christians are all yippin' about all the time came from his mama takin' a left turn on the extramarital mattress path. You gotta admit, take a whole lot of faith to believe that other story. Don't believe there is that much faith. Stupidity, yes. Faith, no."

"I'm not sure. I mean it was a great event."

"That's what they say. But think on it. And if you do think on it, and I mean serious-like, it seems a might tainted don't it?"

"How? It was God's doing."

"Does it make a difference if she danced the carnal polka with a local camel comber or the high hard one himself? She didn't have no conjugality contract with either of 'em. Leastwise not in the book that I read."

"But it was a holy event."

"I'll bet it was. Just ask mindless Joe."

"You mean Joseph."

"One and only. Think about it. Poor bastard comes home from work one day and his dearly semi-devoted tells him she is papoose packin' for some other bone salesman. Such a deal. Remember old Joe hadn't even wandered into the wanton well of womanhood yet and already some pioneering pilgrim had ventured into the virginal alley and apparently, did some paternal planting during the expedition. So, you gotta figure even slow Joe might be a bit upset about the prurient practices taking place in his absence, and that's when she lays it on him. 'It was God, honey.' Man, you talk about inventions coming along a few thousand years too late. Can you imagine having a tape recorder at that little face to face?"

"Hmm," Wasyl mumbled in thought.

The wagon bounced hard over a particularly nasty rut, raising all of its riders several inches off their perches and replanting them in the same spots.

"Damn," Jasper said, rubbing his right buttcheek.

"That's a lot to brain toss, that's for sure," Wasyl said, leaning forward from the back of the wagon and positioning himself on his knees with his head between Myron and Carla in front.

Myron said, "Sure is. And what about the aftermath of that matrimonial discourse? Pretty much only two things coulda happened, way I see it anyhow. Old jilted Joe just says, "Okidoke, no big deal as long as it was a one night stand and it's over." Myron then turned his head to his right and looked at Wasyl. "Or does he do what most fellas would do? Have showdown with Sky King. Calls him down from his cloud couch and says, 'Hey, have you been doing the fertility fandango in my forty wide?' Big boy would probably have said, "Yeah, but I wouldn't call it that because I don't do it exactly like you do." And Joe says, 'More 'n likely not,' cause I ain't never done it yet.' The Maker then tosses down the ultimatum, 'So you gonna do something' about it or what?' Joe thinks for a minute and tells him, 'I ain't quite decided yet.' Kind of a standoff until old Yahweh says, "I'm God, you know." Old Joe just kicks a rock and says, 'Well, you got me there.'"

"Kinda disturbin' when you think about it," Wasyl said.

"Then of course The Almighty, being the loving and merciful superhero that he is, makes Joe Bob cart his wayward, weight-gaining, and unfaithful partner all over the treeless sand dunes in search of a Camel Hump Inn to hatch God Junior at. They end up staying in a livestock stall and put the kid in a giant food dispenser for critters."

"Wow, I've never looked at it like that."

"You're a Christian, ain't ya?"

"Yes sir."

"Ain't your fault then. But anyway, the folks back at the church yonder just figure if the Lord above carried on like that, well they just suppose it gives them a little leeway in their services. So, a bit of drinkin' shouldn't hurt and the naked part, well what's good for the God is good for the gaggle, if you catch my meaning."

"Thank you spiritual adviser," Jasper said, shaking his head.

Carla was brushing an insect off her lap. At least now she had clothes on for the insect to land. They all did, thanks to Myron. Jasper had to admit, for an oddball, he had come through on threads, and quickly.

Earlier, Myron had stopped the wagon when they were out of sight of the compound lights and presented his passengers with numerous items of clothing. He had retrieved the clothing from a brown, oblong box sitting in the bed of the wagon that had a label attached to it on the side that read, "Beene's Funeral Parlor and Crematorium." Strangely enough, the items of clothing seemed to fit them pretty well and were actually a little on the stylish side for their current situation.

Carla was dressed in a dark blue women's business suit jacket, blouse, and knee-high skirt. Jasper found himself in an all-black suit and white dress shirt, while Wasyl wore a beige suit that was just a bit on the tight side so he wasn't able to snap or buckle the trousers.

It seemed odd to Jasper that an old coot like Myron would be able to come up with such quality attire, or at least semi-quality attire. That's when he noticed the label on the box.

"Say, uh, Myron, you got these clothes from a funeral home?" Jasper asked.

Myron gave a slight nod, "Yep. Get a lot of clothes there. Reasonable prices, too."

"So, you're what, a friend of the funeral director?"

"Old man Beene, yeah, we're well acquainted. He's been the attendant of the dead around here as long as anyone remembers. Folks call him Billy Beene they Burying Machine."

"That's really nice," Jasper said with a head shake.

"He used to have this little ditty on the radio when he advertised. Now, how did that go?"

"I can only imagine."

"Oh yeah, it went like this: "If'n you decided to pull the trigger, come see me before the rigor. I'm Billy Beene, the World Class Digger."

"Very engaging," Jasper said.

"Surely is. Old Billy's got style. Yep, he used to be head of the local chamber."

"Of what, horrors?"

"No, 'course not. Chamber of Commerce. Come to think of it, around here, might not be a whole lot of difference."

"So, I take it he has some kind of clothing store there at his funeral home to provide clothes for unprepared dead people. That seems a little odd, doesn't it?"

Myron reached into his chest-high coveralls pocket and retrieved a flat round container of some type of chewing tobacco, popped open the lid, took a sizeable pinch of the crushed leafy product between the natural vice of his thumb and pinkie and put it in his mouth behind his bottom lip.

"Yeah," he said. "You're right. That would be an odd way to do things, if that was what he was doin'."

"That's not what he's doing?" Jasper asked.

"Course not. These are clothes from his crematory business."

"What do you mean, his crematory business?"

"Well, folks, dead folks that is, wear those funeral fittings for three or four days while they is all laid out and everybody is gawkin' at 'em. Then when all the festivities is done, and right before he slips the stiffs in the oven, old Beene strips 'em down."

"You're kidding. Tell me you're kidding."

"Wouldn't kid ya about something like that. Fact is, I was standing right there when he stripped these here duds you all are wearing, off of three future ashtray fillers and tossed 'em to me."

"Jesus. Have you people ever heard of respect for the dead?"

"Highly overrated. It's always amazed me that we trash each other, steal from each other, and molest each other while we're alive, but as soon as somebody's body temperature drops about thirty-degrees we all develop a new respect for 'em."

"It just seems a little morbid and...wait a minute. Did you say he tossed these clothes to you directly from a fresh corpse?"

"I wouldn't say fresh. Been in the viewing room for a spell."

"Please tell me, please, that you washed them."

"The dead folks?"

"No, damnit, the clothes!"

"Oh, the clothes, why didn't you say so? You got nothing to worry about."

"Oh, thank you. So, you did wash them."

"Hell no, I didn't wash 'em. Them folks sure wasn't doing nothin' that would dirty up them outfits. Wasn't like they was workin' out in 'em."

The conversation was unexpectedly interrupted by the appearance of two large human figures standing in the roadway. One was holding a lantern with sufficient glow from its flame to light the immediate area and show the shotgun the second person was holding.

"Deweys," Myron said, pulling back on the leather reins.

"Deweys?" Carla asked.

"Ones I mentioned earlier. They're all a little on the far side of mean ass."

"Are they dangerous?" Jasper whispered.

"Can be. The one with the lantern is Dalton. Shotgun holder is Dete. On the brighter side of things, Darlene ain't amongst 'em. She's the bad one."

"She?" Jasper said.

"Be them boys' sister. She's tougher than a four-legged Frankenstein in an ass-puntin' contest."

"Hey Myron," the lantern-holder said in a high, twangy voice as the wagon came to a halt about thirty feet away and directly in front of him.

Myron gave a short greeting nod, "Dete. Dalton. Evenin' boys."

There was a short silence as if both sides were evaluating the situation before the man cradling the shotgun spoke, "Got some new meat there with ya, huh Myron?"

Myron nodded once.

Dalton said, "Course, ya know you're draggin' ass on a private road, Myron."

"Nope," came Myron's response, "don't believe so."

"Well, let's see Myron," Dete said. "I believe ya are, so let's just settle this trespassing problem amidst ourselves."

The two men in the road were so similar in appearance they could have been twins right down to their unkempt beards. They were even dressed alike in greasy-looking blue jeans, plaid shirts with long sleeves and dirty brown boots. It looked like some bizarre backwoods uniform the duo wore with the only difference being the filthy green baseball cap the shotgun holder was wearing.

Wasyl stood up in the back of the wagon to better observe the scene.

"Howdy boys," he said. "S'pose you could move aside a bit so we could head on down the road?"

"No, don't s'pose," Dalton said as Dete giggled.

"Please gentlemen," Jasper said. "We certainly don't want any problems. We just want safe passage."

Dalton and Dete looked at each other and then back at the wagon.

"You talk funny. You're from out of town?" Dete asked.

"Ya know what he sounds like?" Dalton said smiling.

"What?" Dete asked.

"Man kisser. Yep, he sounds like a man kisser."

"Oh yeah, one of them Ho-mo-sapiens."

Jasper cut in, "You mean sexual."

"Sexualsapien?" Dete said, scrunching his forehead.

"Hushup," Myron said quietly to Jasper.

"Myron," Dete said, "let's settle up this trespassing. You got yourself a fat one, a girlie one, and a sexualsapien. We'll be fair about this. We'll take two. You can keep one."

"Best move on boys," Myron said.

Wasyl whispered, "I Believe I can take one of them if we can get closer. Carl, I mean Carla, how about you?"

"If I get a good..." Carla started.

"Hold tight," Myron interjected. "No need, just hold tight."

"Why?" Jasper said. "Are they bluffing or are we gonna make a run for it?"

"No, they ain't bluffing and we ain't running."

"Well then..."

"Damn son, just hush the hell up," Myron said.

"Myron," Dete began, "I has lost my good nature for ya. Deals off. So, just have all three of them hop on down here now."

Silence.

"Myron," Dalton said, deepening his voice, "if you don't have them do what we say, I might just take a mind to yank out your good eye."

Myron spit on the ground. "Good eye has already been yanked. Bad eye is what I got left."

"Huh, so ya don't see none too good."

"I see good enough to pick out two worthless shit sniffers on a dark road."

Dete leveled the shotgun and pointed it directly at the wagon.

"That's it, Myron. Done talked yourself into a bad deal," he said.

Dalton chimed in, "You three hop on down here. Now!"

Jasper started to rise from his seat.

"Stay put," Myron said, still looking straight ahead.

Dete yelled, "Now! We ain't got all night!"

"You are surely right about that," Myron said.

"Right about what?" Dalton said, tilting his head to the side.

Myron retrieved a chewing tobacco container from his vest pocket. "About not havin' all night. Your night's about done."

CHAPTER 37

"How's he doing back there?" Biff said to Herbie who was seated in the back of the van.

"How's he doing?" Herbie said. "For Christ's sake, he's dead. He ain't doing worth a shit!"

Biff shook his head as he drove and glanced over at Danny who was speaking on the phone in the passenger's seat.

"I'm the one you assholes should be worried about," Herbie chided. "All this hanging out with Carlos Cadaver could give a guy colorectal failure."

Danny turned off his phone. "We need to make a stop," he said.

"Where?" Biff asked.

"Clothing store."

"A clothing store?" Herbie said. "What the hell for? Oh, wait, I get it. You told Wanda about my Hawaiian wardrobe, didn't you?"

"Yes, I told her about it."

"And now the Supreme Empress wants me to change, doesn't she? The arrogant..."

"No, she didn't say you had to change."

"She didn't?"

"No. She did say you're a horse's ass. The change of clothes is for our passenger."

"What the hell? Are you kidding me?"

"No, we're supposed to get him a new suit."

"I don't mean that! She said I'm a horse's ass?"

Biff interrupted, "She wants me to dress up in new clothes?"

"Nope, not you. The dead guy," Danny said. "And she wants him fitted."

"Uh huh, so nothing off the rack," Biff said. "So, what store is it that will let us carry a dead body in for a fitting?"

"Just stop at Walmart around midnight, hell, he'll fit right in. Might even get a job," Herbie said.

"No, no Walmart stuff," Danny said. "It has to be a tux. Very formal attire."

"Formal wear," Biff repeated.

"A freaking tux?!" Herbie said. "What the hell for?"

"Do you want to call the boss lady back and ask her?"

"No. She called me a horse's ass. I'm all up in my feelings."

Danny was looking at the screen of his phone. "Twenty minutes straight ahead. Blondie's Bridal Wear and Groom's Attire."

"That's a wedding place," Biff said.

"Can't get any more formal than that."

CHAPTER 38

Explosions seem never to be anticipated. Especially for those that are about to be exploded. The intended never see it coming. They never see it going. That is the nature of things. And, so it was for the Deweys.

Myron had nonchalantly tossed the small tobacco canister he pulled from his pocket to the ground near the two male interlopers blocking the wagon's path. However, the tobacco tin did not contain tobacco. Myron, a man of multiple talents and even more surprises, was prepared for just such a human intervention and had brought along a few deterrents of his own. Being a man of discretionary actions, Myron was the only person present who was not startled at the event or the outcome.

"Holy Mother of God! What the hell was that?" Jasper exclaimed from his new position on the floor of the backboard, peeking out over the front of the frame toward the epicenter.

Myron was disengaging one hunk of chew from his cheek while adding a new one from a different tobacco can. Wasyl was still in the back of the wagon, but was now crouching instead of standing. Carla remained seated in front as they all attempted to focus through the dust and smoke generated by the explosion.

"Army surplus?" Carla asked, squinting.

"Nope," Myron answered, chewing his fresh cud. "Homemade batch. Good for clearing trees, rocks, and the occasional Dewey."

"Hoo wee," Wasyl said. "Man, that was something."

"Uh," Jasper said, rising slowly, "Are they, uh, well are they..."

"Dead?" Myron said.

"Yeah, I guess that would be the proper term," Jasper said.

They all continued to examine the scene as the post-blaze haze and debris began to clear. Visible now were a couple of boots, the greasy baseball cap, shotgun, and still lit lantern now laying on its side. But, no Deweys.

"Might be," Myron said in an unconcerned voice. "More'n likely not, just blowed off into the trees somewhere yonder."

"But, how could they survive that, I mean how?" Jasper asked.

"'Cause they're Deweys."

"Do we go look for them? I mean, offer first aid or something?"

"Nope."

"Why?"

"'Cause they're Deweys."

"Okay, I guess."

Myron spit to his left, wiped his chin with his left arm and said, "We best be movin' on. I expect after them two finally hobble their blistered asses home, Deweys will be thicker than shithouse flies in these here woods."

He shook the reins and the horses began to move. The wagon riders could smell the odor from the blast as they passed the scene and rolled down the road slowly. Still rocking. Still bouncing.

"Pretty good stock you got there," Wasyl said, nodding toward the horses. "Didn't hardly jump or even flinch as best as I could tell."

"Used to it," Myron said.

"They're used to explosions?" Jasper asked.

"Yep. Done a fair share of blastin'."

"Is that how you got your uh...injuries?" Wasyl asked.

"Injuries?" Myron said. "Oh, fingers and such. Yeah, years back, had one pop a little early on me."

"So, you had one that didn't work, huh," Jasper said.

"Apparently, it did," Myron said, holding up his mangled hand in the air towards Jasper. "Just worked a bit early."

"I have to ask you, why don't you wear a patch over your eye?" Jasper asked.

"How would I see, only got one."

"No, I meant...never mind."

Carla said, "Any chance we can pull this rig over. I need to visit the ladies tree."

Myron drew back on the leather reins and the horses stopped. Carla got up, stepped in front of Jasper who had retaken his seat, hopped to the ground and walked into the darkness of the tree line.

"You know Carla long, Myron?" Wasyl asked.

"Not long," he said. "A short spell is all. How about you?"

"Well, you could say I have. But, been lots of change since I knew him a ways back."

Carla had returned and was climbing back into the wagon.

"Him?" Myron said.

"I used to be a guy," Carla interrupted as she was sitting down.

Myron started the rig going again and said, "Do tell. Heard about that. Not you in particular. Just in general like."

"Guess it's goin' around," Wasyl said.

"Christ," Jasper mumbled.

"Just didn't feel right in your boy skin, huh?" Myron said in a serious tone.

"Hard to explain," Carla answered. "But that's about the best reasoning I've heard so far."

"Well, you're a brave soul," Myron said. "Got to give you credit for that. Had your peter cut off and eveythin', did ya?"

Carla smiled while looking straight ahead, "Yep."

Myron continues, "What would you do with something like that? Devote it to science?"

"Not exactly," she said.

"Probably be a good conversation piece, no pun intended, not to mention what a taxidermist

might be able to do with it."

"Good Lord," Jasper said. "Let's talk about something else."

"Kinda hard to think about somethin' else right at the moment. I believe I'm havin' them what ya call sympathy pains," Myron said chuckling.

"How about this," Jasper said. "Where are we headed? Someplace safe I hope? Like someplace where I can get a hold of a phone and call Washington?"

"Don't get itchy, son," Myron said.

Wasyl cut in, "Hey Myron, did you say earlier that you came out here from Hollywood?"

"Yeah, I was there for a spell. Movie business."

"What did you do out there? Were you an actor or somethin'?"

"No, no, nothin' like that. I was in wardrobe. Really liked that job."

Jasper turned to look at Myron, "You're kidding, right?"

"Kind of a negative sort ain't ya?" Myron said.

Wasyl said, "Why'd you leave that job if you liked it so much?"

"Wife left me. Truth be told, she was the main reason I stayed in that job so long. Once she left, there was no cause to hang around."

"Don't follow you," Wasyl said.

"Well, it's a bit personal."

"Probably should keep it to yourself then," Jasper said.

Myron said, "My wife at the time was Bernice. A fine specimen of a woman. Tall gal, over six foot. Stronger than a state fair ox. Had these big old feet, coulda water skied on them pontoons of hers."

"Thanks for sharing all that, but really..." Jasper said.

"Bernice had this odd little marital bed fantasy about different movie characters."

"There is no God," Jasper whispered to himself.

"Anyway, I'd borrow some outfits from the various movies I was working on, or go to the warehouse and snoop around for old movie stuff and take it back home and the next day, I'd take it all back."

"So what was the problem?" Wasyl asked as Jasper gave him a cold stare.

"Problem was, one day I happened upon the old abandoned stage for the Wizard of Oz. Man, they had some outfits for that movie. Well, knowing Bernice like I did, I brought home a special outfit from the Oz collection, which was all fine, mind you, except Bernice got especially attached to it and wanted me to keep it and not take it back. Kept it for quite awhile."

Wasyl said, "Did someone find out?"

"You might say that. One night, I was all outfitted up in the Oz suit and we somehow ended up out by our cement pool. We got all wrapped up in a moment of passionate bliss and apparently one of the neighbors called the police. Figured Bernice as being ravaged or something by some unknown. You know city folks."

Jasper said, "Oh, sweet Jesus, your neighbors looked out and saw the Tin Man or the Scarecrow having sex with your wife?"

"No, neither one of them," Myron said.

"Oh, wonderful, that just leaves the Cowardly Lion, that would be the ultimate weird."

"Hell no son, where'd you get that idea?"

"Well..."

"I was a flying monkey."

CHAPTER 39

After driving for what seemed like days, the maroon Lincoln with Skeet, Paulie, and Olga arrived at what they hoped was their destination.

"Does this place have a name?" Skeet asked.

"Cooter's Bog," Paulie answered.

"Fits. Sure ain't much of a town."

Paulie pointed ahead through the windshield. "Up ahead looks like the schoolyard. Appears abandoned like they said."

Skeet said, "Look around. I don't believe there's anyone in the whole place."

There were eight houses, all small, all painted white with blue shingled roofs on both sides of an old county blacktop road. At the end of the rows of houses was a rusty iron bridge near a grove of trees traversing a small creek that ran swiftly over some rocks, the gurgling water providing the only noise in the area. Skeet drove his car ahead to the open area next to the schoolhouse about fifty yards past the bridge. The building looked like something right out of a "Little House on the Prairie" set with a peaked roof and a belfry complete with a copper colored bill. Unlike the nearby houses, the school looked like it had recently been painted. The windows were intact and the yard had the smell of fresh cut grass. But just like the dwellings, there were no people around. Skeet parked in the small gravel lot in front of the building and shut off the engine.

"Well?" He said.

"Well what?" Paulie answered.

"Do we just sit here?"

"I guess. Place is kinda weird, isn't it? I'm glad it's daytime. This whole area might creep me out in the dark."

Skeet opened his door and got out.

"Where are you going?" Paulie asked.

"Inside to take a peek. Tired of sitting on my ass."

"I wil go too," Olga said from the back and climbed out.

"Fine. You coming, Paulie?"

"No. We're supposed to watch for our contact. They're supposed to be flying in here. I'll just wait. Might get another call, too."

Paulie had received three calls from his contact on their trip with travel directions and instructions. All the messages had been in code, which delighted Paulie as he rifled through his code book, relaying his findings to a bored Skeet. So, Paulie was satisfied to remain seated in the car, cell phone in one hand, code book in the other.

Skeet and Olga had wandered to the front door of the house and had just walked up the three wooden steps to the front porch when Paulie drew their attention.

"Hey guys," he said.

They turned to see their companion standing outside the car with the passenger door open facing them. But there was a change. He was not alone. There were three men standing with him. Two of the men were dressed in expensive-looking dark business suits. One man had short dark hair and was slim built and about 6 feet tall. The other suited man was about the same height but looked to be a bit heavier. He was partially bald on top with some brown hair on the sides. Both men looked to be in their late thirties, and each wore sunglasses. Neither had facial hair.

The third man was different in every aspect. He had a long grayish black beard while his head was completely bald or shaved. His clothing consisted of blue jeans with numerous dark stains and a rip on the knee of the left leg. He was over six feet tall and wore no shirt over a heavily hair-matted chest and large stomach, both of which were partially covered by a buttonless vest that appeared to be made of the same material as his pants. Where the other men wore polished black shoes, he wore scuffed brown boots. Around his neck was a chain. Not a necklace chain, but a short section of log chain, which Skeet thought went well with the seemingly endless rambling of tattoos on his upper body and neck.

Skeet walked down the steps with Olga following and strolled over to the gathering. As he got closer, it became clear that this was an adversarial group and not a friendly one. He could see that the semi-dome topped man in the suit had latched his hand securely to Paulie's right arm.

"Hey fellas," Skeet said.

There was no response beyond Paulie raising and lowering his eyebrows in an expression of helplessness. Everyone stood and stared momentarily.

"So, you fellas need something? You from out of town? Need some directions?" Skeet asked.

They remained unflinchingly still and mute. Olga stepped up to stand beside Skeet, which caused the first reaction from the strangers.

"Grr!" Growled the man dressed like an extra from "Easy Rider."

"Grr? What is grr?" Olga asked Skeet.

Skeet shrugged, "Best I can figure, it's either a customary local greeting, he's trying to scare us, or he has gas."

"Oh, grr to you too," Olga said with a nod of her head.

No one spoke again for a moment.

"So, that's it?" Skeet said. "I'm supposed to figure out what you guys want from grr?"

"Grr!" The large man said again, scrunching his face and gritting his teeth.

"You said that already. Be careful your face doesn't freeze that way," Skeet said.

"You will address me. I am the supervisor," the dark-haired man finally said.

"Supervisor?" Skeet said looking at the growler, the bald man, and then back at the man speaking. "Okay supervisor, what's up?"

Again, silence befell the group as everyone stood and looked at each other.

"Alright, here's how we'll do this," Skeet said. "I'll tell you who we are, then you tell us who you are." He waited a moment for a reaction, getting none, he continued, "My name is Skeet, my female friend here is Olga, and that bug-eyed fella you're hanging onto is Paulie."

More silence.

"It's your turn. See, that's how it works. So how about it?"

The dark-haired man said, "I am called.. Mr. Death."

Skeet looked at Olga, then back at the man. "Mr. Death? You're shittin' me, right? Mr. Death? Who the hell would name you that? Your mom? Is she some kind of James Bond freak or something?"

"Grr," the bearded man said.

"Yeah, yeah, I got that," Skeet said, then looked at the partially bald man in the suit who had not yet spoken. "How about you? You have a name tag?"

Immediately, the man started gesturing with his hands emphatically in apparent motions of signing.

Skeet said, "Well, at least now we're getting nowhere."

"I...think they want something." Paulie stammered.

"Really?" Skeet said. "I thought they just wanted to hang out here flippin' fingers, growling, and using scary names."

"Enough talk," Mr. Death said.

"Okay, so, if my friend here is right and you do want something and if there's no more talking, we have what I would call a quandary."

The non-speaking man tapped the dark-haired man on the arm to get his attention then started on a massive signing barrage. When he was done, they both looked at Skeet.

"So, what did your buddy say?" He asked.

Mr. Death gave a slight shrug. "I have no idea, I don't read sign language."

"Awesome," Skeet said. "Well, what about you Grrr? You read sign language?"

"Uh..., grr?"

Everyone stood looking at each other for a moment.

"Well, this has all been grand, but I think it's time we headed out," Skeet said.

"No," Death said. "You have some documents. We want them."

Olga clutched a handful of Wanda's brochures tightly to her stomach. Seeing this, Mr. Death reached out and grabbed them.

"So," he said, "now we have the documents."

"Yes, you do," Skeet said.

Olga gave the man a stern look. "These cannot be kept by you. I am keeping."

"Oh, a Russkie, huh?" Death said.

"Russkie? Really? People actually say that?" Skeet said.

"Well funnyman, let's see who laughs now," Death said and put on a pair of dark-framed reading glasses he had pulled from the inside pocket of his sport coat. He stared down at the first, the second, the third brochure in disbelief.

"What is this?" He said, raising his voice holding the brochures out towards Olga. The title, "It's Not the Size, it's The Driver" visible on the front.

"Is very good. Has cute drawing of tiny penis on the top," Olga said pointing, "You see tiny penis?"

"Yes, I see a tiny penis!" He barked.

"Probably every day," Skeet said.

"Where are the documents?!" The man demanded, gritting his teeth.

"We don't have any documents," Skeet said. "So how about we just go now?"

That's when the guns appeared. Both suited men pulled semi-automatic handguns from their jackets and pointed them at Skeet and Olga. The bald man pushed Paulie over by his friends.

"Ow!" Paulie said, rubbing his arm where the man had gripped him. "I think I'm bruised.," he said looking at the man, "You're mean!"

"Very brave of you, Blumie," Skeet said.

"Thank you."

"Just who are you guys anyway?" Skeet asked.

Death stared at him. "We are your worst daydream."

"I think you mean nightmare."

Grr said, 'Grr," and flexed his upper body.

"Nah, you're probably right," said Skeet.

"This is over. I must dispose of all of you. First, I shoot the feminine one."

"I am not afraid to die," Olga said, raising her chin in defiance.

"No, I mean this one," Death said, pointing his weapon at Paulie, causing Paulie to put both of his hands out in front of his body in a defensive gesture.

"Whoa! Wait a minute, wait a minute. Unlike her," he said, "let me say unequivocally, I am extremely afraid of dying. I have no idea what happens in the great beyond or even if there is a great beyond, but I don't like pain or surprises. So, if I have a vote on this shooting idea, let me cast a big NO."

Death leaned towards Paulie, pressing the barrel of his pistol against Paulie's forehead and smiled. Skeet searched for an angle to help, but the second man's gun was trained on him. He knew he still had to make some kind of move.

Then it happened. Just like in the movies. A last second intervention of salvation. Except, totally unlike the movies, Mr. Death, the bad guy, became the accidental savior when, with his wicked smile still intact, he pulled a stringy item from Paulie's front shirt pocket.

"Oh, what do we have here?" He said. "Candy? The spoils of war." And he took a bite out of ...the licorice.

Instant whack. Death fell flat on his back on the ground. Everyone looked down at him for a moment.

"Wow," Skeet mumbled, "that shit really works."

Grr just stood there, wide-eyed, as the other suited man began making elaborate hand gestures that meant something like, "I dislike you greatly and because of how these events have unfolded, I must terminate your lifecycle" but probably in more direct terms. He then took a turn at pressing his weapon into Paulie's skull while vibrating in a most disturbingly hideous, but totally muted, laugh. Multiple things happened at that very instant. Skeet jumped at the bald man while simultaneously Olga let go with a vicious NFL-style punt to Grrr's groin. Oddly, the man Skeet lunged at, collapsed unconsciously to the ground before Skeet made contact. However, Olga did make contact with an earth-shaking thud, driving Grr into a fetal position on the ground next to his supine partner.

"Goddamn!" Grr yelled, clutching his crotch. "What the hell! Damn near kicked my sack off!"

"Hey, he talks," Skeet said leaning down to see a silver dart hanging from the neck of the bald man next to him.

"What is this?" He said to himself out loud.

Paulie sat down hard on the ground.

"I think I'm gonna be sick," he said.

"You'll be fine," Skeet said, still looking at the dart. "You know what that looks like?"

"Oh, no," Paulie moaned. "Look, more company."

Skeet turned to see what Paulie was looking at. Walking toward them from an area behind the school were two men. One was gray-headed, short, wearing coveralls and what looked like a white lab jacket. The second man was dressed in black trousers, a white shirt, and a round dark hat. The man with the white jacket was also carrying a small weapon of some sort, but he was handling it in a very non-threatening, casual manner.

"This doesn't look good at all. Another gun," Paulie said.

"Cool it, Blumie. This'll be fine I believe," Skeet said.

The two men walked up looking over the scene as they approached.

"Howdy," White Jacket said.

"Hey," Skeet said looking at White Jacket's weapon. "I believe that dart in this fella is yours."

"Surely is," the man said, smiling.

"You must be a vet."

"A vet?" Paulie asked.

"Veterinarian," the man said. "Dr. Sloop. First name, Truly."

"Truly Sloop?"

"Long story made real short, Dad had a sense of humor." The man said then nodded at his partner. "This here would be Eli Yoder of the Yoder clan, whose property we are all standing on."

"Sorry," Paulie said, getting up.

"Nothing to be sorry about," Yoder said. "This is the Lord's land. I am only his groundskeeper."

"Amish?" Skeet asked.

"Yes, my friend," Yoder said.

"Well, a good thing you two happened to come along. By the way Dr. Sloop, that was a hell of a shot. I'm much obliged."

"Thanks, but we didn't just happen along," the Vet said.

Grr suddenly rolled over on the ground to his other side and moaned.

"Anyway," Sloop said, "we're here to tell you, plans have changed. I believe, Mr. Blumenshine, you should check your book."

Paulie looked at both men. "What do you mean plans have changed? And who are you anyway?"

"We are who we said we are," Yoder said. "We are friends, you might say. Beyond that, we can tell you only this, "Slip noodle crossed the bird wire at noodle slip."

Paulie quickly moved to the open passenger door of the car and pulled out his code book and flipped rapidly through the pages.

"He really likes this secret agent stuff," Skeet said. Both men smiled back.

"Wow, this is something," Paulie said.

Ignoring him, Skeet said to his two visitors, "So, someone got a hold of you about these three hombres. How did they know?"

"Your cell phone was compromised," Sloop said. "And only those two in the suits were supposed to be waiting for you. That was our intel."

"What about him?" Skeet said pointing at Grr, who was now sitting up.

"I know nothing of that one. What are the names of the two lying there?"

Skeet said, "That one was unable to talk and the other one is Mr. Death."

"No kidding?" Sloop said, bending over looking at the prostate figure. "Well normally I would say a dumb name, but in his case it now fits. Maybe not." He then pointed at an item in the man's hand.

"Ah, the licorice," Yoder said. "He will be fine. It might take a few days."

"But I thought eating the licorice was fatal," Skeet said.

Sloop took a white rag from his pocket and wiped perspiration from his forehead. "It would be except for the usual governmental oversights."

"Like?"

"Like, some government contractors overcharged and under-performed by watering down the poison and, of course, they're way beyond the expiration date. Anyway, with the dose for a ruttin' bull I gave the other fella, they'll both be sleeping it off for a while."

"Wait a minute, if there was only supposed to be two people showing up to mug us, then who are you?" Skeet said, nudging the tattooed man with his foot as he attempted to sit up.

Sloop interrupted, "Hey, aren't you the guy that tends bar down at Littleton Tap? What in the world are you doing with these two?"

"I just tagged along," he said, groaning. "These two came into the bar and offered me fifty bucks to act tough."

"And grr was the best you could do?" Skeet said.

"Hey man, it was only fifty bucks. Hell, I'd a turned 'em down if I'd know'd I was going to get scrotumized."

Skeet grabbed onto the man's arm and helped him to his feet.

"Are you gonna make it?" Skeet asked.

"I think so," the man answered. "Can I ask you all something?"

"Sure."

"What's this all about?"

"Can't tell you."

"Good enough," he said, staggering away.

"Oh, and you might just want to forget about all this," Skeet said.

"No shit," he answered.

"Grr!" Olga said, waving as he left.

He turned, looked at her, waved back and said "Uh, yeah, sure."

"Well, it's time we left," Yoder said. "God travels with you my friends."

"Good luck," Sloop said. "And don't worry about those two," he nodded toward the men on the ground. "We'll check in on them periodically."

As the two friendly men walked away, Skeet, Paulie, and Olga opened the doors to enter their vehicle.

"Well, where to, Secret Agent Paulie?" Skeet asked.

"Washington."

"D.C.?"

"That's the one."

CHAPTER 40

"So, he needs to be fitted for a tux," the man said, looking into the back of the van.

"Yes, sir. That's what he needs," Biff said. "Fitted for a tux."

"He's dead, you know," the man said.

"Yes, sir," Biff answered. "He surely is. And, he needs to be fitted."

"For a tux."

"Yes, sir. For a tux."

The slender man in a black sport coat and pants was bald except for black hair on both sides of his head. He stood quietly studying the situation as Danny and Biff studied him. Herbie was looking at a bridal mannequin in the store's front window.

"This is for a wedding?" The man finally asked.

"Uh, well, sure. That's exactly right. It's for a wedding." Biff said, shrugging at Danny.

"Is he the father of the bride or something?"

"He's the groom," Herbie called out.

"The groom," the man said.

Biff glared at Herbie then looked back at the man. "Yes, sir. He's the groom. He's getting married...posthumously."

“A bit odd, isn’t it?” The man asked, folding his arms.

Herbie walked over. “It’s just like guys in the army. They get medals posthumously all the time. Same thing.”

“Except…different,” Biff said.

“Different,” the man said.

“Come on, buddy,” Herbie said. “Ain’t got all day. Gotta get to the church on time, ya know.”

The man looked at Herbie for a moment then looked back at the corpse.

“Is the bride, uh, is she…?”

“Nope,” Herbie said, “She’s alive and kickin’.”

“Is she aware that her fiancée is…”

“She will be tonight when they get to the postnuptial honeymoon activities,” Herbie chuckled. “Where do you think they came up with the saying ‘lucky stiff’?”

“Sir,” Biff cut in to stop Herbie. “We know this seems unusual.”

“Yes,” the man said. “I believe unusual would be an excellent term. Bizarre, ghoulish, horrifying, would all fit as well, but we’ll go with unusual.”

“Can you help us out?” Danny implored.

“I don’t think…”

“We’ve got a government credit card.”

“Well, let’s not keep the bride waiting.” The man said, pulling a tape measure from his pocket and climbing into the van.

CHAPTER 41

Temple opened the door to his apartment, pushed a button on the wall and a dark light came on giving his apartment a haunted atmosphere as his wall speakers unleashed the sound of Ray Wiley Hubbard's "Choctaw Bingo" in the background.

"Home already?" Voice said.

"I brought homework," Temple answered.

"Ah, you had a need for a more suitable work environment."

"And some of the leaf of introspect."

"On the table by the beanbag," Voice said. "I Thought I would help, so I rolled three new ones for you."

"From which container?"

"Near the foot of your bed."

"The Brazilian batch. Good choice. Did you try one?"

"Surely, you jest."

Temple picks up a joint. "Excellent roll job. So, you did this?"

"Who else would do it? I'm the only one here."

"But you're not exactly here, if you know what I mean."

Voice laughs. "Sometimes, you're not all here yourself, my friend. Now tell me, what's this homework you've brought? Anything that will require my opinion?"

"You're very sure of yourself," Temple said.

"I am many things, of which being sure, is certainly one."

Temple lights the joint and lowers himself onto the beanbag seat. "They plan on shooting them."

"Who?" Voice asked.

"Who, as in who is shooting, or, as in who are they shooting?"

"Begin with the former, end with the latter."

Temple takes a deep drag and releases it.

"The former is a mystery. The latter is the courier, janitor et al."

"Surely, you have suspects."

"I suspect every self-centered, underhanded person in D.C."

"So, everyone is a suspect. Any way to narrow it down?"

"Hardly. Anyone could be one of the vile conspirators. So, I consider everyone a member of the suspect club, except you and me...and I'm not too sure about you."

"I've never been a suspect before. At least not in this world. Feels rather stimulating. Maybe checking motives would help."

Temple exhales a thick plume of smoke. "You're kidding right? Politicians have one motive, re-election."

"Then you have a situation on your hands."

"Yes, I would say this is a situation."

"Would it be in the best interest to get the President included? He is in charge."

Temple laughed. "He's no more in charge than the last President."

"I'm not speaking of the President, I'm speaking of the uh, let's say, surrogate President."

"You speak of me, I take it?"

"Of course. Throw around your fictitious weight. See which rats scurry for cover. Make things happen, Mr. President."

Temple's phone interrupts.

"Well, we'll find out right now what I can do. This call is for the Pres."

"You've had it directed to you?"

"All Level One security calls have been diverted to this phone."

"How did you get this done?"

"I used the same guy that deleted Hillary's two million emails," Temple said as he answered the phone.

Temple spoke in the President's voice for two minutes, then disconnected.

"I'm not being discourteously nosey, but did I hear the word invasion?"

"Yes, you are, and yes, you did."

"In context to what?"

Botswana Marines have stormed the beach at Kendall."

"Which is?"

"Small town on the coast of Florida."

"Have they established a beachhead?"

"Yes, but local authorities have them pinned down."

"National Guard?"

"Three part-time cops, volunteer fire department, and a security guard from the local bank."

"Excellent. Any casualties?"

"No. They hosed them down on the beach."

"Homeland Security is a wonderful thing."

"Isn't it though."

CHAPTER 42

The sun had finally risen to treetop level over the eastern horizon when Myron guided the horses into the weed-covered yard of a structure that had once been a barn. Now, it was a rundown building with a few shingles and a couple of broken windows situated in a clearing between two groves of trees. As soon as the wagon halted, the passengers stood to stretch and moan from the arduous butt-slamming trip.

Jasper said, “Finally, a break. So, is this the rest stop?”

“Nope,” Myron said. “Change of transportation.”

Jasper looked around. All he saw was the old building and the remnants of a long ago used tractor sitting in the weeds as tall as the machine’s apex. He looked back at Myron. “So, what? Now we walk?”

Myron was unhitching the horses. “No son, we don’t walk. Wouldn’t get far walkin’.” He turned the horses loose and they sauntered over to a small pond near the closest grove of trees and began to drink.

Wasyl looked at Jasper and shrugged. Myron walked into a bush that was by the entrance to the old building. There were two doors hanging on rusty hinges at an angle of the doorway and Myron leaned against one with his left hand while he bent over and pulled a leather carrying case out of the shrub on his right.

"Carla," he said, reaching inside the case and pulling out a phone and tossing it to her. She caught it with one hand, nodded a thanks, and walked off in the opposite direction while tapping on the phone.

"Hey, I need to use that," Jasper said.

"Don't think so, son. Carla will be making the calls," Myron said.

"But I have people to call," Jasper griped.

"We all got problems," Myron said, removing a couple more items from the bag and walking inside the old building.

Carla was talking into the phone, then turned back to Myron. "Is the plane ready?"

"I expect so. I'll check it again for pre-flight, but it should be," echoed his voice from inside the barn.

"Plane? What plane? Is there a plane coming? "Jasper rattled off.

"Plane ain't coming. Plane's already here. Around back," Myron said, stepping back out of the structure.

Jasper jogged around to the backside of the building, followed by Wasyl. In a field adjacent to the structure was a plane...sort of.

"Oh God," Jasper whispered.

"Whew boy, how 'bout that?" Wasyl said, now standing next to Jasper, staring at a flying machine that might have been the only thing in the area in worse shape than the barn. By now, Myron had wandered up next to the duo while Carla was still standing in the distance talking on the phone.

"What do you think boys," Myron said proudly.

"What do I think?" Jasper said, pointing at the machine. "I think that is not a plane. It's a rusty beer keg with wings."

Myron said, "Well some people see the glass as half full, some see the glass as half empty."

Jasper stopped pointing. "Oh really? And how do you see it?"

Myron smiled at him, "Hell son, half the time, I can't even see the glass."

Carla walked up to the trio and stood between Myron and Jasper.

"Change of plans," she said.

"Thank God," Jasper said. "I thought we were going to have to get in that dilapidated kite."

"Transportation stays as-is, location changes," she said looking at the plane.

"Shit," Jasper said. "Please, can I use the phone?"

"No," she said, then turned to Myron. "Is that Pitstop Parkinson's plane?"

"Yep, sure is. God rest his soul."

"Oh great," Jasper said. "A dead guy's plane. Even better."

"We're not stopping at our previous landing point," Carla said.

Myron said, "Okay, where am I flyin' us to then?

"Wait a minute!" Jasper screeched. "Where are you flying us! You can't be serious! You're not a pilot!"

"Sure am," Myron answered, "or as they say; a reasonable facsimile thereof."

Wasyl said, "Wow, you can fly a plane too, Myron?"

"I'm not just eye candy, ya know."

"We're going straight in," Carla said.

"Straight in where?" Wasyl asked.

"Straight into the ground," Jasper said.

"It could be worse," Wasyl said.

"We're going to land in Washington," Carla said.

"Airport?" Myron asked.

"White House lawn."

"That would be the worse part," Jasper said.

"Bet that draws some attention," Wasyl said. "You know how excited them secret service folks get sometimes."

"Why can't we just call and get picked up by someone from my department or CIA or something?" Jasper asked.

Carla turned to face him. "Listen, there are people all over Washington and all over these woods that don't want those documents to get back. I have strict contact orders and you'll have to follow along. Actually, Wassie has to follow along because is now the official courier. You can probably do what you want at this point."

Jasper looked around the area. Remote, was the word that came to mind.

"Parachutes. How about parachutes?" He said to Mryon. "At least we might have a chance if we had parachutes."

"You ever jumped out of a plane before?" Myron asked.

"No," he said. "But what if the plane goes down?"

"Be too late, son. By the time you figured out how to use one of them silken sky skimmers, you'd be a big pile of splattage on some rock. Bugs would be draggin' your remnants off for a fiesta."

"Just a thought."

"Nervous sort, ain't ya?"

"Only when I'm getting ready to die."

Myron patted him on the back as Jasper stared at the ground. "Hell, dyin' ain't hard. Besides, the plane will do all the work for you." Myron cackled a laugh and walked around the plane with his three passengers slowly following.

The plane was a small, dirty white machine with a few numbers on the side and faded red lettering on the back end of the tail. Myron opened the door on the passenger side for everyone to view the interior.

"Two seats up front, two in the back. Everybody pick a spot and squat, put your seatbelts on in case the takeoff bumps a bit. Might be a little rough, this ain't exactly a runway here in this field."

Jasper points at the seats. "These aren't regulation airplane seats, they don't match, and what is the deal with the seatbelts?"

The seats he was referring to were cheap plastic and aluminum lawn chairs in various colors of white, green, and red. The seatbelts were long skinny woven chords.

"Chairs will work fine. Seatbelts got chewed off by raccoons or something. Probably had some food stains on 'em."

"So, what are those things replacing them? Colored rope?" Jasper asked.

"Fish stringers. Might smell a bit, but they should serve their purpose."

"I really can't do this," Jasper said, taking a step back from the plane as Wasyl and Carla stepped up and into the rear seating area. Myron walked around to the pilot's side and climbed in.

"Maybe I'll just take my chances with walking or with the horses," Jasper said reluctantly.

"Whatever coils your rope, son. Fine with me."

"Yeah, well..."

Jasper was interrupted by numerous popping noises from somewhere in the woods behind him.

"What's that noise?" He asked.

"That'd be shootin'," Myron said calmly, tying his fish stringer seat belt together.

"Hunters?"

"Deweys."

"What are they shooting at?"

A small puncture mark suddenly appeared on the backside of the airplane wing Jasper was standing near.

"That'd be us," Myron said. "Best come to a conclusion, son. This old plane can't afford to have a stray bullet nick a spot of the Elmer's glue holding it together."

Jasper took another look at the plane, then one more look in desperation for an alternate route of escape. He said, "Maybe we could take one more try at reasoning with these people."

Another round hit the top of the wing.

"Let's move, youngster. That shootin' ain't some friendly form of mountain greetin'," Myron said.

Jasper quickly climbed into the plane cabin and took the front passenger spot next to the pilot seat where Myron was starting the single engine up. After a moment of stalling, shaking, and various disturbing noises, the motor came to life.

"How high up will this thing fly?" Wasyl asked from the backseat.

"Don't rightly know," Myron responded. "Ain't got it off the ground yet."

Myron revved the motor a couple of times then started the plane in motion. It moved ahead slowly, then made a one hundred eighty degree turn back to the direction in which the shooters came. With the single propeller on the plane's front spinning, causing dust and debris to hit the air, the group peered through the windshield at a mob of a dozen or more people at the edge of the woods coming towards the plane at a trot. The Dewey's were still in the distance but the space was shrinking rapidly as the people moved toward the airplane and the plane motored toward them. Most of the crowd, which was dressed like a bunch of paramilitary hunters, were armed with long-barreled weapons. Periodically one of them would stop running long enough to fire a round in the flying machine's direction. The plane started to pick up speed rapidly and the crowd came to a halt, at first just staring at the oncoming vessel, then some standing, some kneeling, they all began to shoot again.

As the plane's speed increased, it started to leave the ground.

"Tell me when we get close to the trees," Myron said to Jasper.

"Tell you what? Just look. They're straight ahead of us!"

"I can't see for shit, son, just tell me."

Jasper just stared, alternating between the approaching tree line, the timber-dwelling militia, and his one-eyed pilot. The plane sped up and the people who had been firing at it threw themselves to the ground face down in hopes of not being run over by the approaching fuselage. Just as the plane reached their location, it started to rise a little. Very little. The trees ahead were looking too close, and Jasper realized that his pilot may very well not have been joking about his vision, or lack thereof.

"Pull up! Pull up!" He yelled.

"Okidoke," Myron said as he pushed the plane's speed even more and guided it upward. As the plane rose, its wheels grazed the tree tops causing the cabin to shake and the craft to tilt slightly before it lifted and was airborne.

"Shoulda said somethin' sooner," Myron said, smiling. "Told ya my sight ain't none too good, what with losing one eye and the other one is glass."

"Glass?!" Jasper squealed, turning to face the pilot.

"Just playin', son," Myron said. "Sit back and tighten up your fish stringer."

The plane gained altitude, then leveled off as the passengers all gazed out their windows to the background sputtering of the engine.

Jasper looked out the window for a moment then looked back at Myron.

"How high are we?" He asked.

"Check the dashboard gauges," Myron answered.

Jasper looked at the dash and located a clock-like glass-covered screen that was labeled 'Altimeter' on top.

"It says zero. The hand on it is flat on zero," he said.

"I expect we're a bit higher than that. Must be broke," Myron said.

"It's not working. Why didn't you check it? Wait a minute, the fuel gauge says zero, too. What the...they all say zero!"

"No operational info, huh? Make for an interesting fight, won't it?"

"I thought you said something back there about a pre-flight check or something."

"Wasn't time. I don't believe the Dewey clan was gonna cease fire, and I figured if we had a flight plan we'd be okay as long as we followed it."

Jasper sighed, "Well, I guess as long as we have a flight plan. I guess that's something positive, at least."

Myron said, "It surely would be something positive. Ifn we had one."

"You mean we don't? I thought you said..."

"I said if we had one. We don't and we don't have no gauges and we don't have a pilot with two good eyes neither. But we'll make do. I've been through some rough times, and I've always came out of it just fine. Look at me,"Myron said, turning to smile at him. Jasper looked at his scarred forehead, missing eye, bent nose and hand where fingers used to live and sighed.

Wasyl called up from the backseat, "He's just a little on the frazzled side, Myron. He's concerned about dyin' and being considered a failure and not leaving a lethargy."

"Legacy," Jasper corrected.

"Yeah, legacy, mostly on account of the fact I'll get all the credit for having him shoved some stuff up my butt."

"Do tell," Myron said. "Gotta be careful with that kind of activity. Man's got to poop right, ya know."

CHAPTER 43

Paulie was sitting in the passenger side of the Lincoln, cruising down a late afternoon highway. With the sun directly behind them causing an ever-lengthening shadow in front of them that the car could never seem to be able to overtake.

He pulled his cellphone from his pocket and looked at it for a moment while from the dashboard speakers Bonnie Raitt was crooning about being outside someone's window with the radio on.

"You calling somebody?" Skeet asked.

Paulie turned the phone over in his hand a few times as if he were examining a fossil.

"You know, that was a near-death experience I had back there by the schoolhouse," he said after a pause.

"Yep. No question," Skeet answered.

"I could have died. Seriously."

"Yes, sir. And I believe seriously is the only way you can die."

"Have you ever had a near-death experience, Skeet?"

"One time. Walt Timmer came home early one day and found Eileen Timmer and yours truly testing the TV commercial claims of comfort and coil support of their new Posturepedic SleepMaster."

"I don't think that's the same thing."

"I don't know. Walt's a pretty fair shot. Fortunately, I'm a pretty fair ducker, leastwise if I wasn't, we wouldn't be having this conversation."

"Well, whatever. I guess that incident has made me do some analyzing. I'm thinking maybe I've been a little hard on my family. A little too judgmental. You know, a little quick to criticize. I think I'll just give them a call and see what's going on in their lives. Maybe give them some supporting words."

Skeet shrugged a 'whatever' and Paulie made the call. The phone rang a number of times, which was unusual, but finally it was answered.

"Hello? Hang on just a second," Ruth said then yelled at someone. "Get off my damn leg and wipe that marshmallow goo off your face! Sorry, hello?"

"Ruth, is everything okay?" Paulie asked with sincere concern.

"Hey blubber bubble! Okay? Everything is great. If it was any better it probably wouldn't be legal."

"What took you so long to answer?"

"Had to wrestle the damn phone away from Jerome."

"Who?"

"The neighbor's orangutan. Just got back from the monkey hospital yesterday and between the pain meds and cherry vodka, he's all geatered up. Keeps calling into that damn Sean Hannity show. I told him it's off the air right now, but have you ever tried to reason with an anthropoid? They always got to have the last word."

"Jerome? Why is he there, anyway?"

"Kind of hard to turn him down, Fudgepuppy, considering it was your mammy by marriage that gave him the super close Schick shave with the ten horse John Deere beard trimmer."

"Whatever you think is best, Ruth. I was wondering, has my wife called by chance?"

"Does the Pope shit in the woods?"

"I thought there might be a possibility."

"She's gone, buttquaker. Let it go. Happens all the time. All sorts of guys lose all sorts of wives to all sorts of guys."

"I suppose you're right."

"Of course, not usually to an unbathed, toothless desert-dweller with a patch over his eye, driving a rusted-out pickup. Got to admit, that's a tough one."

"She might come back," Paulie said.

"Yeah, she might. And you might be Lebron's long lost twin, but it ain't likely."

"Thanks for the encouragement, Ruth."

"Hey anytime, but the big news is, I've got the poop."

"Poop? This doesn't have something to do with Jerome, does it?"

"On Junior's new job. His career. His destiny, the profession he so long sought. His lifetime's eternal calling, some shit like that."

"Oh, that. What is it?"

"Uh, let's see. What was it? What was the word he used? It sounded like...it had something to do...with...was it pans?"

"Pans? He's a dishwasher? That's it?"

"No, no that's not it. Pans with...handles or something, maybe."

"Panhandling?! He's out begging? That's a job?"

"No, wait, that's not it...was it Pandas? The sounds about right. Something to do with Pandas..."

"He's working at the zoo? Is that it? I guess..."

"Got it!"

"What?"

"Pandering!"

"What?"

"Isn't that great?"

"He's pandering? What in the world is so great about that?"

"No, I mean my excellent recall."

Paulie sighed, "He has quit school to become a pimp? He's offering human flesh for rent? He's marketing a bevy of baudies, a harem of harlottes, a congregate of concubines from the bowels of back alleys, indecently, dealing in the dark side of mankind and the weakness of the mortal soul?"

"Jesus. What the hell was that?"

"It just came out."

"Well cut that off at the neck. Besides, there was a hangup right at the beginning, Great Fatsby."

"What was that?"

"Think about it. He's your son. A real spray from the old can of female repellant."

"You're saying that's good?"

"No self-disrespecting woman would ever come near him."

"In this case, I guess that's good."

"Good is the operative word here."

"So, I guess he won't be doing any pandering."

"Yes, he certainly wouldn't have."

"What do you mean, wouldn't?"

"Fortunately, for prince pimple popper, he has me for an aunt and I have connections in the world of..."

"Entertainment."

"Yes, that is correct."

"Oh Lord, some of those people are, well, you know..."

"Quit sniffing the septic, Senor Stout."

"What's he getting involved in?"

"Don't worry, it's totally ethical, procedurally appropriate and one hundred percent legal. Mostly. By the way, all my torturously diligent work paid off and the wedding was a complete success, thank you for asking."

"Oh yeah, I guess I should have inquired. I'm sorry."

"Yes, you are."

"So, they actually got married."

"Eloped."

"Eloped? I thought you said the wedding was a success?"

"It was. Just one of them eloped."

"I'm not following this."

"Only the medieval mama blasted off. Buffalohead stayed and played with his band, The Rashkissers, at the dance."

"Ruth, I believe it takes two to elope, the last I heard anyway."

"Yes it does, Uncle Unctuous. Frank is back in the building."

"What the..."

"My sentiments exactly. Right at the moment Reverend Harry asked the crowd if anyone had any injections..."

"You mean objections."

"Had to be there. Anyway, that's when Frank made his move. Came running down the aisle at full gallop, stopping once to mark his territory on Skinny Landister's pew, then continued right up to the front where the almost betrothed stood and began gnawing away on Granny Gristle. Finally drug her out giggling like an escaped nun to the background of soloist Raspy Thornpicker singing "Chapel in the Moonlight." Would have made a hell of a video.``

"Why would Frank do that?"

"Theories abound. The most popular is that his actions were the result of a deep unrelenting love that suddenly surfaced from a submerged place deep in Frank's soul to his heart and mind, causing him to take immediate and forceful action to ensure his life's passion mate and he would no longer be separated from their obvious predestination, therefore, maintain a physical and emotional attachment through all perpetuity."

"That's amazing."

"Personally, I think it was the prenuptial bacon grease body rub the old skinhanger partook in."

"Do you think she's okay?"

"She was never okay."

"What I mean is, have you heard from her?"

"Not directly, but I'm pretty sure she's alright. We got a call from some small-town preacher asking for a billing address for his midnight marriage services. He apologized because he had to charge twenty-dollars extra for the domestic quadroped rates, but he did say it was cheaper than feral."

"I can't believe she married Frank."

"Don't be so judgmental."

"But Ruth, he's a dog."

"And she's a peach pit with arms. I think it's a good match. At least he didn't piss all over the house plants before he left, which is more than I can say for the Rashkissers."

"Oh, well. Ruth, I was just calling because, well, because I had a close call with death."

"Holy shit! Were you near the hallway closet last night when that thing went off?"

"What thing?"

"Never mind. By the way, what does conflagration mean?"

"Why?"

"Some leftover Jamaican from the wedding keeps yelling,' conflagration, conflagration!' from upstairs."

"It means fire."

"Really? Well, gotta go," Ruth said then yelled away from the phone, "Turn the hoses back on Jimmy!"

CHAPTER 44

The plane's engine popped and groaned, and the craft's altitude changed faster than a yo-yo at times, but they were still airborne and that was all that mattered to Jasper. Carla was on the phone again in the back next to Wasyl, who was gawking delightedly out the window like a Japanese tourist wishing for a camera. Jasper just sat tensely, staring straight ahead through the windshield hoping that the view remained sky blue and didn't suddenly turn grass green. Myron, meanwhile, seemed content to steer with one hand and he used his other to emphasize the thoughts he was regaling Jasper with on life's possibilities.

"Hey son," he said. "Did you ever think about this: Compared to car crashes, there ain't hardly any plane crashes. No sir, hardly none at all. So, calm yourself a bit. Of course, the bad part of that theory is that in car wrecks, it's quick. Whap! Done. Not much you can do, no sir. But we're high enough right now that if this little mudskipper goes down, we'll have time to sing a dozen choruses of 99 Bottles of Beer on the Wall and probably throw in a hand or two of pinochle before we hit Mother earth in the butt and become an early stage of fertilizer."

"Myron, do you have to talk about that kind of stuff? You are creeping the hell out of me," Jasper said.

"Sorry...Just a habit. Like they say, you can lead a horse to water but you can't make him dance."

Carla leaned forward from her seat and put a hand on Myron's right shoulder. "We need to put down somewhere and hang out for a while. Wanda says everyone needs to arrive at the same time so events will be coordinated."

"Got it," he said.

"Who's coming and what events need to be coordinated?" Jasper asked.

Myron rubbed the back of his neck and stretched slightly in his seat and ignored the question.

"Might be a good thing. Give me a chance to practice my landings. If we get a chance to land on the White House lawn, sure don't want to spiral into the ground. Be embarrassing as hell."

Jasper stared at his pilot. "That won't happen, right? You've made plenty of other landings, right? And there's been no problem, am I right? So, uh, how many landings have you made?"

"Counting this one I'm about to make?"

"Do we need to count this one?"

"Probably would be best. At least I'd have one then."

"What the hell? We could all die!"

"Yep. But my policy is what doesn't kill me, I just ignore."

Jasper turned in his seat to look at Carla and Wasyl.

"How did we get a pilot that's never flown before," he said.

Myron said, "Bells and britches, son, I never said I ain't flown before."

"So, you have flown before...No wait, don't answer that."

"That would probably be best too."

Wasyl called from the back, "Hey Myron, where are we gonna land?"

"A small, flat piece of land with some trees by it."

"So how far is it?"

"Don't rightly know. Ain't never seen it."

Jasper said, "What do you mean you ain't never...I mean, haven't ever seen it? You've never been to this place?"

"Kinda goes along with not ever seen it before, don't it?"

Jasper said, "What kind of plan do you have?"

"We see a spot like I mentioned, and we take it down."

Jasper said, "Do you think you *can* take it down?"

"Hell, gravity and the weight of the plane will take care of all that, I'll just try and make sure that it don't come down too hard. But right now, my job is just like my 90-year-old Uncle Ned's job on his wedding night. I'm just trying to keep it up."

Wasyl said, "Well, it might not hurt if we all did a little prayin'. Wouldn't hurt to ask for a little divine assistance during this time of need."

"Go on ahead, think I'll pass," Myron said.

"I'm not trying to offend your or nothin'. Just a little help is good when you need it," Wasyl added.

"Ain't offended one bit. Just don't believe in Hocus the God of Pocus or any of that fable faith, like I said before. Nope. Only one thing in this whole world makes me think that maybe, just maybe, there might be a God."

Wasyl unhooked his fish stringer seatbelt and leaned forward to hear his pilot better over the loud hum and vibration noises of their transport craft.

He said, "You mean like a newborn baby, or the sun rising in the morning, or the stars on a clear night?"

"No, none of that stuff."

"Well, what is it then?"

"Orgasms."

"Orgasms?"

"Sure. Think about it. Nature don't give a rat's ass about something like that. It's just a tantalizer to get you to procreate and keep your species goin'. As far as nature's concerned, you don't do the spastic spunker occasionally, you're extinct. End of story. Nature don't care and it happens all the time. On the other hand, folks like to say we are produced in the Heir Holy's image. If that's the case and there is a God, he probably came up with the Big O. Make the entire thing worthwhile, otherwise the whole thing is messy and disgusting. And of course, he had that thing with Mary. So, he probably wanted to get a little jingle for his jangle. Nothing wrong with looking out for yourself."

"We're doomed," Jasper said.

CHAPTER 45

The landing went off without a hitch. In a hectic sort of way. They came in a bit low over a large herd of milk cows, who after a day of feeding, were making their way back home to be dejuiced, causing a rather excited bovine bolt for the bushes. The subsequent escape from the sky bandit, who the cows were certain was coming in on a strafing run, put some intensely protuberant pressure on the black and white bossies' already pressurized udders, launching opaque squirts and sprays of unpasteurized essence of cow on every living and nonliving object within teat striking distance.

The plane touched down and bounced through an open field rather rapidly to the background chorus of screeching fleeing birds and Jasper's very loud prayers of deliverance and salvation. This was followed by a distinctly panicked refrain from the trio of air commuters requesting that Myron bring their spiritedly bouncing carrier to a halt. Mostly due to the fact that they were getting precariously close to a very large and very swift moving river.

Myron managed to bring the vessel to a stop in extremely close proximity to the waterway. So extreme that the tiny aircraft's front tire rested in the water.

"Whew," Wasyl whistled. "I thought we were going right in the river."

"Me too," Carla said.

"Certain death," Jasper moaned. "In some strange turbulent river."

"What river?" Myron asked.

"That river!" Carla, Jasper, and Wasyl said in unison pointing at the water ahead of them.

Myron leaned toward the windshield and squinted with his one remaining eye.

"Oh, that river. I wondered what all the yellin' was about."

The landing area adjacent to Mother Nature's plumbing project was a relatively flat pasture with trees of various types and sizes bordering the field on opposite sides of the giant waterway.

Some of the previously worried warblers were returning to their favorite pine tree perches hoping the evening's entertainment had been completed.

Meanwhile, after a moment of silent reverent petition of thanks to a deity or two, and a few under-the-breath expletives, the crew of the tiny cloud crusader disembarked. While they stretched and looked around, the sun was lowering itself behind the nearby oak, maple, and evergreen trees allowing just enough light through the leaves to provide a minor glowing effect.

Myron had gone back into the rear of the plane behind all the seats and was pulling out blankets and various other items and tossing them onto the ground.

"Got stuff here to make beds with. I'll start a fire once one of you rangers gets some wood," he said.

"I'm on it," Wasyl answered and trotted off toward the trees.

Carla and Jasper followed Myron as they carried everything to an area that was fairly clear of vegetation about ten feet from the forest line.

"Should be pretty warm tonight," Myron said.

Jasper asked, "Then why start a fire? For light?"

"That and a little smoke will help keep the skeeters down a bit. I lost my last bottle of feline bug repellant in all the commotion before we took off."

"How unfortunate," Jasper said.

The trio went to work putting together their makeshift camp dwelling and clearing away natural debris to form a sleeping area. Wasyl returned with a couple of armloads of dry wood and made a pile in the center of the clearing. Myron then added some crumpled paper he'd lit with a match to the center of the wood and soon a glow began. The small but growing flame was the only light on the quickly darkening moonless night aside from a massive array of overhead stars and two small flashlights that Myron had. He tossed one to Carla and following the beam of the second, he returned quietly to the airplane. When he reappeared, he had a green duffle bag from which he drew some plastic bags with sandwiches, hot dogs, and pickles in a jar. He also handed around a few bottles of root beer and longnecks of Prison Pickers Pale Ale, all of which was gratefully accepted by his fellow travelers.

Everyone sat quietly for a few minutes, savoring the simple fare while they watched and listened to the night life all around them. There was a level of relief and exhaustion that was settling in on everyone, but no one was ready to venture into silent sleep yet.

"Good thing you had all this stuff, Myron. You always carry all this along?" Wasyl asked.

"Depends what I get my hands on. This was a quick trip, so this was all I could get."

Everyone was seated on their blankets gazing at the now sizable fire, the reflection making their eyes tiny mirrors of the flame.

"Hey Myron, you got any more of that chew? Wasyl asked.

“Sure do,” he answered and slipped the canister from his pocket and flipped it to Wasyl on the opposite side of the blaze. Wasyl nodded a thanks and opened it.

“You’re not going to put that in your mouth, are you?” Jasper asked.

“That’s what I asked my prom date,” Myron said.

Carla and Wasyl snickered while Jasper just stared.

“It’s a joke, son,” Myron said to him. “Besides, a little bit of that stuff ain’t gonna hurt him.”

Jasper shook his head. “But you don’t even know what is in there.”

“Sure I do.”

“Okay, what is it?”

“Rotten leaves.”

Wasyl took a pinch and put it behind his lower lip. “Hey Myron, what is the deal with them Dewey’s? Are they just Hillbullies? Can’t be much bullying work out there in the middle of that soggy bog like they are.”

Myron pushed at the fire with a stick to move some of the unburnt wood into the flame. Sparks floated up from the disruption and into the darkness like tiny rocket ships leaving for distant exploration.

“They do some work for Reyes. He’s the fella that owns the ground back there. Security work I’d guess you’d call it. Most folks is afraid of ‘em.”

“You don’t appear to be. And they’re big.”

“Just like the saying goes, the bigger they are, the more room they need to land in. We was lucky that sister of theirs wasn’t there, though. She’s meaner than a centipede with athlete’s foot.”

“She’s that bad, huh?” Wasyl said.

“Yep. Big and bad-tempered to boot. Made a name for herself at the county fair some years back at the horseshoe throwin’ contest. She got a bit perturbed at Shiny Walters, the contest judge, over some scoring. Well, Shiny ain’t no fool and he knew he couldn’t whoop her, so he took off runnin' for the grandstand hoping to get lost in the crowd gathered to see a hog wrestling tournament. Well, big old Mount Dewey slung four horseshoes at him trotting away at about thirty yards and got him right in stride."

"That's a far toss for horseshoes."

"Especially considering the horse was still attached."

Carla's phone was flashing next to her on the blanket. She picked it up and put it to her ear.

"Yes?" She answered. "Okay...where?...Alright...A decoy?...Got it."

Jasper said to her, "Please, ask whoever you're talking to if I can use the phone to call the State Department."

Carla looked at him then spoke into the phone. "Did you hear that? Yes...if that's best...I have the code," and then hung up.

"Well?" Jasper asked, reaching for the phone.

"No," she said, putting the phone back into her pocket. "You are to call no one."

Jasper stood up, "Well maybe I will just take the phone. How would that be?"

"First of all, I would kick your ass. Second of all, if anyone besides me touches this communication device, Myron has explicit instructions to blow them up," she said.

Jasper looked over at the one-eyed man who was smiling and tapping a round tobacco container identical to the one that had detonated earlier.

Myron said, "Why don't you just sit and relax. We're on your side, and besides, if I have to blast you in such close range it'll set off the rest of these little powder packets and we'll all end up looking like week old salsa and pancake batter."

"Does that go for all of us?" Jasper asked. "About the phone, I mean?"

"Absolutely," Carla replied. "Sorry Wassie, but I'd have you blown into tiny Wasyl specks too, no offense."

“Oh, none taken,” Wasyl said. “We understand completely. Don’t we Jasper?”

“Yeah, whatever,” Jasper said, sitting down hard onto his blanket. “Look, I don’t even know who you people are. As far as I know, you might kill us here in the middle of the night, dig the papers out of Wasyl’s ass canal and take off.”

Carla took a sip from the soda can she was holding.

“If we were going to kill you, we would have done it a long time ago. Let me explain a couple of things to you. How do you think you got out of your commode of custody so easily?”

Wasyl said, “I’ve been wonderin’ about that. No lock or nothin’. Was it you?

“No,” Carla said. “The Sagger twins. They work with us. One of them kept the person watching you busy, the other unlocked the door.”

Wasyl said, “How did she keep the guard busy?”

“No! Don’t answer that!” Jasper said. “Whatever you say, I basically have no choice anyway.”

“We’ll get you to Washington and get you delivered,” Carla said.

“All by ourselves? Just the four of us?” Wasyl asked.

“We have help,” Carla said. “Myron, there is one change. The disc jockeys are bringing down two more to the meeting spot.”

“Backup?”

“An infomercial personality and a dead guy.”

Jasper said, “That’s your help?”

“That’s all I can tell you...good night,” Carla said as Myron cackled.

CHAPTER 46

The sun had risen through a blue sky with only a dot or two of clouds as Wasyl helped Myron load the plane. When they finished, they walked back to the spot where Carla and Jasper sat finishing a breakfast of root beer, crackers and hot dogs.

"We leave as soon as the call comes in," Carla said.

Myron pulled out a map from the plastic holder, then put it back in the holder and put the holder back in his pocket.

"Never could read them things," he said, then took a dab of tobacco from his ever-present container and handed it to Wasyl who had taken a seat on the ground. Wasyl took a chew and handed it back.

"Hey Carla" Wasyl said, "Whatever happened to Mona Kline?"

"Nothing happened to her. Why?"

"I was just wonderin'. You two were boyfriend and girlfriend back in the day. Pretty tight as I recall. Most folks through you'd probably walk the matrimonial aisle."

"We did."

"Really? I didn't know you two got married."

"Yup. You'd gone off to school by then."

Wasyl shook his head. "I never knew you two were lesbians."

"We weren't."

"Oh, I see," he said. "Well, maybe I don't. So, you weren't lesbians?"

"No."

"So, you broke up, huh."

"No. We're still married."

"But you weren't lesbians?"

"We weren't."

"But you are now?"

"We are now."

"So, you weren't gay back then because you didn't want to be with no fellas, but you are gay now because you don't want to be with no fellas."

"Yep."

Carla's phone flashed. She answered and hung up in one quick smooth motion.

"Let's go," she said.

Everyone got up except Myron.

"Damn," he said, rubbing his face.

"What's wrong?" Carla asked.

"I think I've scratched my eyeball."

"Awesome," Jasper said.

CHAPTER 47

"So. what do we do now?" Jasper asked.

"About what?" Myron answered as they stood near the plane.

"About what? About flying out of here."

"We can still fly out of here."

"Oh really?" Jasper said. "How? I'm not a pilot. Carla is not a pilot. And Wasyl? Good Lord, we might as well just set the fuselage ablaze and wait inside for the explosion."

Myron spit some tobacco juice. "Calm down, son. You got your brain pulled tighter than a gnat's ass stretched over a rain barrel."

"Okay, okay, so I'm calm. Just so I can remain calm, what's the answer to my question?"

"What's your question?"

"What's my...who is flying us out of here?"

"That's simple."

"Good."

"I am," Myron said.

"You? But you scratched your eye. That has to be a major issue for your ability to, and I use that term loosely, fly."

"How?" Myron asked.

"Well, let's review. You have one eye. You scratched it. You can't see."

"Oh hell, that eye works as good as ever, which granted, ain't all that good," Myron reached into his pocket and pulled out an object. "It's this eye that I scratched. Dropped it, getting supplies out of our homemade jet."

Jasper looked down at the object in Myron's hand.

"Is that...is that a fake eye , I hope?" He said.

"Course it is," Myron answered.

"Holy moly," Wasyl said," Could I take a look at that thing?"

Myron tossed the small sphere to him.

Jasper shook his head. "Why in heaven's name don't you put that into the hideous empty eye socket you have? I'm certain it would be an improvement, aesthetically speaking."

"Nope," Myron said," Ain't comfortable. Only time I put it in the eye crater is when I go to a dance to pick up women."

"This helps you pick up women?" Wasyl asked.

"Surely does."

"Because it makes you look more sophisticated and sexy when you put it in?" Wasyl asked.

"No, nothing like that. Already got the sex appeal. But this here glass eye surely is a chick magnet."

"Oh, I can just imagine the women can't keep their hands off of you and your fake eye," Jasper leaning back against the plane.

"How does it draw 'em in then?" Wasyl said.

Myron took the eye back from his hand. "It's a simple but surefire process. All I do is put it in place in the empty hole, then I troll around the dance hall until I find Miss Right, then I make my approach and strike up a conversation.

"About what?" Wasyl said

"Oh, about the weather, the rising cost of linseed oil and the recent scientific developments on ear wax removal treatments, things like that."

"I see."

"That's when they usually start playing hard to get."

"Difficult to believe," Jasper mumbled.

"So what do you do?" Wasyl asked

"Well, as soon as my lady friend turns to walk away, I get ready to close the deal. As soon as she's turned the other way and can't see me, I pop out my eye and hold it in my hand. Then I say Miss, I want you to know that you are the one woman I've been looking for all of my life! Then when she turns around I take her hand and say "In fact I've been keeping an eye on you, and put the eyeball right in the palm of her hand."

"Holy Hooters! I bet that gets a reaction," Wasyl said.

"It could register on a Richter scale," Myron said, smiling.

Carla interrupted, "Just got a call. We're meeting up with all the operatives." She hands Myron a piece of paper. "Here's some instructions. We'll leave as soon as you're ready, Myron."

"Who are we meeting?" Jasper asked." Military, CIA, State Department?"

"A couple of disc jockeys with cargo, a fat guy and his friend from Iowa and a Russian chick."

"You call those operatives?" Jasper added.

Myron said,"What's the cargo the radio record spinners are toatin'?"

"A dead guy," Carla said.

Myron Nodded.

"A dead guy?" Jasper said."What the...

"Let's go," Myron said. "We got us a far piece to go. We'll be flappin' wings a spell."

"Do we have enough fuel?" Jasper asked.

"Hope so," Myron answered.

"Hope...are you going to check?"

"No reason to. Ain't no place to fill up around here if'n we was low. We'll stop down the line. Besides, you might recall the gauges don't work."

"But if the gauges don't work, how will you know if we're running out of fuel?"

"When we nosedive into an oak tree," Myron laughed. "Load up!"

CHAPTER 48

The sun showed off the sunglasses Wanda was wearing as she sat on the hood of the Jeep Wrangler. She was dressed in dark workout clothes as she sipped a can of Shanked Beer.

The meeting location she had selected was deep inside a federal game reserve. An open field of knee high grass and shrubs hundreds of yards in length straight ahead of her provided an entrance for the group she was waiting for.

Paulie, Skeet and Olga had already arrived. Olga was sitting in the grass reading a copy of "Sex Change for Dummies", while Skeet was leaning against his Lincoln. Paulie was still sitting in the front of Skeet's car reading his codebook and jotting things down in a small notebook.

The van with Danny, Biff, Herbie and their deceased passenger had just pulled in and the live occupants had exited and two walked over to where the rest of the crew was waiting. Danny introduced himself and Biff to the others then said hello to Wanda while Herbie waited by the van.

"What's wrong with Pineapple Pete?" Wanda asked.

"His feelings are hurt,"Danny said.

“Really.”

“Yeah, he’s pouting because you made fun of his Hawaiian clothes and called him a horse’s ass.”

“Sensitive.”

“That he is.”

“So, if I don’t apologize, he won’t talk to me.”

"Pretty much.”

“Works for me,” Wanda said.

“Where’s the rest of the group and the item?” Danny asked.

Wanda nodded toward an open field straight ahead of her. “They’ll be coming in by plane. I hear some sputtering, that may be them now.”

Everyone turned to look in the sky at a small object in the distance that rose and fell and sashayed from side to side.

Paulie got out of the car and walked over to where most of the group was standing and staring skyward.

“What’s that spitting, popping noise?” He asked.

“Apparently, it’s the plane’s engine,” Skeet answered, squinting skyward.

As the small crafty came closer to them, it bounced, fluttered like a butterfly then started to descend.

“Good lord,” Paulie said."Do you think the pilot will be able to land it?”

Wanda nodded slowly. “Oh, he’ll be able to land it. The question is, in how many pieces?”

Herbie had finally left the van and headed over to the gathering where Skeet handed him a beer while holding his gaze at the activity above. As they watched, the vessel glided lower and lower until its wheels made contact with the ground. Dust flew into the air as it bounced off the field a couple times, then slowly spun in a circle and headed straight for the van.

"This'll be interesting," Herbie said.

"We left our passenger in there," Biff said.

"I'm sure he's really worried, being dead and all," Herbie said.

The plane accelerated, then suddenly came to a halt just a few feet from the vehicle. The forward motion raised the tail of the plane in the air and pushed the nose into the ground with the spinning prop throwing dirt and debris everywhere.

As soon as it had come to a complete stop the passengers started scrambling out of the plane's cabin. Carla dusted herself off as Jasper threw himself on the ground and began mumbling a prayer. Myron and Wasyl were digging a fresh chew out of one of Myron's canisters as they walked away.

"Great piece of flying," Wasyl said.

"Hell, nothin' to it," Myron answered.

"Don't be modest. I don't know how you maneuvered us to the ground like you did, especially with all that crosswind."

"I didn't," Myron said.

"What do you mean you didn't?" Jasper said.

"Just what I said. Had nothin' to do with me. We ran out of gas a couple a thousand feet up, so I just treated her like one of my horses."

"What do you mean?" Jasper said.

"I let go of the reins, turned her loose and hoped she'd take us home."

"My god!" Jasper exclaimed as he jumped to his feet. "Do you mean to tell me that you were not controlling the flight during descent?"

"If'n you mean I wasn't drivin' on the way down, that's exactly what I mean."

"You just let go?"

"Well, it wouldn't have done me no good to hang on, the steering handle broke a couple of minutes before we started coastin' on vapors."

Jasper buried his face in his hands as Washyl put his arm around his shoulders.

“Dear salvation, I have barely escaped death, yet again,” Jasper said.

“Listen Shakespeare,” Myron siad,”You ain’t escaped nothin’. It’ll just come a bit later than you figured.”

Jasper looked up at him.”You don’t understand at all, do you? I could have been killed.”

Myron spat on the ground. “For being a Christian sort you don’t put much stock in divine intervention, do ya.”

“I refuse to board that cardboard box again...ever!” Jasper said.

“Not to worry,” Myron said. “The old gal’s had the meat. Probably headed for an eternal resting ground. I figure the Smithsonian.”

“Really?” Wasyl asked.

“Yep. I picture her hanging on the wall between the Wright Brothers display and the non-stick frying pans

that they sell on QVC.”

“Myron!” A voice called from the distance.

“Well, crease my jeans,” Myron said.”Over yonder is Wanda. Best head on over, it’s meetin’ time.”

CHAPTER 49

Jasper, Myron and Wasyl stood looking at the stolen Mexican van, except it didn't look like it had before. It had been repainted a bright yellow with big black letters on the side.

"You're kidding, right?" Jasper said.

"How else would you carry a diplomat from south of the border?" Myron said.

"The question is not really how, it's why. Why would we carry a deceased Hispanic into the capital with this van?"

"Because he's playing the part of a Mexican Ambassador."

"He's a dead man full of holes packed in ice."

"We're gonna de-ice him," Myron said.

"I don't care if you wrap him in tinfoil, put a Zorro mask on his face and a wine goblet in his hand, they are not going to let you drive him into a secured area in this van," Jasper said.

"Why not?" Myron said. "The van's got the embassy seal right on the side. Looks good to me."

"It's misspelled," Jasper said.

"What's misspelled?"

"The seal. It says Maxican."

"Huh."

"Kinda sounds like a south of the border feminine product," Wasyl said.

"Well, gotta make due. Maxican it is," Myron said. "If'n they ask, just say it's a woke thing."

"No, no, you don't get it," Jasper said. "Diplomats always ride in limos. Always. Tell him Wasyl."

"That is true," Wasyl said. "I think they even take limos to the shitter."

"So Myron, how do you plan on explaining the van?" Jasper said.

"I don't need to explain the van."

"You don't?"

"Nope. You do."

"Me? Are you...I don't even speak the language."

"No problem. We'll get an interpreter."

"Who?"

Myron rubbed his beard.

"Well, we already checked out the background of the entire group," he said." A couple took highschool German, one speaks purty good French, and of course Wasyl here speaks fluent Nilo-Sharian."

Jasper looked at Wasyl. "He what?"

"Iwi Selami newi," Wasyl said.

"Wait...what?" Jasper said.

"It's a greeting,"Wasyl said. "Nilo Saharian are languages spoken primarily in the upper reaches of the Chari and Nile Rivers."

Jasper stared at him.

"You gotta admit, I do make an interesting traveling companion," Wasyl said.

"Uh, okay, so, who is driving?" Jasper asked.

"That'd be me," Herbie said as he walked up to the trio.

“Any chance you speak Spanish?” Jasper asked.

“Una paloma blanca, buckaroo,” Herbie answered.

“Why do I feel this mission is going from bad to horrific?” Jasper said.” And again, why am I going along?”

“We all get jobs here,” Myorn said.” Wasyl is of course carrying our buried treasure, Herbie drives and you are here because we need someone who looks like he belongs in the capital.”

“And you, Myron?” Jasper said.”Why are you here?”

“Because of my vast knowledge of Tibetan levitation,” he said.

“You’re absolutely crazy.”

“Nuttier than squirrel shit,” Myron said, getting into the van.``It’s just too bad the plans changed. I sure woulda liked to have landed right on the White House lawn. Bet that would put us on cable news.``

“And in the morgue.”

Everyone took their places with Myron and Herbie in front and Jasper, Wasyl and the body in the back.

“Before we drive on, may I ask what exactly is the plan?” Jasper said. “What I mean is, if something goes wrong, and it most assuredly will, what do we do?”

“Don’t worry, there’s always plan two,” Herbie said.

“Which is?”

Myron said, ”Ain’t exactly figured it out just yet. But it’s fair to assume it will involve lots of yelling and screaming and some explosions.”

“Sounds very exciting,”Wasyl said.

“I like the way you think,” Herbie said.

“We’re doomed,” Jasper moaned.

Myron cackled, “Head ‘em up and move ‘em out Herbie!”

CHAPTER 50

Paulie, Skeet and Olga walked with the other people in the guided tour as the young lady in charge pointed out objects of interest, or at least objects that were supposed to be interesting.

"This is very exciting," Paulie said.

"I don't see exciting," Olga said. "Just pictures of old men and carpet."

"I'm with her," Skeet said.

"How can you say that? We are in the very bed of history," Paulie said. "And remember, we are here on a mission that will save our country, maybe even save the very existence of the world as we know it."

"Breathe deeply and slowly. Your eyes are starting that bulging thing again,"Skeet said.

Paulie stopped walking when he felt his phone vibrate in his pocket. "Oh, geez, it's the hotline."

"Just answer it, 007," Skeet said.

Paulie looked at the phone screen. "It's the number from the White House. I wonder."

Skeet sighed," Just answer it."

"Uh, hello," Paulie said.

"Hey, Pudge Pooch," the voice answered.

"Ruth? What...who...why...?"

"Need to work on your public speaking skills, my bountiful brother," Ruth said.

"Ruth, where are you? I mean the number you're calling from is the one I was told would be from the White House."

"That's because I'm in the White House," she said.

"But how? And what are you doing there ?"

"The how is simple, I walked in. The what is starting to drain me. I'm hanging with the Vice."

"Vice squad?"

"Nothing that good. I'm here with the Vice President."

"Why?"

"Because I said hi to him, and he being a Vice President has no one to talk to, so I'm stuck with him. Let me tell ya, this guy is a religious ranger. All he wants to talk about is divine intervention, God, Jesus, yada yada."

"But..."

"Listening to him has made me realize something."

"What's that?"

"If there is a God, he needs to get his holy ass down here and bitch slap this guy. This dude could set organized religion back centuries. How are those steeple builders gonna collect money from teary eyed old ladies and bang those altar boys if this guy puts everyone to sleep? Damn, ten minutes with him and I feel like I've spent a night on the melatonin express."

"But..."

"Quiet King Cholesterol, I've got instructions for you. Got your little secret agent decoder ring handy?"

"Decoder ring?"

“Code book, dumbass.”

“Uh, yes. Right here,” Paulie said.

“Shut up for a minute, top heavy tap dancer. Here we go. Little Robin RedBreast sitting on a pole, wiggle waggle went his tail, bang went his hole.”

“Uh, that’s the code?”

“Just made that up,” Ruth cackled. “Just look at the picture in front of the book.”

“The one with OBama and Jay Z?”

“Peel that off.”

Paulie said okay as he pulled back the picture.

“What’s underneath it”, Ruth said.

“A picture of Woopie Goldburg and Judge Judy mud wrestling.”

“I’ll bet that’s something. Peel it off and look at the back.”

“Okay, ”Paulie said, “It says booger.”

“That’s your password to get in.”

“Get in where?”

“The White House.”

“Booger?”

“Yeah, heh heh. Fitting ain’t it.”

CHAPTER 51

Temple walked past the secretary speaking on her phone and into the Secretary of State's office. Harberts turned away from his TV to face him.

"Temple! "He said. "It's about time you finally got here."

"It is, sir?"

"I suppose you know why I called you here."

"No and no, sir."

"No and no, what?"

"No, you didn't call me sir, and no, I don't know why, sir."

"Why , what?"

"Why you called me sir, but you didn't."

"I didn't?"

"No, sir."

"Huh, I wonder who I called?"

"No idea, sir."

"Oh well," Harberts said. "At least we got that straightened out." He then turned back to his television.

Temple said. "What did you want, sir?"

"Want?" Herbert said glaring back at him.

“Apparently you wanted something, sir. You said you called me, but you didn’t call me, you called someone else, but now I am here, so now you can tell me what you wanted without calling me.”

Harberts looked blankly at him then back to the TV.

“Isn’t that the Jeopardy show from last week, sir? Why are you watching that?”

Harberts shook his head as if to clear it, then spoke. “I’ve been watching it and studying it all week.”

“Why, sir?”

“I’m trying to correct a national tragedy, Temple.”

“Tragedy? On Jeopardy, sir?”

“Temple, where the hell have you been? You’ve got to get up on your current events.”

“Of course, sir. Which tragedy do you speak of, sir?”

“Well, I’m talking about that boy who was about to break the consecutive win record for Jeopardy. He got beat, but he didn’t really get beat.”

“How is that, sir?”

“Temple, he got beat by a woman. Don’t you get it?”

“I’m not sure, sir.”

“They set it up for her. Had to. That boy was from the upper intellectual strata of our American educational system.”

“I thought he was a professional gambler, sir.”

“Exactly, now you’re getting it.”

“I hope not, sir.”

“Getting beat is one thing. I mean Temple, if a Bass fishing pro or a McDonald’s franchise owner beat him I could say okay, that’s the way the Jeopardy jizzes, but a woman?”

“But, sir....”

“Hell, the only woman that would have a marshmallow man’s chance in a bonfire would be Goldie Hawn or maybe Vanna.”

"Vanna,sir?"

"Vanna White, son. That woman has turned over a lot of letters."

"No doubt, sir."

Harberts turned his seat to face Temple who had sat down across from him at the desk.

"Bottom line is this, "Harberts said. "The producers of that show thought they were pulling one on the American people by having a woman win that game. Well, you gotta roll out of the right side of the hammock to pull the foreskin over my eyes. You see where I'm coming from, Temple?"

"From some isolated planet in a far away galaxy that is extirpating the very essence of human intelligence from the craniums of our world leaders, sir?"

"Huh?"

"Nothing, sir. Back to our original topic. You said you wanted me for something, sir. Does it have to do with the President?"

"Uh, let's see, oh yeah yeah, that's it. The imperial pain in the ass has been calling me all day, wants to know what those weird flags are that are flying over the Washington Monument."

"One is the national flag of Botswana. The second is the West Cocoa Beach city flag."

"Is this for some new holiday?"

"No sir, Cocoa Beach is the city that was under seige."

"Under what?"

"Siege sir, you know, attack. Remember the Botswanian beachhead in Florida? Well, once the two sides got together the locals agreed with the Botswanian cause. Then after an afternoon of softball, brats, burgers and beer, the army of Botswana brought their new allies to the capital to continue their struggle. "

"What's their plan?"

"To take over Washington D.C."

"Huh. How'd they all get here?"

"In pep buses from the high school, sir. As I said, they plan on taking over the capital. The General from Botswana has decided to claim the U.S. in the name of his country, so, he somehow got to the top of the monument and placed their flag there."

"Huh, what's the other flag for?"

"Apparently West Cocoa Beach felt it necessary to place their flag there as well. Actually, they don't have a city flag, so they used their highschool flag with their mascot on it, The Fighting Clams."

"The Fighting Clams?"

"Yes, sir."

"Hmm. Well, we need to do something about this."

"Obviously. And what would that be, sir?"

"We need to get all the flags down."

"Yes sir. Is that all,sir?"

"No. We'll launch an all out assault on Boatswamper."

"Botswana, sir."

"Aircraft carriers, Abram tanks, tomahawk missiles, the whole gambit. Maybe even drop some nukes on them. That oughta get those flags down."

"Or we could just have the grounds keepers take the flags down," Temple said.

"No, we need a full military thrust. We need to crush their military and move onto their capital."

"But sir, their entire military is here."

Harberts placed both of his hands on his desk and stood up. "Good lord, how many are there?"

"Eight sir. "

"Eight? Eight what? Eight divisions?, Eight..."

"Eight soldiers, sir. Actually, if you count the General and his secretary , it would be ten. Total."

Harberts sat back down. "Well, then get them the hell out of here."

"Certainly, sir. What about their demands?"

"Demands? What demands?"

"The General wants to be taken to the remote island where Elvis is living, his secretary wants to see "Cats" on Broadway and the rank and file want to smoke a few joints with Martha Stewart and Snoop Dog."

"You're kidding me!"

"No sir, those are their demands."

"No, I mean Elvis is really living on an island?"

"Uh, moving on, sir. What I came here to do initially was to update you on the

dossier and the actions of our operatives."

"Operatives."

"Yes sir, operatives."

"Always liked the sound of that word... operatives, "Harberts said, leaning back in his chair.

"Uh, yes sir. Anyway, they have arrived in Washington and should be able to deliver the dossier sometime later today."

"Operatives," Harberts said again, putting his hands behind his head.

"Provided, of course, that we can get this done without any interference from any political figures, or news media,and hopefully there will be no security issues."

"Operatives. Kind of like that secret agent James Harden when I say that, doesn't it."

"I think you mean James Bond, sir."

"I do?"

"Yes sir."

"Then who the hell is James Harden?"

"He's an NBA star, sir."

"No kidding."

"None, sir."

"Does he ever say operatives?"

"No idea, sir."

CHAPTER 52

Temple leaned back in his bean bag seat while a THC cloud swirled slowly overhead. In the background Lou Reed was singing "Busload of Faith" as Temple folded his hands across his stomach and closed his eyes.

"Appropriate time for this event," Voice said.

"Agreed,"Temple responded.

"I have to admit, I do not know how you pulled it off."

"Intelligence, fortitude, detailed planning..."

"Luck."

"Yes, luck. That's the word I was searching for."

"I'm exhausted," Voice said," And I didn't really do anything."

Temple shrugged.

"You're supposed to say that I am wrong and that without my boundless energy and support, the mission would have failed," Voice said.

"Consider it stated," Temple said.

"My ego remains intact," Voice said.

"I'm relieved."

“You do realize that you didn’t need all the participants to accomplish what you set out to do.”

“Probably true,” Temple said. ”However, I wanted to see who could be counted on. After all, this is just shy of a revolution we are involved in.”

“A hanging offense as well.”

“I’m not worried about getting my neck stretched. Are you?”

Voice laughed.

“I thought not, “Temple said.

“So, is everyone in place?” Voice asked.

The phone interrupted their conversation. Temple looked at the number. It was the Oval Office calling.

“Hello Madam President,” he said into the phone.

“Yes,” Voice chuckled ,”Apparently they are.”

CHAPTER 53

The special broadcast to the nation was made that night in primetime. Viewership was limited because most people were livestreaming a Taylor Swift Concert or watching a tearful Pat Sajak spinning the wheel for the last time. But those that did watch were introduced to their new President and Vice President.

The country was informed that the Constitution clearly stated in Amendment 8675309, that any time a self consumed pathological liar was running against a clueless and doddering old man for the country's highest office, then the Secretary of State's top aide and a selected female business woman could independently appoint the next President. So, it was up to Temple and Wanda to paddle the national canoe.

There was one change in the original plan. Because of a feeling there was a need for a hero as a second in command, Wasyl was named Ruth's Vice-President, instead of the deceased Hispanic. Yes, Ruth was now President. .

The public response was light, or maybe slight, or maybe nothing. A couple of MSNBC and FOX hosts tried to make a big deal out of what they called a "Coup", but the MSNBC viewers were too busy celebrating the intentional fouling of a heterosexual women's basketball player by a lesbian player and the FOX viewers didn't feel like looking up the word "coup", so any supposed uproar died quickly. CNN, in an attempt to not lose any more viewers, ignored the entire event and instead had their top reporter interview the surviving members of the band Chicago about their favorite chili recipes.

Ruth's first acts as President was to sign executive orders legalizing marijuana, mandating sleeveless spandex uniforms for airline security workers and ordering 3 day work weeks for everyone except truck stop waitresses. She felt they had done enough and were allowed to stay home, fully paid.

Myron and Carla were sent to Russia and China as special envoys to work on a new world peace agreement. They took the Dewey's older sister with him as an advisor. After a week at the Kremlin, they secured an agreement that Russia would cease all nuclear activity, withdraw from Ukraine and become part of Bosnia. In turn the U.S. promised not to send the rest of the Deweys to Moscow. In China, young Miss Dewey defeated the reigning Yokozuna and became the first female sumo champion to the delight of millions of chubby Asian girls.

Paulie was named head of the CIA, Secret Service, FBI, Homeland Security and Jelly Roll's security detail. He was given a new code book, a fake mustache and disguise kit. His wife asked him for a divorce. In the settlement he gave her the cars, the house, custody of her mother and a picture of him line dancing in a Washington nightclub with Rachel Maddow and Megyn Kelley.

Mr. Amaya, the deceased Mexican was honored for his part in the mission by lying in state in the Capitol Rotunda. Over the course of several days, thousands passed his coffin murmuring prayers and genuflecting while wondering who the hell he was, and why they hadn't buried him yet.

Olga had received an annulment from her marriage to Boris due to his mental state. He was now completely incoherent and sat in his padded room at the Mental Health Institute in Independence, Iowa, hugging a roll of Charmain and mumbling various Russian children's verses.

Olga declined Ruth's offer of Chief of Staff and went back to Wanda's School of Passionate Discipline and Leathercraft Emporium as Sales Director. She eventually married one of the civil war ravagers from Wanda's, a one legged bearded gent named Cuspis and together they started their own place of business Olga's Big O. She also wrote a bestseller "60 Tints of Red, How Cuspis Cured the Scourge".

Jasper was beside himself when he found out that the entire thing was basically a test. When told he would be given a role in the new government he said emphatically ,NO!" When told that the new position would be White House Press Secretary, he stated "Well, uh, maybe, hmm, I should, uh, reconsider."

"You need to work on your speaking skills. Hell, who cares. The job's yours," Ruth said.

Biff and Brian decided that they had had enough of Washington, at least for now. They started a chain of combo funeral home/gambling casinos called Cards and Cadavers with Mike Davis. They even opened one in Juarez that offered a "buy two get one free" burial special if you made reservations at least 30 days in advance. You were also given 100 slot machine tokens if you knew the deceased's names or had usable aliases.

Secretary of State Harberts was the only cabinet member that was kept on. President Ruth said he was too valuable to let go. After all, how many people knew who played MIlburn Drysadale's stepson Sonny on The Beverly Hillbillies and all the words to the theme song from The Flintstones in three languages.

President Ruth was unhappy with the slow movement in world events, so she named Herbie The U.S. ambassador to the UN. It did speed things up. When his first speech about endangered Ugandan Wood Ticks was interrupted by the Ambassador from Zimbabwe. Herbie was not happy.

"Hey, asswipe, sit down. You got nothin' I want to hear, especially from some country that starts with a Z. Who the hell names a country with a Z anyway? I heard you guys eat cats over there, or is that the French? Yeah, that might be the Frenchies, but no matter. You'll get your chance to speak alphabetically. Z is last you know and as long winded as some of these abortion escapees are, it might be years before you're up."

CHAPTER 54

Temple took the smoldering joint handed to him and took a long satisfying drag.

"Well, the world is safe now," Wanda said, exhaling as she leaned back in Temple's bean bag chair next to him.

"It might not be safe, but it's gonna be more fun," He said.

"I'd say we did well."

"Very well."

"May I join the celebration?" Voice asked.

"Sure," Temple said, then turning to Wanda he said," You'll have to excuse that, I'm just speaking to something in my head that no one else can hear."

"Oh, I can hear him,"Wanda said.

"You can?" He said.

"Yes. As a matter of fact I can see him ,too. He's right there."

Temple squinted and looked. "Holy shit, so, that's who you are."

Voice laughed and was then joined by Wanda and Temple. Their laughter soon drifted out the open window and into the capitol night.

www.ingramcontent.com/pod-product-compliance
Lightning Source LLC
Chambersburg PA
CBHW051141190726
48290CB00006B/1943

* 9 7 8 1 7 3 4 7 5 1 5 4 3 *